The Catalog

By Maaya Brooker

Also by Maaya Brooker

Fiction for adults:

Within These Walls

Children's Horror Series:

The Danger Kids: The Haunted House and other stories

You can find Maaya Brooker on the following social media channels.

Twiter: @maayabrooker

Instagram: @maayabrooker

Tiktok: @maayabrookerauthor

Email: maayabrookerauthor@gmail.com

Trigger Warnings

Dear reader,

Firstly, thank you for reading my book, I hope you find it to be engaging and deserving of your time.

I must, however, point out that there are a number of trigger warnings in this book. It is not a book that should be read without knowing what these warnings are first. So, below is a list of the horrendous things that my main character Serena and her fellow prisoners must endure.

- Sexual abuse
- Rape
- Physical abuse
- Torture
- Death
- Miscarriage
- Drug abuse

If you choose to read on, I really hope you enjoy the story- and not the horrible things that happen. You've been warned.

Maaya Brooker

Acknowledgements

I would like to thank the following people for your help, advice, and guidance in writing this book. Without, which, this book would be pretty rubbish!

My friends and honest proof-readers, Rachel, Harriet and Jemma- who were able to find errors and give notes on the plot and character development that I missed out on even after a number of re-reads.

My friend, Catherine, who has selflessly given up time to read and edit this book- the second you have done for me- I am forever grateful for your words of encouragement, and your keen eye.

Thank you to my ARC readers- without your honest reviews, and keen eyes for any mistakes, it wouldn't be the book it is today- something I am supremely proud of.

My writing coach, Karen Guyler, who was there when the first 5 chapters were created in class ready for critique- you showed me how to get Serena up that tree and throw so many rocks at her, so she had to fight her way down. Your guidance is what has moved my writing on this far.

Thank you to all my ARC readers that took on reading my book (with a few errors in) and giving me valuable feedback and great reviews on TikTok, Amazon and Goodreads. I appreciate you all.

Chapter 1: Now

The harsh glare of the fluorescent light made Serena dizzy; the man she was facing made her terrified. A million thoughts raced through her mind as she struggled to adjust to the light and the pungent odour of cheap aftershave. She'd been blindfolded, but why? Where was she? How did she get here? Who was this man?

Serena blinked, her eyes felt heavy, and her body mirrored this. She swayed where she stood and felt a hand press against the small of her back, steadying her. She looked to her right, Dominik was standing next to her, looking paler than she remembered, and his eyes no longer radiated that confidence she fell in love with. He glanced at her ever so slightly and quickly looked back at the man sitting rigid at the mahogany desk in front of them. Everything seemed out of place. Unreal.

"What is this?" she said her voice no more than a whisper, "where am I?"

"We will get to that in a minute Serena," said the man.

A jolt of fear cleared her mind. He knew her name. How?

His voice was deep and full of authority. She forced herself to focus her eyes and look at this dangerous stranger properly. His deep voice matched his appearance; he wore a dark grey suit that stretched across his broad shoulders. Every time he moved the suit threatened to tear under the strain of his muscles. His face was set, his thick dark eyebrows were furrowed, and his angular jawline couldn't be hidden by his well-groomed beard. His hands were large, and Serena spotted a ring on his finger; a simple gold band, a stark contrast to the clearly expensive watch that sparkled from his thick wrist.

"Serena," his voice demanded attention.

Serena looked at him, his eyes drawing her in.

"Yes?"

"Serena, do you know where you are?"

Serena shook her head, her eyes unable to leave his own.

"Speak when spoken to."

"No, I...I don't know where I am," Serena said her heart pounding in her chest and her skin prickling with sweat.

He nodded. "Do you know the man standing next to you?"

Serena glanced at Dominik, his eyes straight ahead and not moving from the figure in front of him. She looked back at the man.

"Yes. I know him. Dominik. He's my-"

"That's enough," he said holding up his hand, "what you may not know is that Dominik works for me."

Works? thought Serena confused. "But he goes to college." Her voice was little more than a whisper.

"Well, that is what I told him to tell you. Do you know why you're here?"

Serena's eyes glistened with tears as she shook her head.

"Speak," he growled his voice hardening.

"Sorry, no I don't know what's going on. Please can you tell me?" she looked at Dominik and reached for his hand which remained hanging limp by his side, "Dom what's going on?"

A hand slammed against the desk; Serena jumped, and Dominik flinched.

"Do not speak to him," the man boomed. "You will speak to me only. Do you understand?"

Serena nodded, "yes."

"Good," he said, his smile forced and menacing.

Serena could feel the air in the room fizz. Her mind raced and she tried to recall what she last remembered but the empowering stench in the room and her fear made everything fuzzy. She remembered going to a party with Dominik, it was one he had told her about. It was a small gathering Serena vaguely recalled, with a few of Dominik's friend's that he had introduced to her. They all had girls with them, all around Serena's age, but none she recognised. She remembered laughing, dancing, kissing Dominik; nothing that seemed out of the ordinary. They had even smoked some weed although she remembers some of the boys didn't. She frowned reaching for the memory. Why was that again?

"Serena," a voice called, pulling her out of her memory.

"Yes," she replied feeling small and very scared.

"Do you know what is going to happen?"

"No, who...who are you?"

"Me?" he laughed, a dangerous cold glint in his eyes, "just call me Bishop. But let's talk about you."

Bishop waved his hands over the large desk in front of him drawing Serena's eyes to what he was showing her. She gasped. Her breath caught in her throat, her eyes widened, and her shoulders shook. She was looking at dozens and dozens of photos. All of them of her.

"What?" she muttered in disbelief, her hands instinctively reaching out to them.

"Ah these," Bishop said a smile reaching across his face, "these are beautiful, aren't they?"

Serena's eyes moved from one photo to the next: pictures of her walking to school, looking at her phone, talking to her friend, some of them with her standing in front of her house in her uniform. Her movements for months all documented and printed out in black and white. She scanned her life laid out in front of her, a timeline of what she had been up to all the way up until she had met...Dominik. She looked at Dominik, the person she had fallen in love with, who was still standing rigid next to her, his eyes glued to the table and the photos of her.

"Dom?" she whispered her voice cracking, "what's all this?"

"He won't talk to you until I tell him to," Bishop said sneering at the panic appearing across Serena's face.

"Dom?" Serena tried again, this time shaking his arm, tears streaming down her face and panic rising in her voice, "Dom, talk to me. What's going on? I need you to tell me."

Dominik allowed Serena to shake him, but his eyes never left Bishop. His once handsome face was contorted into an expression of anguish, his bottom lip trembling.

"Dom!" she screamed at him, holding on to his face and forcing him to turn and look at her.

"Serena," he said, his voice cracking, "do as he says. Listen to him."

A wild rage came over Serena and she spun to face the man she was to call Bishop. She lunged towards the table he was now standing in front of and reached for him. A hard sudden slap caused Serena to stumble backwards. Her lip stung and she tasted the copper of blood inside her mouth. Her face burned and she looked up at Bishop through tears.

"That," he said all humour lost from his voice, "that was for disobeying me and thinking you could confront me. You will not make that mistake again, am I understood?"

Serena nodded; the imprint of his strong hand still hot on her cheek. Bishop turned to Dominik who was shaking.

"Dominik, leave us."

"No, Dom," pleaded Serena, clear terror in her voice.

Dominik nodded at Bishop, glanced briefly at Serena and left the room head hanging and shoulders slumped.

"Right," said Bishop stroking his beard and walking straight in front of Serena, "let's start again."

Chapter 2: Now

Muffled grunts, soft cries and whispers lulled Serena out of a disturbing and confusing dream. Her head felt heavy, her back cracked as she moved, and her face throbbed. Serena groaned and slowly lifted her hand to her face, an attempt to rub away the sleep. A sharp sting forced Serena's eyes to open quickly. She frowned; her mind was foggy. What had happened? She bit her lip, a nervous habit her dad always admonished her for, and winced.

"Ow," she said raising her fingertips softly to her lip. It was sore, and cut, and her face felt puffy too.

"Oh god," Serena's eyes widened as the memory of the night before crashed into her. Dominik. The man called Bishop. The photos. The slap.

Serena shook her head slightly and forced her eyes to focus as she took in her surroundings. Her heart raced. She looked at the cold concrete floor that her bare feet touched. It was barely covered by an orange rug with brown stains, that once would have boasted comfort, but now cried emptiness. The walls of the small room she was encased in were coated with an old cream wallpaper; remnants of a brown velvet pattern peeling off it.

Serena's nose twitched, the rancid smell of old sweat, urine and something else sickly lingered in the air. Her throat closed trying to protect her from the stench, and Serena found herself patting her lap to make sure she hadn't been the cause. She was dry.

"Where am I?" she whispered her mind still groggy.

Her head whipped towards the door where a cry came from the other side. She leapt up and instantly stumbled; her thighs screaming from the loose springs inside the mattress she was just laying on.

"Ow, shit," she said limping towards to door.

The door wasn't a typical bedroom door, it was metal and had a small window to see out of. Or into. On her tiptoes, neck straining, Serena peered through the dirty window trying to see where the noises were coming from. There was a lot of movement and commotion happening outside of the room; strange men walked up and down the corridor, carrying piles of what looked like clothes. They walked in and out of rooms. A glimpse revealed that there were at least five other rooms in this corridor, maybe more, and they were all looking as dark and cold as the one she had woken up in. All the rooms were occupied.

A loud clank and scrape made Serena jump backwards and stumble. Someone was at the door. She scrambled back to the bed on the other side of the room, her eyes never leaving the door. Knees brought up to her chest, arms wrapped around them, and trying to make herself as small as possible, Serena held her breath.

The door creaked open, and in the shadow of the frame stood a silhouette of a man, he was smaller than Bishop. As he stepped forward in the dimly lit room, Serena's shoulders relaxed, her eyes blurred with tears.

"Dom," she breathed instantly moving towards him but the look on his face made her suddenly stop and step back.

"Dom, what's going on? Where are we? What's happening?" A deluge of questions fell from her lips.

"Serena," his voice was alien, distant and cold. This wasn't the Dominik she knew.

"Dom...?"

"Sit down."

"Why?"

"Sit down and I'll explain everything."

"What have you done? Where have you brought me?" her voice was shrill.

"Calm down," said Dominik, his confident demeanour faltering a little.

He shut the door behind him, and Serena heard the door lock again. Why were they locking the door? And from the outside? She looked at Dominik standing awkwardly in the middle of the room. Serena's hands twitched, they wanted to reach out to him, and she wanted his familiar arms around her. But he knew something, and she needed answers.

She frowned, "what's going on?" she asked her voice calmer than she expected it to sound.

"Sit down, let me explain."

"What did you do?"

Dominik winced as if those words had slapped him hard across the face.

"I'm sorry, but I had to. It's my job."

"Had to what?"

"Bring a girl to him."

"To Bishop?"

Dominik shrunk back at the sound of his name.

"Yes, Bishop. I work for him. My job was to collect you."

"Collect me?" Serena said, reality slowly dawning on her situation, "collect?"

"Yes."

"That's not what it's called Dom."

"Serena-"

"No, call it what it is Dominik," Serena felt anger build up inside her, "you've kidnapped me."

Dominik took a step towards her, "Serena, look..."

"Don't come any closer, or I'll scream," she hissed. Her body felt electric, and her skin tingled.

"I'm sorry," said Dominik no longer able to look at Serena, "but it was my job to collect you for Bishop. He's my boss."

"And I'm your girlfriend."

Dominik swallowed hard and cleared his throat, clearly distressed, "No, you're his property now."

"What?"

The panic began to rise again in Serena, like bile burning her heart.

"You belong to Bishop now. You all do. Do as he tells you, and you'll be fine. I can protect you."

"Protect me?" said Serena, a small, strained laugh escaping her swollen lip, "like you did when he slapped me?"

"You disobeyed him."

"You kidnapped me."

Dominik shook his head, "I collected you for him. I can protect you if you let me. I do care for you."

"Then take me home. Why do this to me? Let me leave."

"You can't leave here Serena, not until he says so. This is your home now."

"My home?" Serena cried, her eyes wild with panic and her voice filled with hate, "my home? You took me from my home, you bastard! You took me and brought me here. For what? Why am I here Dom?"

"Bishop will-"

"No, you explain it to me. This is your fault. Tell me what's going to happen?"

Serena breathed heavy, she wanted to scream and shout at Dominik. She wanted to thrash at him with her fists, but the look in his eyes and the truth she was beginning to understand was draining her fight.

"Dom?"

"Do as you're told; I can protect you. No one will touch you unless I say."

"Touch me?" Serena choked, her hands covering her mouth and her body shuddering.

"You'll have visitors," continued Dominik as if he needed to say his piece, "do as they say and what they've paid for, and you will be protected."

"Visitors? Paid for?"

Dominik looked anxiously at the door, "play nice and I'll protect you. I have to go."

He turned and knocked on the steel door. It opened and a burly man stood there, with a pile of clothes, staring at Serena with a smile on his face. He threw them on the floor, looked at Dominik and walked away. Dominik watched the man leave and turned back to Serena.

"Serena, do as you're told. No arguments. Obey them and I can protect you."

Serena's mind raced as she watched the man she loved walk out of the room and bolt the door behind him trapping her in this hell. Tears raced down her cheeks and she fell to her knees sobbing violently. As she curled up on the floor, she looked up at the window.

"But I trusted you," she whispered.

Chapter 3: Now

Sifting through the pile of faded clothes that had been left on the floor for her, Serena's stomach heaved. Her head pounded, her mouth was dry, and her ribs ached from the relentless waves of sobbing that had possessed her for hours. Voices sounded through the metal door; some small and shrill, others deeper and more dangerous. Serena stared at the door hoping she would hear the scrape of it opening, hoping that someone would come in with a glass of water, maybe even some paracetamol to help curb the incessant thud in her skull.

She jumped a little as her hopes were answered and the door was noisily opened. There, standing in front of her, was a shadow that swallowed up the light that was spilling from the corridor into her room.

"Please," Serena whispered, her throat scratching, "please can I have some water?"

The silent mass stepped forward looming over her frail figure, he had something in his hands. A tray of some sort. He walked over to the small table that sat beside the bed and awkwardly placed the tray down. Serena watched him, too scared to breathe or move. He looked over at Serena and pointed at the tray.

"Jesti," he grunted looking at the tray and motioning to his mouth and then he walked out.

Confused, Serena stared at the door expecting him to come back in, she hadn't heard the scrape of the bar or lock. She tilted her head and frowned. Something sweet in the air made her mouth salivate instantly. She turned to the table and the tray that had been delivered. Slowly, Serena crawled over to the table. She pulled herself onto the thin mattress and looked down at the table. Food. He had brought food. And a glass of water. And some pills.

Heart thumping, Serena stretched out her shaking hand towards the glass, placing the pills in her mouth. Bringing the water to her lips she gulped half of it down before choking and coughing at the odd taste. Looking into the glass, Serena recoiled and gagged. Floating just above the bottom of the glass was what Serena could only describe as sand. Gritty, brown grains were mixed into her water. It was tinged orange, and it took a moment, but she realised the odd taste in her mouth, was rust.

Smacking her lips together, trying to get rid of the metallic taste, Serena picked up the small plate that sat beside the glass. A solitary buttered roll sat on it. She picked it up and gave it a sniff. It was stale: but it was food. And the smell of butter made her tongue pulse and her mouth fill with saliva. Hungrily, Serena devoured the roll and licked her finger to pick up the crumbs that had fallen from her mouth. Closing her eyes and savouring the taste and the happy reaction her body had to being fed after such a long time, Serena lay back on the bed and breathed deeply.

Voices talking from the corridor brought Serena back to her prison. She remembered that the door hadn't been locked. Picking herself up from the bed, Serena carefully tiptoed across to the door; holding her breath and ready to run back to the safety of the bed if needed. The voices became clearer, and Serena realised whoever was out there, wasn't speaking English. She stretched her legs and craned her neck to see out of the window but a sudden cramp in her thigh made her shrink back. Massaging her leg, Serena looked at the door handle. He hadn't locked it. Maybe she could open it?

Her hand hovered over the handle, good old-fashioned fear stopping her from yanking it open in a flourish. She had to be careful. She needed to learn what was out there and where she was. Serena held her breath as she shakily turned the handle and pulled the door open.

"Just an inch," she whispered to herself, "slowly, carefully, just an inch, and look out of this room."

The door creaked. The voices suddenly stopped. Serena winced, one eye closing, the other looking out. She held her breath and her heart raced. She could just make out the two men standing near the end of the corridor on her left, they turned and looked in her direction. Serena pressed her lips together, her limbs shaking from the tension in her body, and watched certain that they could see her. After a moment, the men turned back and continued to talk. Serena breathed, relief washing over her. She edged her face closer to the opening of the door to see better. Just to her right was a room on the other side of the corridor.

Serena leaned in close to try and understand what she was seeing. The door was open, and she could see that the décor was similar to her room; a small bed against the wall and a table with a lamp on it. Her heart stopped and her skin instantly became clammy. Standing at the foot of the bed was a man, his shirt open and his trousers down. His eyes were shut, his body glistened with sweat, and he was gripping the hips of a girl on the bed and thrusting ferociously inside of her from behind.

Serena's stomach lurched; the girl was about her age, maybe younger. Serena's eyes widened with fear and horror as she watched the girl being man-handled and groped; her clothes had been torn off and her back was red with lacerations. Serena's tears matched the streams that were running down the girl's face. She felt helpless. What was going on? Why was he doing that to her?

Suddenly, the girl's head snapped up and their eyes locked. The girl's eyes widened, and her mouth opened. Serena's body cramped and her lip trembled. She brought a shaky finger to her lips begging the girl to be silent with a shake of her head. A desperate whimper escaped the girl's lips. Petrified, Serena's eyes flicked up to the man.

He was looking straight at her.

Any shock he felt was instantly replaced with a smug smile. Holding Serena's gaze, he gripped the girl tighter, his nails digging into her hips, making her cry out in pain. Thrusting harder and deeper he didn't look away. Serena let out a gasp and covered her mouth with her hand. He smiled and licked his lips. The whole time driving hard into the girl and looking deep into Serena's eyes.

"Oh god," she whispered. She quickly stepped back from the door and closed it, no longer caring about the noise it would make.

Scrambling backwards into her room, Serena closed her eyes and held her face in her unsteady hands.

"Oh god," said she to herself trying to control her breathing.

The look of terror on the girl's face was burned into her eyes.

Breathe in...

The hands gripping onto her hips.

Breathe out...

The grunts from him as he thrust harder and harder.

Breathe in....

The look of satisfaction and excitement in his smile as he locked eyes with Serena.

Breathe-

Serena gasped, her eyes widening and her body wobbled.

She turned, looking for the bin and quickly ran to it, emptying out the roll she had eaten just moments ago. Her eyes streamed, her throat burned, and her stomach twisted.

She looked around the room for something to wipe her mouth with and saw the pile of clothes she had been looking at.

Serena picked up a small cloth and dabbed at her lips. She frowned and looked closely at the clothes she had been given. Her skin prickled as she realised these weren't just clothes for her to change into, these were the clothes they wanted her to wear. As a uniform. For them. Her eyes glanced from one thong to the next and she picked one up, her fingers traced the fake diamonds across the tiny material.

Tears fell openly as Serena realised her fate was the same as the girl who had clearly just been raped.

Chapter 4: Then

The swirls and curves relaxed Serena's eyes and the rhythmic movement of her pencil across the paper soothed her. Serena needed something to distract her mind a little from what she could hear. She was in art class and a group of girls she loosely regarded as friends sat on the same table as her talked in excited and hushed tones. One of them was her best friend, Amy.

Amy was the only friend that Serena had that she truly believed cared for her wellbeing and whether or not she was ok. Amy had been her best friend for years and many people mistook them for sisters, but it didn't take long for people to know which of the two had more charisma and style: Amy was the popular one. Serena bit her lower lip and frowned, even she wasn't sure why or how they were still best friends. Amy was the confident, outgoing and flirty one; and Serena was awkward, shy and found it hard to talk to people, especially boys.

She watched Amy's mouth move as she rattled on about whatever she thought was important and the girls on the table needed to hear. Amy was like that; so easy going and relaxed. Never letting anything get to her and never taking things personally. For best friends, they had little in common other than their dark skin and thick long black hair. Amy's skin was a fraction lighter, and her eyes were a deep blue. Her skin wasn't dotted with darker freckles or marks like Serena's and Serena was jealous that Amy was the one the boys looked at twice.

"So, what was the kiss like?" asked Hannah one of the girls. She was pale with bright red hair and striking blue eyes.

They all leaned in towards Amy, hanging on every word. Serena rolled her eyes.

"Well, it was, to be honest...a little sloppy," said Amy grinning.

The girls all erupted in giggles, covering their mouths with their hands, all covered in multi-coloured painted nails and patterns drawn on with a biro.

"So, what did you do?" said Alice shaking and tilting her head.

Serena knew that Alice disliked her – she wanted to be best friends with Amy- and she hated that years ago Amy had picked Serena over Alice. Even though they were close, Alice always gave the impression that she and Serena were in the wrong roles.

"Well," said Amy, "I put my hands in his face and told him to hold back on too much tongue." She smiled knowing the girls around her were hanging on every word of hers. "He said he had never kissed anyone before, so it was clear to me that I had to teach him how to kiss properly."

"And?"

"So, I taught him," giggled Amy pouting her lips and winking, "I showed him how to kiss."

Again, the girls giggled and muttered to each other how funny and amazing Amy was. Serena looked up as she felt a nudge on her elbow. It was Amy looking at her and smiling for approval. As if she needed it from Serena. She smiled and looked back at her artbook with her doodles across the page.

"And, well I have to say, once I taught him how to kiss, everything else came easy to him."

"Everything else?" said Hannah whose eyes were wide.

"Yeah, had to show him how to do all the other things us girls like," Amy winked, "stroke and kiss our necks, and kiss and touch us in those...hard to reach places."

"Amy, you didn't," gasped Hannah laughing.

"What else happened?" asked Alice, her face more serious as if she were taking mental notes.

"Well," said Amy loving the attention, "we did oral."

"What?" said Hannah.

"I taught him how find my clit and play with it until I came."

Serena looked up at her friend in shock. Amy looked at her and grinned.

"And I showed him what a good blow job is like."

"My god," said Alice shaking her head, "did he...did you...?"

"Did he come? Yes. Did I swallow? Yes."

Amy shrugged her shoulders and smiled at her friends.

"It's what we do, you should always swallow. It shows him you care."

"That's disgusting," said Hannah laughing.

"It's what they like, and it's what's expected of us," said Amy.

Serena's fingers gripped her pencil. She stared hard at the doodle of a rose she had just shaded in. "Why would you even do that?" she whispered.

"What?" said Amy snapping her head towards her best friend who hadn't spoken this whole time.

Serena breathed, "I said why would you do that? You don't love him. You shouldn't just give it all to the first guy. You've only ever been with one guy. And you didn't even have sex with him. So, what's so special about this one?"

A silence fell among the group as Serena's words hung in the air. Serena looked at Amy. Her face changed, and her eyes flickered with something Serena didn't recognise. Hannah and Alice were silent, their eyes looking to find something to focus on instead of the awkward tension that was building between Serena and Amy. Amy shook her head and smiled. A forced, fake smile with something else darker lurking behind it.

"I know more than you Serena," she said through gritted teeth, "have you even ever kissed a boy? No. You won't even let them grab your arse."

Serena's face burned as Hannah and Alice tried to hide their smiles. They couldn't.

"I just wondered why you'd do that to someone you don't even like that much," said Serena looking directly at Amy, "it's a personal thing and you just-"

"Just what?" said Amy her voice hard, "No one follows your high and mighty standard of love these days, Serena. I liked him and so gave him head. That's it."

"He used you," said Serena.

"I used him," retorted Amy.

"It's wrong."

"You know what, let me do my thing, and have fun. You're not my mum so don't worry about me alright?" Amy was red in the face and her voice was like venom, "how can you judge me anyway, you won't even wear a thong."

Serena's eyes widened. Amy had gone too far. That had been a secret she had told Amy when all the girls in their year had been going on about thongs and how sexy they were. Serena hated them. Hated how they felt against her skin, hated how uncomfortable they were and hated how her body looked in them. Amy had promised to keep that a secret. So much for that. Serena looked at Alice and Hannah as they laughed, no longer feeling the need to hide their joy at witnessing this argument between friends. Serena looked at Amy who was grinning.

"You won't wear a thong?" asked Alice grinning maliciously.

"There's nothing wrong with them," added Hannah.

Serena said nothing.

"They probably don't look good on her," said Amy turned to the other two and smiling, "anyway, as I was saying before we got interrupted by Miss Frigid over here, give them head, it's what they love and it's what is expected of us."

Chapter 5: Then

"Serena, are you listening?"

Serena cleared her mind and blinked.

"Looks like you were in a daydream young lady, did you hear my question?"

Suddenly realising where she was Serena looked at her teacher in embarrassment. She could feel everyone around her looking at her and she began to sweat. Someone giggled behind her.

"Sorry Miss," Serena said feeling her face heat up, "what was the question?"

"Ok," said Mrs Morris glaring at the students around Serena who were snickering, "I asked what the structure of the poem says about the poet's state of mind?"

"Says she was daydreaming," called a voice from her right.

Another chorus of laughs.

She looked down at the poem in front of her searching for the answer, all she could see were the doodles of flowers and 3D cubes. Looking back at Mrs Morris waiting expectantly, Serena bit her lower lip and gave a small shrug. Her eyes stung as the fits of laughter and snide comments echoed in her head.

"Ok, class," Mrs Morris said clearly seeing the discomfort Serena was in, "settle down. You all laugh, but do any of *you* know the answer?"

The class grew quiet.

"I thought so," said Mrs Morris looking at Serena, "right, let's all focus and I'll go through it one more time."

** ** **

"Wow Serena, that was totally embarrassing for you," laughed Amy as she sat down next to Serena at lunch in their usual spot just outside the Drama studio.

Serena shook her head, a tight smile on her face, "Yeah I know, don't remind me."

"Like, everyone was looking at you and laughing."

Looking at her best friend unwrapping a thick sandwich and taking a big bite, Serena felt the urge to slap it out of her hand.

"You laughed too."

Amy looked at Serena in surprise. Serena and Amy were never sat together in lessons, the teachers had made that mistake years before. Too talkative, they had said to Serena's dad who had frowned in disappointment in an ever-worsening parents evening. He thought Amy was a bad influence and had requested that in all their classes, they were separated.

"I heard you laugh. I know your laugh, Amy."

Amy swallowed and smiled, "It was funny, come on, admit it."

"No, it wasn't," Serena said picking up her limp homemade sandwich, "I literally couldn't breathe- everyone was staring."

Amy waved her hand in the air dismissively, "Yeah, but like for a second. You're so dramatic."

Serena avoided looking at her friend, she breathed, trying to keep her anger from boiling up and spilling out of her mouth. Something she had perfected since knowing Amy. It had been a couple of days since their argument and now Amy acted as if it had never happened.

"Look, no one cares now. It's old news."

"I care."

"Oh," said Amy, shaking her head she added, "Look, babe, just chill, ok? It's done. We've all been caught out by Morris. She just knows when we ain't listening. Let it go."

Serena nodded stiffly. She took a small bite of her sandwich and forced it passed the lump that had formed in her throat. Amy didn't understand; she could brush off something like that easily, but Serena could still feel how clammy her hands were and even now, her skin prickled with unease. She began to search for a happy memory to calm her nerves, but found that even now, after weeks of practising this technique, she was unable to conjure up even one simple memory to make her smile.

"Ow!" Serena muttered as a sharp pain in her foot forced her to concentrate on Amy. "What was that for?"

Amy nodded to their right, her eyes twinkling with excitement.

"Look," she whispered smiling, "it's Cal and his mates."

Serena quickly glanced to where Amy's look had not left. "Shit," she said turning her head away and quickly packing her lunch away. She could feel her face heat up again and that tightening of her chest making breathing difficult.

"Shall I call them over?" said Amy smiling mischievously.

"No, don't," Serena pleaded.

Amy ignored her.

"Cal!" she said waving to the boy Serena had had a crush on for the best part of the year.

"Amy," hissed Serena feeling her throat close up with panic and her vision blur.

"Don't worry," said Amy smiling as the boys walked towards them, "just be yourself, ok, maybe a little less frigid than your normal self."

Serena breathed, forcing down the mix of panic and anger rising in her. She plastered on a shaky fake smile and turned towards the boys.

"Hey, Amy," said Cal smiling at Amy. He turned towards Serena, "hey Serena."

He knows my name, thought Serena smiling back at him in silence. She nodded and saw her friend look at her with wide eyes, *'open your mouth and say hello dammit'* those eyes were saying but Serena couldn't. Something was stopping her from talking.

Cal frowned and turned back to Amy. His friends smirked at Serena.

"Uh, Cal," said Amy glancing quickly at her friend, "did you see Amber's post from last night?"

"On the message board?" he said grinning, "Yeah hilarious, who do you think she was writing that poem about?"

"Cal mate, you," said one of the boys laughing and slapping Cal's back.

Cal shook his head. Amy laughed flicking her hair behind her shoulder and pouting her lips.

"He's right," she added standing up and brushing non-existent crumbs from her slender torso, her hands lingering on the edge of her skirt and drawing the boys' attention to her thighs. "That was for you, you interested in her?"

Cal laughed and shook his head, his eyes tracking Amy's hands, "Nah, not my type."

"Ah, right," Amy said glancing at Serena and smiling, "so who is?"

"Never gonna tell," said Cal winking at Serena and turning to walk away, his friends following him.

Amy laughed as the boys walked away and sat back down to face Serena. Serena's heart was pounding, and her palms were marked where her nails had dug into them, and she bit her lip, a force of habit when she was nervous or frightened.

"Fuck," she said, angry with herself for not talking.

"Babe, you need to loosen up. Flirt a little. He ain't going to notice you if you sit there all stiff and don't say anything."

"You mean, flirt like you just did?" Serena could feel her voice turn hard.

"Yeah, like me," said Amy smiling, "I just got his attention, and I hardly did anything. You should do that too."

Serena stood up, gathering her rubbish and pulling on her bag quickly. She needed to get some fresh air. Needed to get away from Amy.

"That's not me Amy," she said through gritted teeth and staring at the floor.

"Well, being you isn't working at the moment," said Amy nastily, "better being a bit more like me and less like you."

"I'm not a whore."

Serena turned and walked off fast, leaving her friend calling to her. Her eyes welled up and her lip quivered, as she left the building through the side door, she felt a scream surface to her lips.

Chapter 6: Now

“Quick Serena get up,” a voice hissed in Serena’s ear as she slept.

Serena felt hands on her shoulders shaking her. She moaned and tried to turn her back away but a jolt of pain in her hip from an uneven spring in the mattress she was laying on woke her up abruptly.

“Quick get up,” the voice urged.

Serena recognised the voice as Dominik’s. As she sat up in bed, she heard a loud banging from outside and an array of shrieks and shouts. Her mind flicked back to the previous night; the man and the young girl across the hall from her. His smile and her cries burned into her brain. She looked at Dominik and remembered. He had betrayed her. He had taken her from her safe life.

“What do you want?” she hissed at him.

“There’s an inspection, you have to get up now,” he looked at her.

“I don’t have to do anything you say,” said Serena her courage slowly returning to her as she watched Dominik squirm every time he looked at the door, "go away. I don't want you here."

"I don't care," he said. He pulled at her arm hard, "get out of the damn bed now, or you'll be in serious trouble."

"Fuck you," said Serena yanking her arm back.

"Bishop's on his way," said Dominik standing back and picking up a dress off the floor and throwing it at Serena, "if you're not out there, dressed and ready for work, he'll punish you."

The mention of Bishop's name made Serena's blood run cold and her body tense with fear. Bishop. The boss. The one everyone was afraid of: including her. Serena's eyes flicked towards the door of her room; it was open, and she could see people scrambling around. A man stopped at her door, worry etched on his face as he looked at Serena and then at Dominik.

"Get her out here now," he growled looking over his shoulder, "Bishop's here."

Serena's bravado disappeared as she scrambled to her feet fumbling with her dress. Her body ached from the restless nights and her stomach grumbled. She slipped into the dress which was far too short for comfort; a backless black dress covered in sequins with thin straps only just holding in her breasts. She pulled her hair back into a ponytail as she stumbled out of her door for the first time since arriving.

The sight in front of her, struck fear through her body. The corridor was brightly lit and cold. A faint smell of sweat and tang lingered in the air making Serena wince. As she looked around at the people standing in the corridor, Serena realised she wasn't alone. Her door, her room, was one of about ten along the corridor. Outside each room stood a young female, dressed similarly to Serena with matching faces of despair and fear. Next to each of them stood a man- ranging from as young as Dominik to much older- each of them making sure the girl they were next to was standing straight and standing very still. Serena spotted the man she had seen rape the girl across from the corridor look at her. No smile for her this time. Some looked worried like Dominik did standing next to her, others were angry and slapped their girl into obedience. Serena looked at Dominik.

"What the fuck is this?" she whispered, her voice trembling.

"Inspection," said Dominik looking at her and then at the end of the corridor where a man and woman had appeared, "stand still, look straight and don't say a fucking word."

Serena jumped at hearing Dominik swear, he only ever swore when he was afraid. She looked towards the end of the corridor where his gaze hadn't left and saw Bishop. Her breath caught in her throat and her lip pulsed at the memory of his slap. He looked just as sinister as she remembered, his large body taking up most of the corridor. His eyes looked dangerous, and his movements were slow and deliberate. He looked like he was watching everything carefully and with pride.

The woman next to him, however, was very different. She was wearing a smart red skirt with a black hem, a blouse that showed off her curves and her black laced bra that was struggling to keep her breasts maintained in them. Her legs were golden brown and slender, and she wore heels that emphasised her shape. Her hair was thick and long and dark, not too dissimilar to Serena's, although Serena's hadn't been brushed in a while and was starting to matt against her sticky skin. Sweeping across her shoulders and neck, the woman wore a delicate scarf that tried, and failed, to hide the thick diamond necklace hanging from her neck. She held long black gloves in her hand and her nails were long, immaculate and painted deep red. She walked alongside Bishop with power and purpose.

"Who's she?" she whispered to Dominik.

No answer. She looked towards him and saw that he was standing rigid and looking straight ahead, just as he had been in Bishop's office a few days ago. Like a deer in headlights.

"Dom," she said a little louder, "I said who's she?"

"Shh," he hissed, "stay still, stay silent."

Serena was about to ask why when a squeal from the end of the corridor interrupted. Serena gasped as she watched Bishop and the woman stand in front of a small, frightened girl. Bishop loomed over her, his hands pressing at her small breasts and her hips. Turning her around and feeling her buttocks. The girl shook, and as Bishop spun her around to face the front again, Serena saw she was crying.

"Shh," she heard Bishop say, trying but failing to be soothing, "no noises now during inspection."

The woman stepped forward and stood in front of the young girl. Serena relaxed, surely this woman could see what was going on and see how terribly frightened the young girl was. She could see that this woman would have sympathy and help her. Surely, she would-

Serena jumped. She hadn't seen the woman's hand rise above her head, and she hadn't expected the sound it made as it whipped across the girl's face. Neither had the young girl. She fell into a heap on the floor and fell silent with shock. The woman turned to face the man who had been charged to look after the girl and said something Serena didn't recognise as English. He picked up the girl from the floor who was now sobbing and dragged her into the room they had been standing in front of.

"Dom," she whispered as quietly as she could.

"Stay calm, stay quiet," he whispered back.

Chapter 7: Now

Serena closed her eyes and tried to concentrate on her breathing, but the whimpers, gasps and occasional slaps made her heartbeat too fast. Serena could feel her skin prickle as she felt Bishop and this woman get closer and closer to her. She dug her fingernails into her palms focusing on the pain forming in her hands, she needed to calm down. Everything around her felt heavy, and she struggled to breath.

"And who is this?"

The voice was coming from in front of her. Serena opened her eyes slowly to see the woman in the red skirt standing there her long nails lightly brushing over her scarf. She was mesmerising and her beauty was striking. Serena couldn't take her eyes off the woman. She saw Bishop nod from the corner of her eyes.

"This is Serena," Dominik said, his voice barely a whisper.

"Serena," she said, her voice although quite silky, still had a touch of menace about it. She looked at Serena, "how old are you girl?"

"Fifteen."

"Nice and young, perfect," the woman smiled. She looked at Bishop and nodded.

The air around Serena became thick with Bishop's cologne as Serena watched Bishop step towards her. He smiled and raised his eyebrows. Serena felt dizzy with fear.

"Now, young lady," said Bishop, his accent much more profound than Serena remembered, "I am going to inspect you. Stay still, do what I say, and this will be over soon."

Inspect me? Serena thought but before she could really understand what that meant, she felt Bishop's hand on her face. Her eyes widened and her skin burned where he touched her.

Serena's body tensed as she looked into Bishop's eyes. They were twinkling; he was enjoying this. His hands moved methodically and expertly around her jaw, down to her neck and shoulders. He pressed and prodded her arms and looked at her hands which were scratched and rough. Serena gasped as she felt his large hands cup her breasts. He pressed softly around her nipples and his thumb brushed over her nipples through her dress. Her eyes filled with tears as his hands moved down her body, pressing at her waist and hips.

Serena glanced towards Dominik, her eyes pleading for help, but she found him standing as rigid as before, looking straight ahead. She let the tears fall down her face as Bishop's hands slipped under her dress. Her body burned, every inch of her trying to shrink away from Bishop's touch. His hands moved towards her buttocks, again cupping the cheeks in his hands and squeezing. His fingers stroked along her thighs and towards the small patch of hair above her vagina. Serena's silent tears morphed into small sobs as she felt Bishop stroke her pubic hair with his thumb.

His eyes locked in with hers and he smiled.

His fingers lingered against the knickers she was wearing and pressed gently against her, making her close her eyes and turn her head. Serena's mind desperately searched for somewhere safe, but Bishop's hands pulled her back to her reality. His hands moved down her legs and finished off the inspection.

"All good," he purred in her ear.

"Good," said the woman, "a virgin?"

Serena's eyes flicked open, and she looked at the woman. She was horrified to see that the woman was smiling and nodding, the invasion of Serena's body hadn't phased her at all. It was just business. Her question wasn't aimed at Serena.

"Yes," said Dominik. For the first time looking at Serena and then back at the woman, "she is still a virgin."

"Why?" the woman asked stepping towards Serena putting her hands on her shoulders and slowly spinning Serena around.

"I didn't get a chance to finish the job."

Serena's head turned to Dominik; his face was red, and he was looking down at his feet as if he was embarrassed. *The job?* What the hell did he mean by that? Serena had asked him to take things slow in their relationship, and he was more than happy to oblige. It was one of the things she loved about him. *Had* loved about him. And here he was sounding like he had failed and disappointed mummy and daddy by not taking her virginity. Serena's heart pounded and she felt her ears begin to burn.

"Finish it then," the woman said with a flick of her hand.

"Yes, Sestra," Dominik said still looking at the floor.

The woman nodded at Bishop and continued down the corridor. Bishop followed.

"Ivan," Serena heard her say to Bishop as they walked away, "these girls are fine. Get them washed, fed and ready for the opening bids next week. I'm done for today; you can finish the inspection."

Serena watched the two walk away. Her skin still burned but she shivered standing in the corridor. She looked around and saw everyone that had already been inspected was gone. She could hear muffled noises from those rooms. A hand on her shoulder made her jump.

"Serena," Dominik said smiling at her, "it's over. You've passed."

Serena looked at Dominik and frowned. Standing, smiling and looking like everything had gone to plan, was a man she had fallen in love with. A man she had told secrets no one had ever known. A man she had been vulnerable with. A man she had kept a secret from everyone she loved, because he had asked her to and because he had said he loved her. A man she no longer recognised. She felt numb.

"Serena," he said grinning as he opened the door to her room as if it was a romantic hotel room instead of a prison he had brought her to, "this way."

Serena nodded, looked at the floor and shuffled into the room. She stood, eyes closed, in the middle of the room and her heart dropped at the sound her of door closing with a metallic thud. For a moment Serena relaxed in the silence around her, trying to blank out the humiliation she had just encountered. Breathing in deeply Serena's eyes suddenly snapped open. She wasn't alone. She could smell Dominik's faint aroma as he stood behind her.

"Why are you still here?" she whispered although something in her bones said she wouldn't like the answer.

"Serena," said Dominik. His voice was soft, not unlike the days when they spent time alone together, "you're so beautiful."

Serena felt his hands slide onto her waist from behind and his breath against her neck as he kissed her. A feeling that once used to make her moan push back against him now made her tremble and panic.

"What are you doing?" she stuttered; her eyes wet with new forming tears.

"You heard Sestra," he said gently pushing her towards the bed, "you need to be ready for the customers. I need to help you."

"What do you mean?" Serena's voice was coarse.

"You know what she said," he said tugging her dress up and over her hips, "you can't be...you know, a virgin."

"Don't touch me."

"Serena, I care for you."

"I said don't touch me."

"Serena, listen," Dominik shook his head, Serena could tell by the way he said her name that he was exasperated, "I still love you."

"I hate you. Leave me alone."

"Look," he said his voice hardening and pushing her onto the bed. His hands grabbed at her chin and forced her to look at him, "it's either me or someone else. At least I'll be gentle."

Serena shook her head, allowing fresh tears to fall across her face. She knew Dominik was right, but she was conflicted; she didn't want him to touch her, but she knew he was right, if he didn't take her virginity someone else would. She bit her lower lip.

"But I'm not ready, I don't want to."

"You have to," said Dominik knowing he had the upper hand. He smiled gently at Serena as he unzipped his jeans and climbed on top of her, "it's what's expected of you."

Chapter 8: Now

Serena's head pounded and her body screamed in agony. Dominik had left her room twenty minutes earlier and Serena hadn't moved since he had climbed off her, kissing her dry lips and telling her she was perfect. He had left her a towel and soap and told her to go to the shower room to get cleaned up. He said food and clothing would be waiting when she got back. But Serena couldn't move.

Her thoughts wouldn't let her. She was numb. As far as she understood, her life was over. Would anyone come looking for her? Did anyone miss her? Did they realise she was even gone? How long had she been missing for? Would the police get involved? Could anyone actually find her? These questions plagued her mind and paralysed her body. What was to become of her now? The more she thought about where she was and what she was going through, the less she believed she would ever be free.

A loud knock on the door echoed through the room. The door opened and a deep husky voice called through to her.

"Girl, get up, go shower. Now."

Serena made no move. The voice hardened.

"Now or I come get you and drag you shower. I will even clean you."

The thought of being touched by another man, made Serena move. She shuffled off the bed and grabbed the towel and soap that sat on the floor. As she stood, she noticed something on her inner thigh. She brushed a finger over the mark and gasped as she realised what she had just brushed off. Blood. She was bleeding. She looked up, panic in her eyes and held the towel in front of her, trying to hide her legs. But the man at the door had seen and he smiled at her, his eyebrows raised. He sneered as she padded past him and joined the group of girls heading for the shower room tears falling down her face.

** ** **

Serena stood in a large white room and looked around her in awe. This was the cleanest place she'd seen since arriving here- and that included the shower room she had just been in. She had showered in what could only be described as lukewarm water trying to scrub every inch of her body, but the leering eyes of the men watching them all showering had forced Serena to be as quick as she possibly could.

The three white pills she had swallowed with her plain sandwich as food were starting to take the edge off the cramps shooting though her stomach. She felt lightheaded and swayed in the heels that had been left in the room by

Dominik. Serena never wore heels so walking and keeping her balance was difficult. The tight gold sequinned dress she had been told to wear wasn't helping either. It hugged her slim body so tight that she was only able to take small, hobbled steps and couldn't lift her arms out too wide for fear of tearing through the material.

The room was set up like a professional studio; light boxes, props, screens of different colours and cameras were spaced around the room and the girls were being led from one place to another. The room was oddly calm, and Serena was surprised. So many girls in the room and none of them seemed to notice one another. They moved when they were told to and did what they were directed to do; no noise, no fussing, no crying or pleading. Just obedience.

"So quiet," Serena said, her voice slurring a little.

"They've all taken their medication," a voice said behind her.

Serena turned.

"Dom," she said.

"Come on Serena," he said leading her to an empty screen and camera, "it's your turn."

"For what?" she asked although she allowed Dominik to manoeuvre her where she needed to be. Her legs felt heavy.

"Your photos, you need them before the clients come to visit."

Serena squinted her eyes and tried to focus on Dominik. Those pills were amazing. She no longer felt pain in her abdomen. Dominik, however, didn't look happy. "You're not smiling," she said her eyes blinking slowly.

"I'm ok, let's just get this done."

"Ok Dom...in...in."

"Serena, are you ok?" Dominik asked his warm hands stroking her back like he used to.

"I feel good," said Serena swaying on her feet, "those pain meds you left for me are working. I'm tired though."

"How many did you take?"

"All of them."

Dominik shook his head and waved a man with a camera over, "you shouldn't have taken them all. Not yet."

"It's ok," said Serena, blinking as the stranger with the camera switched on the light boxes.

The screen they were standing in front of was instantly illuminated in bright white lights. Serena swayed. The cameraman looked at her and then at Dominik saying something in a language Serena hadn't quite placed yet. Dominik replied in the same language. The man nodded, looked at Serena and smiled.

"Hello sexy lady," he said, his voice dripped with slime, "come onto stage for me."

Serena smiled and unsteadily moved to where he was pointing. Dominik tried to help but she shrugged him off.

"I can do it," she snapped at him, "you've done enough."

He looked like a puppy being told no and walked off muttering to himself. Serena looked at the man behind the camera, his face was hidden by the tripod and camera. A slow panic began to move through her body, and she swallowed hard, trying to keep the food she had eaten down.

"Sexy, stand here. Do this. The men like this."

Serena's eyes widened and suddenly everything was clear to her again. Where she was. What she was wearing. And what was now expected of her. As she looked around the room, she noticed all the girls were being photographed. These were the photos that the 'customers' would see.

"Put finger in mouth," the cameraman's voice brought her back to her senses.

Serena did as she was told. Bright lights flashed in front of her face and the clicking sound of the pictures being taken deafened her. Each time the cameraman ordered her to stand this way, pout that way, look over there, Serena did as she was told. Her face burned.

"Now," said the man walking towards her licking his lips, "now for honey shot."

"What?" she stuttered.

"Lay on sofa," he said nodding to a sofa that Serena could only describe as one of those sofas she would see on TV in a psychiatrist's office, "open legs and smile."

"What? No, please," Serena pleaded.

"Do now, or I call for someone for help you."

His voice had changed. He was no longer flirting or toying with her. Serena sensed danger in his eyes. Her lip trembled as she unsteadily walked to the sofa, she looked at the man who watched her smirking.

"Now sexy open legs pose," he said one hand moving down to his crotch and the other clicking away at the camera.

Chapter 9: Then

Serena lay on the bed next to Amy; the two of them giggling and listening to music. She had finally been given permission by her dad to spend a few hours after school at her best friend's house on the promise of revising for their exams. Of course, they weren't. Instead, the two of them had snuck a few glasses of wine from the fridge and replaced what they had taken with some apple juice and fizzy lemonade. Amy insisted that her mum wouldn't even notice, half the time the wine only came out after a few gins anyway. The wine had quickly made Serena lightheaded, but she didn't want to admit it to Amy, she didn't need to be teased over that too.

"How's the wine?" Amy asked taking another sip from her glass.

"Good," said Serena copying her friend. She grimaced. If she was being honest the wine was actually quite horrible and tangy.

"Liar," said Amy looking at Serena. She smiled and burst into laughter, "it's horrible, isn't it?"

Serena laughed too, "yeah it's gross, I just didn't want to be rude."

"Don't worry hon, it's horrible," said Amy, "but it gets the job done."

"True," said Serena giggling and taking another mouthful.

The girls lay there in silence for a moment, listening to the music and the sound of each other breathing. Then, Amy turned to face Serena, resting her head on her hand.

"So," she said her breath hot in Serena's ear, "are you going to ever do anything about Cal?"

Serena turned to face her best friend and smiled, "what's the point? I don't think he likes me like that."

"He does."

"How do you know?"

"I've seen the way he looks at you and smiles at you," said Amy sitting up on the bed and fidgeting with her hair, "you just need to take the first step. Let him know you're interested in him too."

"And how do I do that?" asked Serena joining her friend cross-legged on the bed. She reached for the last of her wine, the more she drank, the less horrid it tasted, "all the girls in the year think he's cute so they're always all over him. How am I supposed to get a look in?"

Amy looked at her friend thoughtfully; she tilted her head and chewed on her lip. Serena watched Amy with a mixture of jealousy and admiration. Things like boys and confidence always came easy to Amy, and most of the time she wanted to help Serena catch up with the rest of their group. Suddenly, Amy gasped and jumped off the bed.

"I've got it," she said, excitement in her voice, "I know what you can do."

"What?" asked Serena feeling a little tipsy as she watched Amy jump about.

"Sexy snaps," said Amy turning towards her full-length mirror and placing her hands on her hips.

"What?"

"Take some sexy shots of yourself and send them to Cal."

"No way," said Serena shaking her head vigorously.

"Why not?"

"I don't want to show off my body to anyone."

"It's not anyone, it's Cal. He likes you and you like him, so why not?"

"I don't know him well enough."

"Well, maybe this will help you get to know him better?" said Amy winking at Serena.

Serena shook her head. The thought of taking photos of herself and then sending them to Cal was out of the question. But at the same time, she wanted him to notice her. Could Amy be right? Did like her? Either way, she just wasn't sure.

"I don't think so," said Serena chewing at her fingernail, "I don't even know what kind of shots I would take. I'm not taking nude pictures."

"You don't have to do nudes," Amy laughed spinning around and placing her hands beside Serena's legs on the bed, her words slightly slurred, "just some suggestive ones. Nothing obvious showing. He doesn't need to see everything. Just tease him."

"I don't know how."

Amy smiled. She knew that she had Serena on the edge of agreeing to do what she had suggested. She had to play the next moment sensibly. She brushed her hair out of her face and sat next to Serena. She held on to Serena's hand and looked at her friend.

"I can help you hon. We can do it here, right now, and I will help. You don't need to show anything you don't want to, and I'll make sure they're tasteful and not too slutty."

"I don't know," said Serena, her willpower starting to fade.

"Do you trust me?"

"What?"

"I said do you trust me hon?" asked Amy, a serious expression on her face.

Serena nodded.

"Then trust me when I say I can do it with you, and I promise you won't look like a slag."

"Promise?"

"Yes, I promise," said Amy smiling and getting up and moving to her wardrobe, "come on, let's look at what you should wear."

"What's wrong with what I have on now?" Serena asked looking down at her slim jeans and fitted T-shirt.

"We need you say, 'hey Cal, look at me I'm sexy' not 'hey Cal, I can do your maths homework for you'," said Amy giggling.

Serena laughed and joined her friend at her wardrobe, stumbling a little as the wine continued to make her wobble. "Ok," she said, "but I think I'm going to need more wine."

"Just what I was thinking," said Amy as she turned to leave the room, "you look through some of my clothes and see what you like, I'll go get the wine."

"Thanks," said Serena.

"Just do me one favour?" Amy added at the door.

"What?"

"Don't pick any trousers – you need to show off those sexy toned legs of yours."

Serena giggled as Amy trotted out of the room in search for some more wine. Serena looked at Amy's wardrobe and plethora of clothes: she had so many. Serena's wardrobe in comparison was measly and small and her selection of clothes were very modest; any skirts she had weren't too short and the tops weren't low cut. Serena had to admit, Amy was right, her clothes were boring and not sexy at all.

Serena was looking at a small maroon dress that she had plucked from the wardrobe as Amy walked in with a bottle of wine. She waggled it at Serena who laughed and held out her glass to be filled. It had been a while since her and Amy had got on like this; they had spent too long recently bickering and arguing with one another. It was nice to be relaxed and with the Amy that was her best friend.

"That's a great dress," said Amy nodding at it, "that'll make your legs look like they go on for miles, and it's pretty good at making your boobs look bigger."

"You think?" Serena said holding the dress against her body and looking in the mirror.

"Yeah, definitely. Look, go get changed and we can start taking some photos."

Serena did as she was told. When she came out of the bathroom and walked back into Amy's room, she saw that Amy had changed the lighting. She had used her fairy lights and lamps to create a soft lighting effect and had set up her bed with pillows stacked.

"Here," said Amy pointing at the bed.

"I'm not sure," said Serena who was feeling self-conscious in the dress.

"Look, I want you to pose like I did here," Amy picked up her phone and starting swiping through photos of herself. Serena was shocked: these were quite revealing and left little to the imagination.

"I'm not doing that," said Serena.

Pointing at a picture of Amy laying on the bed, her legs uncrossed and fingers in her mouth, Serena began to giggle. Amy joined in.

"No, you daft bitch," said Amy through giggles and sips of her wine, "I'm not saying do that exact pose- that little sexy shot was for David last month. I'm saying something like this. Just pout a little, flash those sexy long legs of yours that Cal keeps staring at and have fun."

Serena giggled and shook her head. She took a big gulp of her wine, clearing half of it from her glass in one go and flicked her hair.

"Come on then, Amy," she said her eyes glazed and a wobble in her balance, "let's get some sexy shots of me."

Chapter 10: Then

Serena sat on her bed later that evening swiping through the photos she and Amy had taken. It had been a while since she'd had that much fun with Amy and she had to admit, dressing up a little and taking those photos had made her feel good about herself and the wine had relaxed her. The photos they had taken weren't too raunchy or too revealing either, they were glamorous, and Serena had liked the way she looked in them. Amy had tried but failed, to persuade Serena to send them to Cal straight away. Serena needed time to think about it and she needed to be more clear-headed to make that decision.

Looking at the photos, now feeling somewhat sober (with a little headache coming on) Serena wrestled with herself about sending the pictures. She liked the way she looked in them, and Amy said she could choose which one she sent to Cal. And she really did want to impress him, but she just wasn't sure. She'd heard of too many stories where the photos had gone viral and how the whole world had seen the images. She text Amy.

Thanks for this afternoon, was loads of fun. Love the photos too. Xxx

Excellent, yeah snaps were great. Xxx Have you sent one to Cal yet?

No. I'm not sure which one and not sure if I want to.

Do it woman. He'll love the one with you sat on the edge and legs crossed.

I dunno.

Your legs look great and your tits look fab too :)

Serena laughed at Amy's comment. She swiped back to the photo Amy was talking about. Amy wasn't lying Serena did look great in that picture, really grown up too. Serena liked the photo too. She began typing a new message:

Hey Cal. Serena here.

Almost instantly a reply: *Hi Serena. How you doing?*

Good. :) Just going through some photos Amy and I took earlier.

Oh right? Good ones I bet? ;)

Serena smiled. Yet again Amy was right. She had advised Serena what to say to Cal as they sat finishing off the bottle of wine and Serena had changed back into her jeans. She knew it would get a reaction from him. Serena's hand hovered over the keypad: should she say what Amy told her to?

Wanna see? ;)

For sure xx ;)

Serena giggled and threw herself back on her bed. Grabbing a pillow, she squealed into it and pounded her feet on the mattress. She selected the photo and breathed. All she had to do now was press send. Her thumb hovered over the keypad. What was stopping her now? Cal had said he wanted to see the picture, and the one she was sending him wasn't too dirty.

"Come on Serena," she said to herself, "stop being such a wimp and send it."

Serena pressed send and held her breath. She waited. The icon on her phone was flashing telling her that Cal had received and seen the message. He had seen the photo. Biting her lip Serena stared at her phone. Minutes passed and there were no new messages from Cal. She picked up her phone, tears threatening to spill from her eyes and text Amy.

Sent it.

And? Came the reply from Amy.

Nothing. He hasn't replied.

Maybe he hasn't seen it?

He has. It's been looked at.

Don't worry. Give it time.

I knew I shouldn't have done this.

Hon, chill. He's probably just wanking to it ;)

Serena smiled and shook her head. Typical Amy.

That's disgusting.

It's sexy. Hon, don't worry, chill. If he replies then that's cool, but if he doesn't then he's not worth it. You looked amazing in that photo and if he can't see that, then fuck him.

Yeah...

I'm right and you know it. Look, gotta go, let me know what he says ok?

Ok. Thanks.

See you tomorrow. X

Serena put her phone down and closed her eyes. Amy was right, she needed to relax and not obsess over what he thought of the photo. But she knew she wouldn't sleep at all if he didn't reply. Covering her eyes to block out the light, Serena moaned. Her head was starting to throb from the wine. This was the most she had ever drank and she was starting to feel ill. Suddenly, the sound of her phone beeping and informing her that she had a new message made her sit up quickly. She instantly regretted doing that.

"Ugh," she muttered to herself, and she rummaged for her phone, "not drinking that wine again."

She looked at her phone. A message from Cal. Her breath caught in her throat and her heart pounded from nervous excitement. She looked at the message.

Great photo. Xx ;)

Serena smiled and typed out a reply: *Thanks.*

You look great in that. Love your legs. Didn't realise they were that long and sexy.

Thanks – now I'm blushing.

It's true. You look sexy.

Thanks.

Anyone else seen this photo?

No, just for you ;) x

Cheers, I'll enjoy it later on ;) xxx

Serena giggled and rolled her eyes. She bit her lower lip as she typed out her reply: *lol sexy. But when do I get a photo to enjoy? ;) xxx*

I'll send you one later on. When I'm alone ☺

Sounds good to me ;)

Gotta go. I'll text later.

Ok. Chat later.

Serena put down her phone and rolled onto her stomach. She squealed again into her pillow. Cal had noticed her. He had liked that photo of her and said he'd text later on. Things were going just as she had always wanted. All that worry about taking and then sending the photos was all ridiculous. She's enjoyed herself whilst taking the photos with Amy, and now Cal liked them and wanted to chat. Serena wasn't sure what she was worried about in the first place. Things were finally going her way. She needed to tell someone. She picked up her phone and called her best friend.

"Hello?"

"Hey, Amy. He liked it."

"I told you he would. It's a proper sexy snap! That's so cool."

"I'm buzzing! He said he'd chat later on and I'm so…well…you know."

Amy laughed, "what did he say about the photo?"

"He said, and I'm quoting, 'you look sexy'. My god Amy."

"Told you," said Amy, "you looked amazing."

"Thanks."

"No worries, just promise me one thing?"

"What?" said Serena looking at her reflection, she was grinning like a mad woman.

"Tell me all the dirty details."

"Oh Amy," said Serena laughing at her friend's brashness.

"I mean it, if you and Cal get together, I want the details."

"We're just talking," said Serena although she could feel her body warm through with the thought of kissing Cal.

"Details."

"Right, I'm getting off now," said Serena laughing.

"Yeah, you are."

"Amy, you're gross."

"Details, I want them."

"Bye Amy..."

"Dirty details."

Serena laughed again as she cut the call. Things were finally looking up for her.

Chapter 11: Then

When Serena woke up the next day, she couldn't stop smiling. All she could think about was Cal's comment about her photo, how he said she looked great and that he would speak to her when he saw her at school the next morning. And now that the next morning was here, Serena felt on cloud nine. Things were finally looking good, and she had Amy to thank for it. Serena was pleased that Amy had persuaded her to take some sexy photos of herself and send the best one to Cal. He liked it, so that's all that mattered; it could only get better from here on. She applied a little extra makeup to her face and decided to wear her hair down instead of its usual up do.

As she walked towards the year 11 entrance Serena fiddled with her phone. She was checking for messages from Cal: they had agreed to meet under the tree on the hill just to the side of the doors. Serena looked up as she heard someone say her name. It was Amy, waving at her and calling her over. Serena grinned and walked over to Amy- she would want an update on how things with Cal were going, but the closer she got the more she realised that Amy wasn't smiling.

"Hey Amy, are you-" Serena began.

"Have you checked your stories?"

"What?"

"On Snap?"

"No, why?" Serena began to feel uneasy; a tingle began to spread across her body.

Amy motioned her to walk with her, leading her to a more secluded part of the school gates. She looked around and bit her lip.

"Amy," said Serena who only saw that look on Amy's face when something was wrong, "what's going on?"

"I'm so sorry I made you take those photos," started Amy, her eyes wet.

"It's ok," said Serena smiling, "Cal liked them. I liked them. I actually think I looked good."

Amy nodded and looked around them. Serena looked too.

"Amy, what's wrong?" Serena said her voice catching as she saw students from the school all looking her way, pointing and talking, "Amy? Talk."

"Your photo got shared."

"What?" Serena said eyes bulging.

Amy shook her head and handed Serena her phone. Serena gasped and her face became hot as she scrolled through the messages posted under her photo. Message after message of hate and hurtful words all attacking Serena. Serena's vision blurred as she fought back tears.

"Serena," Amy whispered.

"Why did they write this?"

"Cal shared it, the dickhead. He shouldn't have. I'm so sorry hon," Amy watched Serena as she read more and more of the messages, "don't read any more. It's all bullshit."

But Serena was engulfed in the deluge of comments all aimed at her.

Puke, she looks gross.

What was she thinking?

She doesn't even have any tits?

I didn't realise she was so dark!

Wrong colours!

I would not wear that dress if my legs looked like that!

Ugh, cover up that gross birth mark.

What's that mark on her leg? It's disgusting.

Her face is so rank!

Disgusting.

Sad and lame attempt for attention.

Dirty gal. Have some respect whore.

Put those manky legs and that vile scar away!

Ugh, my eyes!

"Serena," said Amy taking her phone from Serena, "hon, come on."

"Whore," Serena muttered to herself, "they called me a whore. Why?"

"Cos they're dicks and they ain't got anything better to do than try to rip you down," said Amy putting a hand on Serena's shoulder.

"And my scar," said Serena her hand unconsciously moving to her right thigh where her birth mark is, "they said it's disgusting."

"They're haters. With no life. They'll find anything to crush someone for. Look half of these are anonymous too. Fucking cowards."

Serena wasn't listening. She looked around the school grounds and watched as more students looked at their phones and then back at her. The photo had gone viral. Her arms felt heavy and her legs began to shake. Her breath caught in her chest as she spotted Cal walking towards her.

"Cal," she said looking directly at Amy for the first time since being pulled aside.

"Fuck," said Amy stepping forwards.

"I need some air," said Serena, panic setting in at the prospect of facing Cal right then and there, "I can't be in school today."

"I'll come with you," said Amy.

"No, I need to be alone," said Serena, tears spilling from her eyes.

"Serena," called Cal, closer now.

"Wait for me," said Amy as she marched up to Cal.

Serena watched as Cal tried to talk round Amy and get to her, but Amy wouldn't let him. Serena looked around and saw a gap in the fence the kids who skipped school sometimes used to get out without being noticed. Looking back at Amy and Cal arguing, she turned and ran towards it ignoring the voices calling after her.

Serena didn't stop running until she saw the little park hidden next to the local shop. She walked into the gated park, and she dropped onto a bench breathing hard. Her legs burned and her scar especially felt on fire reminding her that it was there.

"Fuck!" Serena screamed and then allowed herself to cry properly.

Powerful sobs shook her shoulders and Serena gasped for air. In that moment Serena felt the most alone and outcast she had ever felt. She had made a series of stupid mistakes, trusting the wrong people and now a picture of her was viral and everyone had seen it. She was a laughing-stock. She hated Amy for persuading her to take the photos, she hated Cal for sharing it when it was just meant for him, but most of all she hated herself for being so stupid and allowing herself to be controlled like that. Serena opened her eyes as her phone rang. It was Amy. She cancelled the call. Serena didn't want to talk to anyone right now.

As she concentrated on slowing her breathing and wiping her face, her phone lit up again. This time it was Cal. She held her phone in her hand trying to decide whether to talk to him or not. She didn't know what to say. Actually. She knew what she wanted to say but didn't know how she was going to say it to him. The phone rang again. Cal, again.

Sighing, she answered. "Cal, what do you want?"

"I'm sorry," came Cal's voice sounding smaller and less confident, "I didn't mean to-"

"Didn't mean to what?" Serena snapped, "didn't mean to post and share it when you knew it was just for you? Didn't mean to allow all those people to see it and make those comments? Didn't mean to trick me into thinking you even liked me?"

"I do like you," his voice was smaller now.

"Shit way of showing it," said Serena - the anger inside building layer by layer, "why did you share it?"

"I don't know why I shared it."

"Honestly, that's your excuse? You don't know why you did it?"

"I'm sorry."

"Fuck you Cal, I don't ever want to see you again."

"Serena wait-"

But Serena didn't wait to hear what he had to say. She cancelled the call and threw her phone across the park. A long, painful scream surfaced, and Serena gave into the sobs she'd held at bay whilst talking to Cal.

After what felt like hours, Serena breathed hard. She was all cried out. No more tears for Cal and no more tears for herself. Wiping her cheeks with her hand, Serena looked at her bag laying next to her. As she rummaged through it looking for a tissue and cursing when she couldn't find one, she felt the presence of someone standing in front of her. Looking up, expecting to see that Amy or Cal had found her, Serena was surprised to see a slender man looking down at her holding out a packet of tissues with a look of concern on his boyish face.

"Here, take these," he said. His voice was soft, and Serena detected an accent she couldn't place, "I think you need them more than me."

"Thanks," said Serena taking the tissues and quickly wiping her nose.

"This is yours," he added handing Serena her now scratched phone back, "are you ok?"

"Yeah," lied Serena looking at her phone.

"Ok," he said smiling, "ok, I'll leave you alone then."

"Thanks...what's your name?" Serena called as he walked away.

"I'm Dominik."

Chapter 12: Now

Serena sat shivering in the blazing hot room she was trapped in. Her memory from the previous night was fuzzy and she couldn't remember everything; those pills she'd swallowed took more than the headache away. What she could remember made her heart pound just as loud as her head was. The slow realisation of what was happening to her and where she was, which she had felt mere days ago, had now crashed into her like a fist to the gut.

I have to think of a way out of here, she thought as she looked at the locked door in front of her.

A loud scraping sound and clank made her jump and then wince with pain as her brain threatened to push out of her skull. She watched, shivering and scared, as a hand curled around the door frame and pushed it open.

"Dom," she breathed, her shoulders instantly relaxing. He was the only person she could rely on in this hell she was confined to.

"Serena, how are you?" Dominik looked twitchy.

"I feel like shit," Serena said rubbing her arms. Her skin burned from the inside with every touch, "everything aches. My head is pounding."

"Doesn't surprise me," Dom said quietly.

"Do you have any aspirin or anything to stop my head from exploding?"

"I have something, but not aspirin," said Dominik quietly reaching into his pocket and taking out an envelope.

"Great," said Serena not noticing how uncomfortable Dominik was as he held the envelope out to her, "hand them over."

"Are you sure you want them?"

"Yeah, course I am. I need something to stop the pain. I can barely open my eyes without screaming."

"Just take one."

"I'll take two," said Serena stubbornly taking the envelope and tipping the pills out in her hand, "I'm in agony. Two will help."

Serena reached for the dirty glass with water on the table beside her bed. The glass hadn't been washed since Serena had been there, and water was only refilled once a day. She picked two pills from the four that were in the envelope and popped them into her mouth. Taking a gulp of water to wash it down, she looked over at Dominik. He was watching her oddly and then skulked out of the room. Serena shrugged and lay back down on the bed and closed her eyes.

Serena's eyes flickered as she felt someone shaking her shoulder a while later. She wasn't asleep, everything was just hazy. Her head felt furry, but the headache and shivers were gone.

"Hmm?"

"Time to get up," said a deep voice, "you have five minutes and customer then arrive."

Serena slowly opened her eyes and recoiled at the sight of Olli, the man who guarded the rooms, standing over her.

"What?" Serena mumbled.

"Get up. Get ready."

"Why?"

"Customer will be here, waiting."

"Waiting? For what?" Serena said sitting up and licking her dry cracked lips.

"For you. He has paid for you."

Serena's throat closed. Had she heard him correctly? She looked at Olli and saw he was smirking and looking Serena all over. Her skin prickled.

"But I..."

"He has paid. He will be waiting. You have five minutes to get ready."

"But Dom-"

"Now," Olli said cutting off Serena. His voice had taken a hard edge to it now. He stepped closer to Serena and loomed over her, "this is your job now. Get working."

"I'm…I'm not ready."

"Put dress on. Open legs. Easy." Olli said grinning and waving a hand in the air as he walked out of the room closing it with a thud.

Serena looked at the dress she had worn at the photo shoot then closed her eyes. Tears fell down her numb face and although her mind raced with fear, her body moved much slower. She could hear doors opening and closing and lots of male voices outside of the room; a small knock on the door made her jump into action. She grabbed the dress and pulled it on, picked up a cracked mirror and looked at her face through the grime. Looking around, Serena settled for dipping her hand in the glass of warm water, wetting her hands and smoothing her hair down a little. She wiped her shaking hands over her face pressing gently over her cracked lips. She took a sip of water from the glass – it tasted stale, but she needed some moisture on her lips and looked up at the door as it opened.

"Ready?" Olli said peering in almost gleefully.

Serena looked down at her feet, nodding her head slightly.

"Come in, this is Serena," Serena heard Olli say to someone she didn't have the courage to look at, "she is fresh."

Serena winced at the way Olli said *'fresh'*. She looked at him and realised he was relishing in her discomfort. She turned to look at the man standing next to Olli. A small slight man, with narrow dark eyes. His skin was pale and splattered with scratches and marks. He ran a bony hand through his hair as he looked at Serena.

"Oh, I like them fresh," he said puffing on a cigarette, "dark like is chocolate."

"One hour. Enjoy."

Serena watched the man nod at Olli as he walked out of the room, locking it once it slammed shut. Tears threatened to spill as she stood there trembling, her stomach spun threating to spill out. But she refused to allow this man, this predator, to see her breaking. He walked towards her smiling. Serena held her head high and although a slight breeze could have knocked her down, she locked eyes with the man.

"One hours," said the man in broken English and walking around Serena tracing his fingers along her shoulder blades, "what we do in hour girl. You will be the amazed."

Serena stood still, focusing on her breathing. The man's touch burned her skin and made her flinch.

"What's this?" said the man lifting Serena's dress leaning down so his head was in front of her thigh, his lips mere centimetres away from her skin, "a scar. I like scars."

"Birth mark," said Serena through gritted teeth. She imagined thrusting her knee into his jaw and breaking it but knew there would be no way out even if she did.

"Birth mark," he repeated standing up and facing Serena, his sour breath smothering her senses, "you like?"

Serena watched as the man brought his cigarette to his lips and watched the embers glow. Suddenly anger filled her body, "fuck you," she spat out taking a step back.

A mistake.

She had underestimated this man. Quick as a flash he moved forward making Serena lose her footing and pushed her onto the bed. In an instant he had her pinned down.

"Kurva," he spat at Serena, anger making his eyes glow, "I am going enjoy this now."

He slid her dress above her waist and drew on his cigarette, the end burning red and smouldering. Serena struggled but it was futile; he had her immobile. He smiled, looked down at her birth mark and brought the cigarette end to her thigh. Serena's eyes blazed as she felt her skin sear from the heat. As she cried out in pain, he laughed and pressed the butt against her skin harder. Serena felt dizzy from the smell of burning flesh and the shooting pain she felt along her leg. Her eyes rolled and her body softened, all fight gone. She felt the man shift on top of her, his hands moving around her body angrily, she felt him slide between her legs and allowed her mind to take her somewhere else.

Chapter 13: Now

Months passed and each day played out in the same sickening way; a steady line of men visiting and paying for Serena. Some became regulars, and some even feigned interest in her as a person, but none listened when she begged them not to do what they had come for. She was just property, a plaything for them all. It was her job and now it was her life. Serena relied more and more on the pills that were given to her to cope with everything that was happening; they helped with the physical pain she sometimes felt when a client was rough with her, and they helped with numbing her mind to the hell she found herself in.

Dominik still visited- but his visits to check in with her had gone from every other day to only once a week on what was a day 'off' she was gifted for recovery and cleansing. Each time Serena looked at Dominik he seemed less and less like the man she had fallen in love with. He couldn't meet her gaze or look at her for long. Guilt ate away at Dominik throughout the months and the days when Serena was angry and volatile with him, were the worst for him. No matter how much she loved him, Serena wasn't going to forgive him or give him any relief from what he had done to her and was still doing to her. She needed him to hurt as much as she did.

Serena sat on her bed and looked at the table; a few pills sat next to her newly filled glass of water, alongside a book that Dominik had given her for her 16th birthday a week earlier, sat unopened. In the time she wasn't being hounded by Olli, pitied by Dominik or used by the clients, Serena spent her time thinking about her friends and family, wondering if they were looking for her, wondering if they were even worried about her. Her heart ached for them. She thought about Amy and how much she wanted to hug her best friend and tell her that she was sorry for everything that went on before she was taken. Tears fell down Serena's face and her shoulders trembled as she thought of her dad, her step-mum and her little sister all at home without her.

A knock at the door made Serena wipe her eyes and look at who was walking in. It shouldn't be a client, today was a rest day. Dominik shuffled in staring at the floor and avoiding Serena's stare.

"What do you want?" she sniffed.

"It's inspection day, Serena. Bishop will be coming later on today."

"So?"

"So, you need to get yourself and the room ready."

"What happens if I don't?" Serena said anger rising in her chest.

"Come on, Serena," pleaded Dominik finally looking up at her, "you know you need to do this. If you're not ready, you won't pass the inspection, and then Bishop-"

"Bishop will do what?" said Serena scooting off the bed and walking towards Dominik who looked smaller and more uncomfortable with every step, "make my life miserable? Eh? What on earth could he do to make my life worse than it is now?"

Dominik stood silent and looked at the floor, his hands shaking a little.

"Answer me!" screamed Serena pushing Dominik but he just stumbled backwards.

"You have the rest of the morning to get ready. I'm sorry. Bishop will be here in the afternoon," he said as he stepped out of the room and shut the door.

Serena walked to the door, knowing that on inspection day it wouldn't be locked, stepped out into the corridor and looked at Dominik hurriedly walking away.

"Fuck you Dom," Serena called after him.

She watched him stop at the end of the corridor, glance over his shoulder at her showing that he heard and walk away. Standing there in the corridor, Serena looked around her. As usual on inspection day, the doors were open and unlocked and as usual the girls she had become used to seeing and speaking to were drifting around getting themselves ready for the inspection. Serena's outburst had brought many of them to their doors. Serena looked at them and nodded.

"Hi Jasmine," she said to a girl who had arrived the same day she had, "you ok?"

Jasmine nodded. She was the same age as Serena but much shorter. She had pale skin which was a stark contrast to her long dark hair and black eyes which were always darting about, as if a deer looking out for danger. She absently moved her fingers to her face and traced a scar under her right eye that she received after the first week from Olli for not being quick enough. Serena averted her eyes, the scar on Jasmine's face making her own one on her leg pulse.

"What about you Serena?" asked a plump girl who occupied a room next to Serena. She was older than Serena, but her round face made her look more innocent.

"I'm ok, Tia," shrugged Serena.

There wasn't much to say or talk about with these girls. They were all prisoners together, but it wasn't like in the movies where they could sit together and have moments of normality, looking at one another was a reminder of what was happening to each of them and there was no way of forgetting about it.

"How long have we been here?" asked Jasmine absentmindedly scratching at her arms that were dotted with needle marks.

"Must be at least 6 months now," said Serena, "I've turned sixteen in here- Dominik gave me a book for my birthday."

"I remember turning sixteen," said Tia with a small sad smile on her face, "went to London with my mates. That's when I met David."

David was Tia's guard and the one who had brought her to Bishop. Tia dropped her head and wiped away a stray tear.

"I was so stupid," she muttered as more tears fell from her face, the thumped the heel of her palm repeatedly on her forehead.

"Stop that," said Serena walking towards Tia and placing a hand on her shoulder, "it isn't your fault. It's theirs. They did this to us. We've done nothing wrong."

Tia nodded and wiped the tears off her face with the back of her hand and allowed Serena to give her shoulders a little squeeze. Jasmine joined them and patted Tia on the arm, her eyes darting along the corridor.

"I'm ok," said Tia.

"How long have you been here?" a voice from behind them made the three turn.

It was the girl who Serena had seen Lady Bishop slap hard across the face during her first inspection- Kerry.

"Two years now," said Tia.

Serena turned to face Tia again, her mouth wide open, "two years?" she said her voice small.

"Yep. I should be over all this crying shit and know everything, but I can't get over it."

"We understand," said Jasmine nodding at Serena and Kerry, "we were brought here the same time."

"I know," said Tia rubbing at her face, "but you won't be here for much longer. Damn, I need some pills."

"What do you mean?" asked Serena.

"Every month or so, Bishop brings in a new batch of girls."

"So...what happens to those already here?" whispered Kerry her eyes wide with fear.

"You don't want to know."

"We do," said Jasmine her voice cracking, "you have to tell us."

"No, ask your guards. They'll tell you."

"Tia," said Serena putting a hand on her shoulder and looking in her eyes, "You need to tell us. After what we've all been through, we need to know."

Tia breathed deeply and looked at the small crowd of girls that had now congregated together in front of her. "They...they are sold on," she said.

"What?"

"No, that can't be."

"You're lying."

"Why are you still here then?"

Serena held up her hand to the barrage of questions that were flying at Tia to silence the girls. She turned and put a hand on Tia's shoulder again.

"We need to know everything," she said quietly but sternly, "tell us. We have to be prepared."

"Ok," said Tia after a moment, "every month or so, they have a selection. Some of the men we have seen, and some others all come to inspect us and look at us all. If you're picked, then you get sold to the person who picked and paid for you. It's like a catalogue. Bishop has a catalogue of us all- pictures, ages, where we are from- all that. He shows it to his customers and then they buy us. We are his collection."

A silence fell amongst the group as the reality of something much worse than they'd already experienced loomed over their futures. Serena felt her pulse quicken and a knot formed in her chest. She closed her eyes and pressed her hand against her forehead. The throbbing headache she'd kept at bay with the pills was back.

"So," said Serena quietly, "you're telling us that where we are isn't the final stop?"

"No, this is like the holding section."

"Why are you still here then?" asked Jasmine.

Tia looked at the ground, her face turning red, "I've never been picked. Bishop can't sell me, but he knows his regular clients will pay to use me – so I'm still here."

A small murmur spread amongst the girls in the corridor and eventually grew into sobs and panic. Tia retreated to her room, no longer wanting to answer questions or speak to anyone. Some of the other girls followed suit and returned to their rooms. Serena stood in the corridor with Jasmine and Kerry. They looked at one another in shock.

Chapter 14: Now

Standing outside of her room, with Dominik beside her, Serena was overcome with a sudden nervous urge to laugh at how unreal her situation had become. She was one of about a dozen or so girls who were standing in the corridor to attention, like soldiers waiting for a commander to come and inspect them. Some of them she knew, and others were brand-new faces. *A new batch of girls.* Serena thought sullenly to herself. Almost every girl had a male guard, or chaperone (as they believed they were) standing next to them to attention, and Serena realised as she looked at them, that they looked just as scared and nervous as the girls did.

She rolled her eyes and stifled a laugh. Dominik looked at her, eyebrows raised in panic.

"What?" he whispered.

"Nothing," said Serena not matching Dominik's hushed tones. She turned to look at him, "we all look ridiculous, don't we?"

"Face forward," he hissed knowing Bishop could arrive at any moment.

"I know why us girls are scared," Serena waved her arms around, motioning to the others in the corridor, "and we know our punishment, but why are you *men* looking so frightened?"

Serena's lack of discretion had caught the attention of everyone in the corridor. Dom shot her a look.

"Be quiet Serena, you'll get us all in trouble."

"What are you scared of?" Serena snapped at Dominik.

"Shut up, bitch," snarled David from her right, Tia's guard.

Serena looked, Tia caught her eye and shot her a pleading look.

"What are all you big, strong men afraid of?" Serena pressed again.

"Be quiet," said another chaperone, "control your girl Dominik."

"Serena, please," said Dominik.

"We may be objects for sex to you all," Serena continued, anger rising at how her life was unravelling, "but you're all the bitches, not us."

An intake of breath all around, made Serena realise she had hit a nerve. A slight giggle escaped from Jasmine standing across from Serena, but before she could wink or smile at Jasmine, her guard Stefan, red faced, turned on her. Jasmine's face whipped to the side and a cry escaped from her bloodied lips as she lost balance and crumpled in a heap to the floor.

"Quiet bitch," he said his hand turning as red as Jasmine's face.

"Don't touch her!" yelled Serena as she ran to Jasmine's side, holding the crying girl in her arms.

"You," Stefan said, grabbing a handful of Serena's hair and pulling her to her feet, "you bitch." Then turning to Dominik, "control her."

"I'm sorry," said Dominik moving to take the struggling Serena back.

"Fuck you," said Serena looking at Stefan in the eyes, she spat at him, "fuck you all."

Serena watched as a momentary look of shock appeared on Stefan's face, and then shuddered when the expression quickly turned into a sneer. She saw his fist raise above his shoulder in slow motion, ready to slam into her. Serena held her breath and closed her eyes readying herself for the impact.

"Stop," boomed a voice to her side.

Serena opened her eyes and saw Bishop standing there glaring at the scene.

"Let her go. Now."

Serena felt the grip on her hair loosen and as she fell forwards, her legs now jelly, Stefan flashed her a look of pure hatred and pushed her towards Dominik. Serena stumbled towards him; he had stopped midway to her at the sound of the deep voice.

"What is all this chaos?" demanded Bishop as he stepped into the corridor, arms folded across his broad chest.

Serena looked over at Jasmine and Stefan and saw that he was red in the face but had picked up Jasmine from the floor and now stared down at it as if his life depended on it. He winced as Bishop walked closer to them.

"What is going on?" Bishop asked again barely being able to control his anger.

"That bitch- she meddled in my business with my girl," said Stefan looking at Serena.

"You slapped her, she was only laughing," hissed Serena.

"Quiet," snapped Bishop. Even his voice made her shrink back, "Dominik, get her in her room. Wait for me in there. I must finish this inspection."

Dominik nodded as he led Serena towards her room and closed the door once they were inside.

"Stand straight," she heard Bishop say to Jasmine, "Stefan, get her cleaned up. I don't want bruises on her face when they come to collect her. You can punish her later."

"Yes, Bishop," nodded Stefan leading Jasmine into her room, a tight grip on her shoulder making her yelp out in pain.

Serena turned to Dominik anger still soaring through her veins, "what the fuck Dom?"

"Shut up Serena," barked Dominik. His sudden outburst of anger towards her made her step back, "you started all that. Jasmine deserved that slap."

"What?"

"And you're lucky that Bishop came when he did, otherwise Stefan would have beaten you too. And he would have every right to."

"Every right?" asked Serena her eyes widening, "none of you have *any* right to keep us here or *touch* us or treat us like this. Don't talk to me about rights, Dom. I was protecting her, no one else was going to."

"It's not your job."

"Bullshit," spat Serena, her anger returning in full force, "any of you *men* out there could have helped Jasmine. None of you did, so I stepped in."

"Why did you?" asked a voice from behind Dominik.

Dominik spun around and his face paled and dropped. Serena saw that Bishop had entered her room. Bishop stood there, face stern and barely controlling anger.

"Why did you help her?" he asked again.

"She needed help, Stefan, he slapped her," said Serena, "and she needed someone to step in for her."

"That is not your job."

"I had to."

"You wanted to protect her? From Stefan?" asked Bishop walking towards Serena.

His sheer size dwarfed Dominik who was now stepping back towards the door. Bishop waved his trunk of an arm in the air.

"Dominik, leave."

Serena looked past Bishop and saw Dominik scurry out of the room, fear now taking over her where anger and bravado once was. Bishop kept his eyes on Serena.

"Serena, sit down." Serena did as she was told. "Tell me why you wanted to protect her."

Serena gripped her bedsheet with her sweaty hands and looked up at Bishop. There was a look of genuine intrigue hidden among the anger and Serena's shoulders dropped a little.

"She was hit for no reason. It wasn't fair. He is so big, and she is so small, someone had to help her."

"Why you?"

"Why not? No one else was going to help."

"Are you not scared of the guards?"

"Sometimes," said Serena suddenly feeling tired and cold, "I would rather they hit me than her. She's so small."

"What about the others?"

"Are you asking if I would I have stepped in if it was them?"

"Yes," said Bishop folding his arms and tilting his head.

"Yeah, I think I would have," said Serena after a moment of thought, "I know I'm not the oldest, or the one who has been here the longest, but I can't stand by and see this. What you are all doing to us, is wrong, we should be free."

Serena held her breath, the last comments had made Bishop's jaw tighten and she knew she had pushed the boundaries of what Bishop would normally accept, but she needed to get it off her chest.

"You won't be free. But you can make what time you are with us, better for all the girls. Would you do that?"

"Do what?"

"Help us prepare the girls and help us look after the girls."

Serena said nothing.

"What if I said, if you help the girls, like a...a sister, I will make life easy for you."

"How?" whispered Serena, her voice scratched at her tightening throat.

"Less...clients for you."

Serena's eyes widened and Bishop smiled.

"You become big sister, a *Sestra*, for the girls- keep them doing what they should, look after them, and help the guards get them ready for clients. And in return for your work, and loyalty and *obedience*, you will have less clients."

Serena's mind filled rapidly with what Bishop had just said. She could help the girls. But then she would be *working* for him. She could have less men visit her room. But she would be *working* for him. She could look after them and make sure they weren't beaten. But she would be *working* for him. Serena stood to face Bishop, shrugged her shoulders slightly and took a deep breath.

"Sestra?" she said.

Bishop smiled and nodded.

"No more beatings for the girls?"

"Only when they deserve it."

"Less clients for me?"

"Yes."

"Sestra," Serena repeated and extended a shaking small hand.

"Yes, sister," said Bishop taking her hand and shaking it, "welcome Sestra."

Chapter 15: Then

Serena watched her dad and step-mum flutter around the room looking for keys and jackets and wallets. She held her little sister in her arms and stroked her thick dark hair.

"Serena," said her dad patting his jacket to make sure his wallet and phone were in there, "you have the number?"

"Yes," said Serena rolling her eyes, "in my phone and on the notepad."

"Call us if you need anything," added her step-mum walking up to Serena and giving her sister, Danika, a kiss.

"I will."

"No messing about Serena," warned her dad.

"I won't."

"We're relying on you to look after your little sister, ok?"

"Ok, don't worry, dad," said Serena putting down her now squirming sister on the floor and watching her run into the living room, "trust me, I won't let anything happen to her, ok? It's just a couple of hours."

"The girls will be fine," said her step-mum, Katalina pulling Serena's dad towards the front door, "come on, Anu, we'll be late if we don't leave now."

Serena's dad looked at his wife, then at each of his daughters in turn, and smiled. He nodded and began walking out of the house.

"Bye bye daddy," called Danika from the living room who had found her favourite spot on the swivel chair near the window.

"Bye princess, love you," came the reply, "bye Serena."

"See ya dad," said Serena, "happy anniversary. Enjoy your night out."

"Call us if you need anything."

"Bye," said Serena rolling her eyes and shutting the door.

Serena locked the door and turned to face her little sister. She sighed; she was meant to be out with Dominik tonight but was forced cancel as soon as her dad asked her to look after Danika. She was going to lie to her dad about going out, she wasn't telling anyone about Dominik just yet, so it just made sense to cancel rather than try to explain why she couldn't look after her sister; that would just lead into another in a long line of recent arguments with her dad.

Danika was almost 5 years old and a handful. The age gap between them wasn't easy on Serena, especially after her parents' divorce and her dad finding someone else so quickly. Her mum had been fine with it, but Serena felt she'd not had enough time to adjust to her new step-mum before she had to compete for her dad's attention with a new-born.

She loved Danika to bits but sometimes she just needed space, and quiet.

"Right, monster," she said to her sister who had been spinning on the chair and was now looking quite dizzy, "what do you want to do?"

"Film, please," said Danika her legs kicking out in excitement as Serena stopped the chair and tickled her.

Serena looked at her watch.

"It's a bit late for a film, Dani," said Serena, "maybe some cartoons before bed?"

"Yay," said Danika, then placing her hands on her hips and tilting her head, she added, "my name is Danika, not Dani."

Serena rolled her eyes and picked up the TV remote. As well as having the same curly hair as her step-mum, Danika also picked up on Katalina's insistence in calling Danika by her full name. Serena preferred Dani, and always tried to use it, but was corrected by her family.

"Come sit with me, Danika," she said patting a space on the sofa next to her, "one episode before bed, ok?"

'Ok," said Danika yawning and snuggling into Serena's arms.

Serena kissed the top of her sister's head. She picked her phone out of her pocket and smiled; Dominik had left her a few text messages. It had been a few months since she'd met Dominik in the park and things were going great with him; he was more mature than Cal and the other boys at her school and he didn't demand anything from her. Dominik was sweet, caring and always put Serena first. He hadn't pushed Serena for anything physical and was happy enough to spend any time they had, just talking and laughing and flirting.

Serena, had in fact, been the one to instigate their first kiss. She smiled, thinking of that kiss; it was in the park they first met at, and they were on the swings next to one another laughing and talking about school. Serena jumped off the swing and Dominik followed her lead but stumbled. She pulled him up and before she knew it, she was in his arms. They looked into each other's eyes, lips inches from one another and she felt a jolt of something exciting run through her body. She leaned in and kissed Dominik. He kissed back wrapping his arms around her and pressing their bodies together. It had been amazing.

Serena smiled and unlocked her phone to read the messages:

Hey. How are you? Sorry we can't meet up today, but I understand. xx

Give us a call or whatever when you get the chance. xx

Serena thumbed a reply:

Hey, sorry about tonight again. I couldn't get out of looking after Dani. Miss you. X

That's ok, miss you too. So, what you doing right now?

Watching Paw Patrol (blah) with Dani, she's almost asleep.

How old is she?

4. She'll be 5 in a few months.

Sweet. Bit of an age gap?

Yeah, dad remarried, and they have a little girl now.

Your half-sister then?

I guess. I just think of her as a sister. She's so cute- she has her thumb in her mouth and is trying to stay awake.

When is her bedtime?

About now. I'm going to put her to bed once this episode is done.

Aw, you're a good sister.

Yeah, sometimes.

Why, sometimes?

Sometimes she's just so annoying. I can't concentrate on my work.

Have you spoken to your dad about it?

Ha! He would hate that I'm moaning. Dani is perfect in his eyes. I think sometimes he wishes I was with my mum instead of him.

I'm sure that's not true. Don't you get on with your dad?

Most of the time I do. We've been arguing loads recently. He just doesn't get me. I guess that's just typical though-kids and parents just don't get on.

But you're perfect too ;)

Serena smiled at the message and looked over at Danika now fully asleep next to her. She turned off the TV and shifted in her seat.

She's asleep. I'm going to take her to bed now. I'll call after?

Yeah sure. Speak in a bit. x

Grinning at the last message, Serena put her phone down and scooped up her little sister. Danika stirred.

"Ssh" said Serena, "bedtime Dani."

Danika opened her little eyes and looked at Serena, "Danika, not Dani." Then closed her eyes again.

"Ok," said Serena laughing softly as she walked up the stairs.

Ten minutes later and after two bedtime stories, Serena was downstairs and in the kitchen. She licked her dry lips and opened the fridge. As she grabbed a can of Sprite a recently opened bottle of wine caught her eye. Serena grabbed the bottle, took a long swig from it, and placed it back in the fridge. She giggled to herself as she felt the bubbles rise up from her throat and let out a burp.

Moving back to the living room, Serena looked at the clock; 8pm, she still had at least two hours before her parents would come back. She picked up her phone and dialled.

"Hey you."

"Hi. Is your sister in bed now then?"

"Yup, all tucked up. I'm bored now."

"No homework?"

"Can't be arsed. Nothing on TV either. What you up to?

"Nothing, wondering what to eat."

Serena bit her lip, "want to come over?"

There was a silence on the other end for a moment longer than Serena felt comfortable with.

"Come over?" came Dominik's voice, sounding nervous.

Serena smiled, "yeah grab some food and bring it over."

"What about your sister?"

"She's asleep and parents won't be back for a while. So?"

Serena waited for a reply, her skin felt hot, and she was biting her nails again.

"Uh, yeah ok," said Dominik. Serena smiled and let out her breath slowly. "I'll bring pizza?"

“Perfect,” said Serena.

“See you soon.”

Serena squealed as she ended the call. What was she doing? Sensible, boring Serena was doing something bold and rebellious. She was excited. She looked at her reflection in the blank TV screen.

“Shit,” she said running a hand over her hair, “I need to sort my face out.”

A few minutes later, Serena stood at the kitchen counter tapping her fingers. She’d applied some make-up, brushed her hair, changed out of her baggy T-shirt and leggings into a pair of shorts and a tank top. She was nervous and looked at the fridge again. After a short pause she opened the fridge, picked up the bottle of wine and poured herself a large glass, gulping half of it down before she even got to the living room.

Feeling a little light-headed, she picked up her phone. She was desperate to call Amy and tell her all about Dominik and that he was coming over, but she promised Dominik that she wouldn’t tell anyone about him until he was ready to. She sighed, put the phone down and waited.

** ** **

Serena listened to Dominik’s heartbeat as she rested her head on his chest. They sat cuddled up for a little while after eating pizza and sharing another glass of wine together; music played, and they sat in a comfortable silence.

"This is nice," she slurred slightly, shifting her leg so it crossed over his lap a little.

"Yeah, it is," said Dominik his hands tracing up and down her arm, making goosebumps appear.

"Dom, can I ask you something?"

"Sure."

"Why haven't you made a move on me yet?"

Dominik stopped stroking her arm and lifted Serena's chin to face him: an odd expression on his face; not amused, not annoyed but a mix. He looked at her and smiled.

"I'm happy to go as fast or as slow as you want. I'm happy to wait, I'm not desperate like other guys."

"Oh," said Serena feeling a twinge of something close to rejection.

"Not that I don't want to," said Dominik giving her thigh a squeeze, "I just think when you've found someone special, like I have, waiting isn't an issue. I care for you."

Before Serena could answer, Dominik leaned down and kissed her. She kissed back, hard. Her hands stroking his face, neck and moving down to his hips and legs. She felt him take a sudden intake of breath at her touch and her hands pressed against his growing stiffness through his jeans. Dominik moaned. Serena stopped kissing and slowly moved towards the floor, her fingers finding his zip.

"Serena," he said breathlessly, "you don't have to."

"I know," she whispered, "I want to."

"That's not what I came here for," he said looking at her on her knees in front of him.

"I know," repeated Serena unzipping Dominik's jeans and grabbing onto him, "I want to."

Chapter 16: Then

Serena looked at the large envelope that was addressed to her dad, turning it around in her hands she felt panic rising in her stomach.

"Earth to Serena, are you even listening?"

Serena looked over at Amy. They were both holding their termly reports in their hands and were walking out of the school gates. Amy was talking and, as usual, Serena had phased her voice out.

"What?"

"I said, what does your report say?"

"Dunno, haven't opened it yet."

"I've opened mine already."

"It's addressed to my dad," said Serena getting frustrated with Amy.

"So? Why don't you open it?"

"What does yours say?" Serena said ignoring her friend's question.

"Just the usual 'talks too much and is coasting by'. I'm going to pass my exams so that's all I want. Doesn't matter if they aren't top grades."

"But you could get top grades if you wanted to," said Serena shaking her head in disbelief.

Amy shrugged and shoved her report into her bag, "Wow, you sound like my mum. Yeah, I could do well but getting top grades isn't everything. You need life experiences too," she pointed to a group to their left, "I'm going to Alice's place to hang. You coming?"

"No," said Serena who felt her phone buzz for the third time since leaving the school building. She knew it was Dominik.

"Come on," said Amy dropping her shoulders and tilting her head, "it'll be fun, Alice has some beer and the lads have weed. You never come out anymore. Stop being so boring."

"I'm not being boring," Serena said through gritted teeth, "I just don't want to hang with Alice and them. They are so immature, and I've got better things to do."

"Like what?" challenged Amy.

"I dunno, just anything is better than hanging with that lot."

Amy looked at Serena, her hands on her hips. Things between her and Serena were getting worse. Since Cal. Amy thought that Serena still blamed her for the photos, but Serena had forgotten all about Cal, now that she was with

Dominik. She wanted to spend every waking minute with him and found her friends at school irritating and shallow. She couldn't tell Amy about Dominik, even though she desperately wanted to, but she also knew the kind of sleazy comments Amy would make about Serena being in a relationship. And Serena didn't want to hear all that- she and Dominik were above all that.

"Serena, what's up with you lately? You don't share anything with me anymore," said Amy a hint of sadness in her voice.

"I just don't want to hang out with them anymore. I've outgrown the idiots in our year."

"Does that include me?"

Serena looked at Amy properly; she looked genuinely upset, and Serena longed to tell her everything.

"Hey," shouted Alice as the group of teens began walking away from Amy and Serena, "you bitches coming?"

Amy looked at Alice and back at Serena, the hurt in her eyes turning into anger in defence, "you coming or not? Last chance, or are we not good enough for you?"

"I'm not coming, I'm going home," said Serena turning away from Amy.

"Fine," said Amy walking away, "I won't bother asking you again."

As Serena walked away, eyes stinging with tears of anger and hurt, her phone buzzed again. She picked it up: it was Dominik.

Hey, you finished school yet? Want to meet up?

Serena typed out a reply: *yeah just finished. Love to meet up. Could really do with seeing you.*

What's happened? Bad day?

Just Amy again. She's pissed me off. I'll tell you all about it later. Where did you want to meet?

Our favourite place?

Sure, see you in 5 xx

Serena smiled, stuffed her report into her bag and walked towards the park.

** ** **

Turning the key in the front door, Serena hoped that her parents wouldn't be too mad at her. She'd been out for hours and was now late home. She quietly clicked the door shut behind her and placed her bag down, taking out her report.

"Serena," called her step-mum from the kitchen, "is that you?"

“Yeah,” said Serena skipping past the living room where she could hear her dad talking on the phone, “sorry I’m a little late.”

“More than a little,” said Katalina looking at Serena and rolling her eyes, “you missed dinner.”

“Sorry,” said Serena feigning her most sorry look.

“Have you eaten?”

“Yeah, I had chips. Not hungry now. I haven’t ruined dinner, have I?”

“No,” said Katalina shaking her head and taking a sip of her wine, “one of us will take it as lunch tomorrow. Your dad’s not happy though.”

“How mad is he?” said Serena grabbing a glass and filling it with some water from the tap.

“Mad,” said a deep voice from behind Serena, making her jump.

“Dad,” she said turning around.

Her father looked like he had been running a marathon; his face was flushed and there were beads of sweat across his forehead. He stood against the kitchen doorway, arms folded, blocking it.

“Where have you been?”

“With Amy,” said Serena surprising herself at how easily she was able to lie to her dad.

“Really?”

"Yeah," said Serena walking to the fridge and opening the door to hide the blush forming on her face. She could never lie to her dad without her face giving it away.

"Well, I just got off the phone from Amy, and she said you left her ages ago."

Serena's breath caught in her throat. She closed her eyes momentarily. Amy had ratted her out.

"I was with her," started Serena, her mind working overtime looking for ways to get out of this situation. "Then I wanted to go, and she wanted to stay at Alice's, so I left on my own."

"It's so late," he said clearly not believing her.

"Sorry."

"Where did you go after?"

"I went to the library."

"Why?"

"I needed to study."

"Why not come home?" her father's questions were laced with anger and disbelief.

"I needed somewhere quiet."

Serena was desperate to get out of the kitchen, but her dad hadn't moved from the doorway. There was no way out. She looked at her step-mum for assistance, but Katalina was staring into her wine glass avoiding getting involved in their argument.

"You're lying," he said gruffly.

"No, I didn't want to go with Amy."

"I don't believe you. You and Amy have been inseparable for years. Why the sudden change?"

"Amy wasn't going to Alice's to study. There was a group of them there- boys included. I didn't want to be a part of it."

"Why didn't you come straight home?"

"I told you; I went-"

"Don't lie to me!" he shouted his face red and neck bulging, making Serena and Katalina both jump.

"I wanted to be alone," cried Serena tears welling up, "I walked around after the library."

"That's so stupid," snapped her dad throwing his arms up in the air and taking the report that was sitting on the kitchen counter, "a young girl walking around town on her own. Ridiculous. Do you want something horrible to happen to you?"

"Nothing would happen to me."

"Come on, Anu," said Katalina.

"No, Kat," said Serena's dad shrugging, "I'm right. She should've come home. I thought we raised a sensible girl. She's reckless."

"Dad, I'm sorry. I just didn't think and wanted-"

"You don't think anymore. You don't use your head. And you lie to us."

Serena looked at her dad. She didn't know what to say. There was nothing she could say to make it better- especially as she was in the wrong and especially with her dad in the mood he was in.

"Sorry."

"I don't believe you."

"Dad, I am," she pleaded.

"Please just go to your room, I don't want to see you for the rest of the evening."

Serena looked at her step-mum, tears spilling down her face. Katalina looked sorry but shook her head: she wouldn't be helping Serena out this time. Serena took a deep breath, squeezed past her dad and walked to her room.

Throwing herself on the bed, Serena screamed into her pillow and cried. Sneaking around with Dominik was not going as well as she had planned, she needed to speak to him.

Chapter 17: Then

The wind was cold, and the sky was grey as Serena waited for Dominik to arrive. She paced around the park and kept looking at her phone hoping that he'd replied to her urgent message. She hadn't slept all night, thinking of ways to get back on track with her friends and family whilst keeping Dominik happy. She was desperate to tell people about the man she loved; a realisation she had come to during the night. But she didn't want to disappoint Dominik or go ahead and tell people until he was ready. He was so sweet, and she knew she would have to be careful otherwise she would lose him.

"Come on, come on," she muttered to herself sitting down on the bench they had first met, "where are you?"

Serena looked at her phone for the fifth time that minute. Her message had been read, she saw the double tick in the corner, but still no reply.

I need to talk to you. It's important. Meet me in the park tomorrow morning. I'll be waiting.

Serena closed her eyes and concentrated on her breathing. Deep breaths slowed her heartbeat and began to clear her mind. She knew what she needed to say, and only hoped that Dominik would listen. The air around her suddenly changed and she opened her eyes. Dominik was standing there, wrapped up and frowning.

"Hey," she said suddenly all confidence dissipating from her.

"What's up Serena? Why aren't you in school?"

"You sound like my dad," laughed Serena, then stopped when she realised Dominik wasn't laughing. "Sorry, I need to talk to you, I had such a bad day yesterday and I can't face school or anyone really today. No one except you."

Dominik's face softened, he sighed and sat down next to Serena. Instantly she leaned her head in his shoulder and felt his warmth as he held her.

"What's up? It sounded urgent."

"It is, kind of," she said sitting up and facing Dominik, "it's a long story too."

"Well then let's get out of this cold," said Dominik standing and holding out a hand to her, "or at least let's walk as we talk so I can stay warm. I'm bloody freezing."

Serena laughed and nodded. Dominik wasn't from here, and although he didn't say much about his past or family or where he was from, she knew it was from somewhere in Europe and somewhere warmer than the UK.

"My house," she said holding Dominik's hand, "everyone is at work, the house is empty, we can talk there."

"Just talk," he said raising his eyebrows.

"Yeah, just talk," she said smiling.

They walked back to her house in a comfortable silence holding hands. Serena's head swam with scenarios of how today was going to pan out with Dominik: was he going to be mad? Angry? Upset? Happy? She had no clue. Glancing over to look at him, Serena realised that she could never tell what he was thinking; his face right now was neutral and the frustration from earlier was no longer visible. He was still an enigma to her.

As they entered the house, Dominik a few steps behind her, Serena called out. No answer, confirmation they were alone. She turned and smiled at Dominik and waved him into the house. Dominik tentatively stepped in, copying Serena and taking off his coat and shoes at the front door. He watched as she walked into the kitchen.

"Want a drink?" she called.

"Uh, yeah, what have you got?"

"I'm making a cup of tea for me, you want one?"

Dominik walked into the kitchen and watched Serena happily move around the kitchen, opening cupboards, grabbing mugs out and filling the kettle.

"Coffee for me, please."

"Of course," said Serena, she knew he would prefer coffee to tea, "how do you take it?"

"Black with two sugars."

Dominik watched Serena make the tea and coffee and grab out some biscuits for them to share too. She was clearly nervous but was hiding it from him through smiles and busy hands. Holding on to his coffee, Dominik followed her into the living room where they sat next to one another on the sofa. Serena took a sip of her tea and held the plate of biscuits up to offer Dominik one. He smiled- wide and forced.

"No thanks," said Dominik placing his coffee on the table, "come on Serena, talk."

Her face fell for a moment then she was back to smiling, a smaller smile now.

"Ok," she said. But then said nothing else.

"You wanted to talk, not me," said Dominik an edge to his voice, "you've skipped school for this, and I...well, just tell me what's going on, I'm worried."

"Oh, it's nothing to worry about," said Serena playing with a strand of hair that had come loose from her usual ponytail.

"Then why all the drama? Talk to me."

Serena took a deep breath, she knew that she couldn't avoid talking to Dominik any longer about what was bothering her, but she hoped that she could buy some more time. Everything that she planned to say the night before seemed to have escaped her mind and now she was drawing a blank.

"So, I had a massive argument with Amy yesterday."

"What happened?" Dominik leaned in closer to Serena, his voice softer now.

"She was asking if I wanted to go with her and the others to drink and smoke weed, and I didn't. She was angry with me, and I said I had better things to do."

Serena watched as Dominik frowned and sucked in his breath.

"Don't worry, I didn't say anything about you. But I really wanted to."

"Serena..."

"I know, I know. But Amy is my best friend and I know she would be really happy for me, and she would really like you and you'd get on. I just wanted to tell my best friend that I had met someone who made me happy."

"Serena, you know I want to keep us a secret."

"But why?"

"What did you tell her?" Dominik said avoiding the question.

"I just told her I had better things to do rather than hanging with them. They're too immature for me and I've outgrown them all."

"Including Amy?"

"No, I didn't say including Amy. But I didn't say it wasn't including her. I was just so frustrated."

"Was this before we met up last night?"

Serena nodded. She reached a clammy hand to her cup of tea, took a sip but no longer enjoyed the sweetness of it.

"What did Amy say?" he asked after an agonising minute of silence.

"She got angry and said that I was acting like I was better than them and she was pissed that I was clearly hiding something but wouldn't tell her. Dom..."

"No, Serena," said Dominik shaking his head adamantly, "I'm not ready for people to know about us."

"But why?"

"You said something about your dad in the message too?" said Dominik reaching for a biscuit and dunking into his coffee.

Serena sighed and sat back on the sofa. She curled her legs underneath and grabbed a pillow to squeeze.

"Yeah, that was bad too," she said.

"What happened with him?"

"Well, he got pissed that I came home late. He knew I wasn't with Amy when I told him I was."

"How?"

"He called Amy."

"She ratted you out?"

"No, she said I was with her for a little while but not the whole time."

"Oh."

"Yeah, so dad was mad about where I had been, I told him the library."

"Good."

"Yep, but I couldn't tell him I met someone, so I had to lie to him. Dom, it was horrible, he was so mad and so disappointed in me. I don't think he's ever been that mad before. I just wanted to tell him I was with you, with someone, and not alone."

"Don't tell him about me, please."

"Why not?" Serena pressed.

"I'm not ready yet."

"But why? It's been months now; we know each other, and I trust you."

"I don't want anyone to know about me yet."

"I want to introduce you as my boyfriend, I am happy, and you keep me safe. I want you to meet my dad."

"No."

"But why? Dom I just don't get it? What are you afraid of?"

"I'm not ready."

"Why?"

"Serena!" Dominik shouted throwing his hands in the air in frustration, "I don't want anyone to know. I have been through all this before, and it didn't end well. It's not always about you, ok? My family are strict too, they don't want me to date anyone they haven't approved first. I could get into a lot of trouble if they found out. I can't risk it. For your sake. I don't want to hurt you, but I can't risk anyone finding out. They'll make me break up with you, they'll move me away from here, they'll send me back."

"Send you back?" Serena whispered in shock at Dominik's outburst of emotion.

"Yes, back to...away from the UK. I don't want that to happen, I don't want to be without you. I...I...love you."

Dominik dropped his hands in his head and Serena stared at him breathing hard. She was in shock. He wanted to protect her. He wanted to stay with her. He *loved* her. She scooted towards him on the sofa and placed a hand on his shoulder carefully. She felt him instantly relax.

"Hey, I'm sorry I pushed too much about all this," she said caressing his hair and kissing his head, "I didn't know. I'm sorry."

"It's ok," he said his voice muffled, his face still in his hands.

'Babe," she whispered lifting his shoulders back and turning his head to face her, "I love you too."

His eyes glistened and his face softened.

"I love you," she repeated softly.

"I love you too Serena," he said kissing her gently, "I promise you can tell everyone soon, just not yet."

"Ok," said Serena breathlessly, "I'll wait until you're ready."

"You're so special," he said holding her face in his hands, "I don't want to be without you. You're my girl."

Chapter 18: Now

Serena stared into the small mirror Bishop had given her as a perk for being Sestra. Her face was thinner than she remembered it looking, and her eyes looked hollow; her hair looked less greasy although it had become frayed since arriving. She realised that working for Bishop, however sickening it was, meant that she appreciated the privileges that other girls didn't. Getting access to more soap and vitamins was worth it. She also only took two white pills a day now, the headaches and longing for them were becoming fewer and further apart. She knew that they were drugs of some sort, and she had been close to becoming addicted to them. A couple a day was enough for her to persuade the men that she wasn't a threat, but also have control over her own mind. She hid the others in a small tin that the mirror had come in. A tin Olli had forgotten to get back from her and was now hidden under a floorboard she was able to pull up under her bed.

Shouts and cries from outside of her room brought Serena back from her thoughts. She frowned and tilted her head towards to noise to decipher what was being said. In the almost 12 months she had been there, she'd picked up on some of whatever language the men spoke. She guessed it was Polish but couldn't be certain. She knew that it was an

Eastern European language but couldn't pinpoint which one. Slowly, she lifted herself off the bed and tiptoed to the door. The floor was cold on her bare feet, and Serena shivered rubbing her arms to keep herself warm.

The voices of men were raised and menacing and in between their slurs of abuse, Serena could hear pleas for mercy from the girls. Something was happening and she knew this would be time for her to step in, as Sestra. The men had been told to call her that as much as she and they hated it. She just wanted to look after the girls and knew that each time she stepped in between the men and their girls, she was stepping towards trouble. Serena cast an eye over what she was wearing- a baggy T-shirt scattered with small holes that she slept in most nights, and a pair of shorts made from cutting the legs off a pair of old tracksuit bottoms she was given. Her hand reached for the door handle- her room was no longer locked (another perk of being Sestra) and hesitated for a moment. The sound of Tia's cry shot her into action. She opened the door, stepped out to observe the commotion.

What she saw would forever be burned into her memory. Tia was laying on the floor, her hands and arms across her, protecting her face and two men, David and Olli, were standing above her. David was red faced and panting hard. He was holding a leather belt in his hand and Serena understood instantly how the deep red welts across Tia's arms and body had appeared. Olli, his arms crossed, was laughing loudly and goading David on. David raised his arm, shouted something that Serena only knew to be a curse and whipped the belt across Tia's frail body.

“Stop!” cried Serena running towards the commotion.

Neither man paid her any attention. David raised his hand again and the sound of the leather ripping into skin echoed in the corridor.

“Stop!” Serena screamed again, pushing David as his arm raised again.

She knelt down next to the sobbing Tia and held her close, feeling the heat from her wounds seeping onto her own skin.

“What doing bitch?” growled David looming over her, “get out my way.”

“You can’t hurt her.”

David laughed, “because you think you in charge?” Not waiting for a reply, he looked over at Olli, “get this suka out of my way.”

Olli reached down, no longer laughing. His eyes were filled with hatred, and he grabbed Serena roughly by the arm and yanked her away from Tia’s limp body with ease, man-handling her like a doll.

“Get back to your room,” he hissed.

“No,” said Serena struggling to free herself, “he can’t beat her.”

“She my suka, my bitch, I do what want,” called David tightening his grip on his leather belt.

“She’s done nothing wrong,” cried Serena wincing as Olli’s fingers pressed harder into her shoulders.

“She got fat like pig,” sneered David looking down at Tia and kicking her in the ribs, “she losing money and must be punished. Fat bitch.”

“Go to your room,” repeated Olli letting her go.

Serena watched Tia sob and cry, she was bruised and bloodied. She saw David’s arm raise to strike again.

“No,” she said anger flowing through her veins, “leave her alone!”

Before Olli could grab her and stop her, Serena jumped towards Tia, covering her defeated body with her own. The sting of the leather strap across her leg knocked the air from her chest. Her eyes rolled and her body tensed. The pain shooting through her body was worse than anything she had imagined. Her leg burned and began to swell instantly, Serena felt herself collapse on top of Tia.

“Serve you right,” said David grinning at the pain he had inflicted on her, “now get up and go.”

“No,” she said looking at David, her eyes streaming with tears, “I won’t let you hurt her anymore.”

“Then you will suffer too.”

David raised his hand again, his eyes wild. Another shooting pain burned through her body as the whip sliced through her t-shirt and into her skin. Serena whimpered.

"Stop," said Olli placing a hand on David's shoulder, "this is enough. We can punish her later."

David turned, ready to shout at Olli for stopping him, but then paused. His frown turned into a smile, and he looked at Serena.

"Fine," he said feeding his belt back into his jeans, "you take the pig to clean up room. Clean her and bring back ready for clients."

Serena stared back at David, refusing to move a muscle. David stared at her for a moment, looked at Tia, shrugged and turned to Olli.

"I need cigarette," he said, and they both turned and walked away, "get the little piggy cleaned."

"Come on hon," Serena whispered, picking up Tia careful not to touch the lacerated skin, "let's get you cleaned up."

** ** **

Serena looked down at her shaking fingers and breathed deeply. The past few hours had been traumatic; not only for Tia who was in severe pain and whose body was sliced from the impact of David's belting, but also for Serena who tried to help. She ignored her own injuries and focused on cleaning Tia's wounds and applying some cooling cream and antiseptic cream without hurting Tia any further. Her ears echoed with Tia's cries of pain and the image of her raw skin would not leave her mind.

Once she had cleaned up Tia, she walked her back to the room, hoping and praying that David wasn't in there waiting for them. He wasn't. She lay Tia down on her bed and stood looking at her friend who lay there whimpering and twitching with pain. Serena walked into her own room, picked up her tin and opened it; there lay about half a dozen pills that she hadn't touched. She picked up two white pills, sighed and went back to Tia. Tia needed those pills more than she did, anything to help dull the pain. Helping Tia to swallow them, Serena swore to protect the girls more, and to speak to Bishop about the men again. Not much had changed since she'd been given her role, and she needed Bishop to listen.

Leaving Tia falling asleep, her eyes glazing over from the effect of the drugs kicking in, Serena walked back to her room. She kept her head down and her hands in curled into fists thinking about what she would say to Bishop. As she walked into her now dark room and closed the door, she felt something was different about the room. The light flicked and her breath caught in her throat. Sitting on her bed was David, grinning. Serena turned to flee but bumped into someone: Olli. He blocked her escape and shook his head.

"I told you to leave David and his girl alone," he said shaking his head.

He turned, left the room and for the first time in weeks Serena heard her door lock. Heart racing, she turned back towards David.

"Your turn to be punished," he said standing, hand on his belt buckle and motioning Serena to the bed.

"Please," Serena said inching towards the bed, scared fresh from the memory of her welt on her leg, "please don't hurt me."

"Oh, I not hurt you," said David unzipping his trousers and licking his lips, "don't want to ruin beautiful chocolate skin."

Serena's eyes widening in horror of realisation of her fate as David pushed her onto the bed and climbed on top of her, pinning her underneath his body.

Chapter 19: Now

Even days after the attack, Serena could still feel her body throb in pain. David had been rough; so rough that she had bled heavily and needed extra alcohol and drugs to numb her from the pain. As he crawled off of her, David grinned, squeezed her jaw in his rough hand, his fingernails digging into her skin, and spat in her face.

"Don't ever get in my way again suka."

Serena nodded, tears falling freely.

"You know this word, suka?"

Serena nodded, her lip trembled, "it means bitch."

"Yes, good dog," he sneered tapping her face and walking out.

Dominik asked her what had happened later that evening, but Serena refused to talk. Her silence confirming her breaking spirit.

"Serena," pleaded Dominik placing a hand on her shoulder as she sat picking at her nails on the edge of the bed in a drug infused haze, "please speak to me."

"Don't touch me," Serena slurred, the hate in her voice sounded muffled even to her own ears.

"Let me help."

"I want to speak to Bishop."

"Serena, you can't-"

"I want to speak to him." Serena concentrated on trying to make her words sound clear.

"You can't."

"Bishop can help."

"He is...look let me help."

"Bishop."

"He won't see you."

"Yes, he will, I'm sestra. Get him."

"He's not...he's away."

"Away?" scoffed Serena, "like on a holiday?"

She let out a screeching laugh that made Dominik wince and rub the back of his neck. He sat next to her and frowned as she scooted away from him.

"When will he be back?" asked Serena shrugging off his hand.

"In a day or two I think."

"I'll wait."

"Serena-"

"Go away," she said turning her back on Dominik and curled up on the poor excuse of a bed she was confined to, "get out. Get out. Get out!"

The sound of the door swinging open stopped the pair from saying anything more. It was Olli, grinning.

"Out, Dominik, she has a client."

"Not today, Olli," said Dominik straightening himself up.

"Yes today. He will be here in 5 minutes."

"But Bishop said she didn't-"

"Bishop isn't here. It is happening. You can stay and watch? You like doing that?"

Olli grinned, Dominik frowned and shook his head, and Serena just sat on the bed her body beginning to tremble.

"Then out." He turned to Serena, "You- get ready."

Serena nodded and walked to her pile of party clothes she had been given to wear as Dominik was ushered out by Olli.

The next two days played out in the same way; Serena had a few moments in the morning with the girls, but not as much time as she had been promised. She made sure their injuries wouldn't stop them from performing, and then they all readied themselves with extra shots and pills for the onslaught of men. Most clients arrived after midday, some of them stinking of vodka and beer, others on their lunchbreak from work. All wanting the same thing. Serena was supposed to have fewer clients but whilst Bishop was away, Olli took it upon himself to give her extra men to please.

As she sat cleaning herself after her final client was gone, there was a knock at the door. Serena frowned, Olli never knocked on the door anymore, he revelled in walking in on the girls hoping to find them naked so he could stare. There was a knock again. Serena grabbed her t-shirt she used as her night shirt and pulled it on over her head. The door creaked open and Dominik walked in.

"What do you want?"

Dominik looked down at the ground, her brown eyes burned into his flushed cheeks.

"Bishop's back."

Serena nodded, too nervous to speak.

"I asked him if you could see him."

"Ok."

"He told me to come get you now."

"Now?"

"Yeah, now. He said he has time now."

Serena scrambled into a pair of shorts and tied her fraying hair up into a ponytail. She stood up and Dominik finally lifted his gaze towards her.

"Ready?"

"Yes," she nodded, "I'm ready."

Serena followed Dominik along to the end of the dingy corridor and to a heavy door that was clearly a way out. It was locked. Dominik knocked on the door and a face appeared in the sliding hatch. A face Serena didn't recognise as one of the guards she had become familiar with. He looked at Serena and then at Dominik, nodded and unlocked the door. The door thudded open, and Serena was temporarily blinded by the bright lights; a stark contrast to the barely lit room and corridor she had been restricted to since her arrival.

"Move," said the man motioning his head towards a series of doors, "he is waiting."

Bishop sat at his substantial desk frowning at Serena and Dominik as they walked in. Dominik stood exactly where he had the first time Serena had met Bishop many months earlier like a terrified boy.

"Bishop," said Serena, "I need to-"

"Speak only when you are spoken to!" boomed Bishop standing so suddenly that Serena took a step back, "have you forgotten my rule? Do I need to remind you again?"

Serena clamped her mouth shut, looked at the floor, and shook her head. The memory of the sting of his slap returned to her cheek.

"Good," said Bishop sitting back down, "Dominik leave us."

Dominik nodded and walked briskly out of the room, not even glancing back at Serena.

"Sit," Bishop said to Serena motioning to a chair.

Serena did as she was told. The cool soft leather of the chair felt like heaven against her bruised and aching thighs.

"Now," said Bishop leaning back in his throne-like chair, "what did you want to see me about?"

Serena swallowed. She had planned what she was going to say- every last word of it- but now, sitting in front of Bishop, with his eyes boring into her, being faced with telling him about David, Serena wondered if it was the right move. What would happen if he and Olli found out she has spoken to Bishop about them? Serena faltered.

"Well?" urged Bishop, "I don't have all day. I have a business to run."

Serena nodded and prayed that her voice didn't betray her fear, "well you and I agreed that I would look after the other girls."

"As sestra, yes."

"Yes, sestra. Well, I tried looking after Tia but David was beating her with his belt-"

"Yes, he would have good reason to do this."

"No, he just said she was getting fat."

"Yes, Tia is fat. No one is buying her- they just want to fuck her."

"But he was beating her."

"So?"

"I thought our agreement meant they couldn't-"

"No," cut in Bishop his voice hardening, "our agreement is you look after them, and you don't have many clients."

"Yes, but he was beating her. I had to stop him."

"Why are you telling me all this?" said Bishop frowning and showing his irritation by tapping his fingers on the table.

"Well, you said the guards couldn't hurt me...and David, well he came into my room after and..." Serena's eyes welled up.

"He punished you?"

"He raped and beat me."

If the word *rape* had made Bishop uncomfortable, he didn't show it. He rubbed his eyes and sighed, "what do you want me to do girl?"

“Just make them stop. Please.”

“They are the guards; I cannot monitor what they do all of the time.”

“But if you could-”

“Tell them not to hurt you anymore?”

“Not just me, the others too. He used a belt. Tia has scars.”

“So?” said Bishop standing and walking towards where Serena sat.

“Scars are...they...” Serena felt less and less like she was helping, “scars are ugly. The clients don’t like them.”

Serena could feel bile rising from her stomach as she said the words. She hated what she was saying but realised that it was the only way to get through to him, appeal to Bishop’s sense of business.

“The clients...they won’t want to pay for her,” she added her voice quiet.

“That is true,” said Bishop and clapped his hands making her jump, “ok sestra, I will talk to the men to go easy on the girls...and you.”

“Thank you,” said Serena looking at her entwined fingers in her lap, “I just-”

“But how will you repay me?”

“Huh?” Serena snapped her head up and looked at Bishop wide eyed. He loomed over her eyebrows raised, “I...I don’t understand.”

“I do this for you,” he said waving his hand in the air, “what will you do for me?”

Serena stared speechless feeling her skin begin to itch.

“I have an idea,” he said stepping closer to Serena, his thumbs hooked into his belt buckle, “I think we can find a way.”

Serena’s throat closed and she felt faint as she watched Bishop rub himself inches from her. She could smell his musky odour and as she looked up at his face, she saw the delight in his eyes.

“Now this,” he said unzipping his trousers and reaching his other hand out to grab the back of her head, “this is how you can thank me.”

Chapter 20: Now

Serena stumbled into the hallway hearing the door to Bishop's office shut heavily behind her. She felt sick. As she stopped and leaned on the wall, she swayed retching. The man who had been guarding the door grabbed her and pushed her.

"Not sick here suka. Move."

He shoved her roughly through the open doorway and into the darkness of the familiar foul-smelling corridor her room was situated in. Over the months she had learned some of the words the men used to describe the girls; suka was bitch. Not the worst thing she had been called. As she fell to the cold hard ground, she heard him laugh and lock the door behind her.

"Fuck you," she whispered as she heaved herself off the floor using the cracking wall for support.

She shuffled towards her room hearing the painfully haunting sounds of grunting coming from many of the rooms; the evening clients were starting to arrive.

"Move," said a deep voice behind her pushing her into the wall.

It was Olli, and he was escorting clients to and from rooms. He looked at Serena's pale face and laughed gleefully. As he ushered a client into Jasmine's room and shook Steffan's hand he turned to look at her again.

"Get ready *sestra*," he said spitting out the last word for emphasis, "you have a new client coming soon."

"What?" said Serena shaking her head, "but I don't get clients-"

"You're wrong. This one is special."

"Special?"

"He requested you. He never fucked a dark girl before. He wants you."

Serena recoiled at Olli's crude words and rushed into her room. She didn't like being out in the corridor when the clients came, preferring to avoid their stares and jeering in the solace of her own room. In here she could cope with the scale of what was happening and the reality she now lived in. Just.

Slamming the door hard, Serena leaned against it, closed her eyes and breathed deeply trying to ground herself and calm her nerves. She jumped as Olli shoved the door open and grinned at her.

"He is coming, get ready."

Serena nodded.

"You look like shit," laughed Olli, "I give you extra minutes to fix it."

Serena walked to the pile of clothes she was expected to wear, the only thing cleaner than the rest of the clothing was a little black and red leather dress that hugged at her body and barely covered anything. She grimaced, she hated this dress, it was the worst outfit out of the whole collection. Stepping into the dress she pulled it over her hips and around her breasts. She slipped on a pair of 6-inch heels many clients liked her wearing and undid her hair, allowing the strands of thick black hair to drape over her deep chestnut shoulders. She picked up the lipstick that was given to her to wear and applied it lightly on her cracked lips, she patted on some dark eyeshadow with her fingertip and eyeliner to make her eyes look dramatic; a look she would never have been seen dead wearing in the life she was ripped from. As she swallowed two of her pills, she heard the door open and turned to see who this new client was. Her breath left her body in an instant.

"Hi beautiful," said a tall thin man looking her, a nervousness in his voice.

Serena stared open mouthed at the man standing in front of her smiling.

"I have been told no names, so you call me Martim."

"Martim," Serena repeated, her throat hoarse.

"Mmm yes I like that," he said moving closer to her, his smile widening, "wow, you beautiful."

Serena forced a smile and took a step closer to him, "you're a...a...police officer?" she looked at what he was wearing in surprise.

He looked down at his uniform and grinned, puffed out his chest and nodded, "you like a man of law? A police?"

Serena's mind raced and she grabbed at his arms, "please, help us," she cried her body shaking, "please help. They've kidnapped us. You can help. Please help me!"

Martim's smiled disappeared.

"Please," said Serena feeling panic overflowing, "help us get out of here. We don't want to be here, they've taken us. Please."

"Look girl," said Martim frowning and prying Serena's fingers off his arm, "I don't help you."

"You can. Please help us get out of here, bring more police. Please help me. Please. You have to- you're police. Please."

Serena tried to lunge at Martim who had struggled to create some distance between them but fell back suddenly. As she looked up at Martim in shock she saw his eyes blazing and his hand raised. The burning sensation of a hard slap spread across her face. She realised that Martim wasn't here to help her. She felt sick.

"You...you're one of them," she stuttered shuffling herself towards the wall furthest away from him.

Martim walked in silence towards her bedroom door. He knocked and waited for Olli to open it, never taking his eye off Serena cowering on the floor. She strained to hear what was being said between the two men in hushed voices. Olli glared at Serena, shook his head and walked away.

“What did you say?” said Serena quietly.

“Business talk,” said Martim turning and closing the gap between them in two easy long strides, “I want for you.”

“Please don’t do this,” she pleaded as he grabbed her arms and pulled her roughly to her feet, “please, you’re a policeman. You’re supposed to protect. A good guy.”

“Oh, I am good,” he said dragging her to the bed, “I show you how good.”

“Please, no,” whimpered Serena.

She watched Martim unbuttoning his shirt, unzipping his trousers and rubbing at his groin in pleasure. He grinned and climbed on the bed, reached his hand out to stoke her leg. Serena closed her eyes, allowing tears to fall down her cheeks. She bit her lip to feel something she was in control of as he pushed her legs apart and pressed his body against hers.

Zipping up his trousers moments later, Martim stroked Serena’s legs and smiled, a hint of affection across his face, “How was that beautiful? Good?”

Serena stared at the wall behind his head and didn’t move. Her body felt alien.

“Never had dark girl before,” said Martim walking towards the door, “dark was good.”

He knocked on the door, signalling to Olli that he was done. Olli opened the door, and the echoes of another evening with clients drifted into the room. He looked at Serena and then smiled at Martim.

"Satisfied, sir?" he asked.

"Da," said Martim leaving the room, "I return, she likes *politzya*."

The two men laughed as they closed the door and walked away, leaving Serena curled up on the bed.

Sleep she commanded herself, *you just need to sleep.*

But the incessant noise from outside rattled through her aching mind. She crawled off the bed, one hand rubbing at her temple, and moved to her secret stash of pills. Moving as quickly as she could, she grabbed another two pills swallowing them dry. Serena sat at the back on the bed, her head in her hands.

"He was a policeman," she sobbed all hope of salvation leaving her.

Serena wasn't sure how long she had been sat on the edge of her bed, but the pills she had taken were starting to work their magic. She felt fuzzy and relaxed. The sudden sound of her bedroom door scraping open made her look up; her eyes struggled to focus on the shapes in front of her.

"Serena," she recognised the voice as Bishop's. She blinked trying to focus.

"Mmmhh," she managed.

"Olli," she heard Bishop say.

She watched as the large shape of Olli walked up to her and stood in front of her, grinning. "Hey kurva."

Serena recognised the word as 'whore', she'd been called it many times before and Dominik had finally confirmed what it meant. She looked up at Olli, his face all blurry, and blinked. The rush of ice-cold water being thrown in her face made Serna gasp. Her head cleared almost instantly, and she wiped at her face and coughed. Olli laughed and walked back to where Bishop was standing.

"Serena," said Bishop again taking a step closer, "are you listening?"

"Yes," she mumbled blinking.

"I hear you have been making trouble."

"What? No, I haven't. I promise," said Serena confused and panicked. She stood shakily, "I've not done anything wrong."

"Well, that isn't what my friend here said."

Serena blinked, cursing herself for taking the extra pills. Her eyes widened when she saw that alongside Bishop and Olli, stood Martim frowning.

Her legs wobbled.

"Yes," said Bishop, "you shouldn't have tried to cause trouble."

"I'm sorry but..."

"You will be," laughed Olli triumphantly.

"Serena, I am disappointed. I thought we had deal."

"We do, Bishop, I just-"

"Your betrayal must be punished."

"But I am loyal."

"Olli," said Bishop turning and walking out of the room, "please see that our Sestra here learns her lesson. Maybe our guest would like to join you? Your visit today is free, of course."

Martim nodded at Bishop and followed Olli into the room.

"Bishop, please," called Serena standing with her arms limp at her sides. Her legs threatening to give way.

She watched Martim and Olli walk towards her, both grinning and eyes wild with excitement.

"Guests first," said Olli motioning towards Serena.

"Please," whispered Serena as she watched his tight fist pull back and before everything went dark.

Chapter 21: Then

"Slut!" screamed Serena lashing out her hand and finding the soft cheek of her best friend again.

"Bitch!" screamed back Amy as she grabbed a handful of Serena's long hair.

Serena and Amy punched and kicked at one another in rage as a growing number of students gathered around them, all cheering on the two fighting girls.

"Fucking bitch! I hate you!" hissed Serena as she and Amy fell to the floor in a heap.

"Fight! Fight! Fight!" chanted the crowd, many of whom had taken out their phones to record the battle between best friends.

Cal pushed his way through the crowd, "what's going on?"

"Cal!" squealed Alice in delight, "It's Amy and Serena, they're fighting."

"What? Why?" said Cal standing at the front of the crowd with Amy and Serena scrapping at his feet.

"Serena's a snake," said Alice grinning and filming the fight on her phone, "it's great, isn't it?"

"No," said Cal stepping forward and reaching out to separate the girls, "you two stop, come on help me Alice-ouch!"

Cal stumbled back as an elbow belonging to a fired-up Amy connected with a crack on his jaw.

"Ow, fuck, Amy! Stop!"

But the two girls weren't listening. Their wild eyes matched and the hatred for each other burned strong. They weren't going to stop beating the hell out of each other.

"What's going on?!" boomed a voice from behind, making Cal flinch and Alice quickly pocket her phone.

Mr Scott, the head of year came hurtling through the crowd followed by another teacher. Although he was a short man, and usually mild-mannered, everyone knew not to mess with him if he was angry. The crowd quickly dispersed leaving Mr Scott and the other teacher to pull apart the struggling girls.

"I said what's going on?" Mr Scott shouted again.

"Alice and Serena were fighting," said Alice breathlessly.

"And you thought you'd stand there and just watch?"

Alice blushed, looked at her feet and began shuffling away.

“I tried to stop them,” said Cal his face already swelling.

“I hate you!” screamed Serena at Amy trying to reach her.

“Snitch!” retorted Amy trying but failing to get out of the grasp of the teacher who had come with Mr Scott.

“Amy, Serena, stop it now!” boomed Mr Scott, forcing the girls to look at him, “come with me right now.”

“But she started it,” said Amy panting heavily.

“I don’t care. Come with me. My office. Right now.”

** ** **

Serena sat sullen looking out of the window, everything appearing and disappearing in an instant, her hair a mess and her face pulsing from the punches and scratches Amy had showered her with. She bit her lip, seething.

“Are you even listening to me?”

Her dad’s voice from the driver’s side of the car snapped her back into reality.

“Yes, I am listening,” she said stubbornly.

“I can’t believe I’ve had to come and collect you from school,” he ranted staring out of the window, the afternoon traffic was starting to build. “And for fighting! With Amy! What the hell were you thinking?”

“Sorry.”

“Sorry? I don’t need to hear sorry, Serena, what in hell happened?”

“Nothing.”

“You and Amy have been best mates for years. What happened between you two?”

“Nothing.”

“Nothing?”

“I don’t want to talk about it ok?”

“Well, I don’t care what you want. We’re having this conversation whether you like it or not.”

“It’s not a big deal,” lied Serena remembering Amy’s poisonous remarks that led to the fight.

“Three days exclusion is a big god-damned deal.”

Serena didn’t say a word.

“You’re in year 11 now, exams are coming up, and this is what you do?” Serena’s dad continued to rant, voice raised, not stopping to allow her to talk, “you’ve been off for a while now. With me, with Katalina. And now with Amy. What’s going on?”

He looked over at Serena who sat staring intently out of the window, avoiding the barrage of questions, stone silent.

"Serena?"

"What?"

"I said what's going on?" his voice softened as he watched his daughter look out the window and wipe away a tear, "talk to me."

"Nothing's going on, I'm fine. I don't want to talk about it."

Her dad sighed and looked back at the road. They sat in silence until they reached home. Serena followed her dad into the house and as she turned to walk up the stairs to the solace of her bedroom, she felt his hand on her shoulder.

"Serena," his voice was gentle, and concern darkened his features, "what happened between you two?"

Serena opened her mouth to repeat her lie but caught the look in her dad's eyes. She shrugged her shoulders and looked at the floor, "we had an argument."

"Well, I know that silly," he said guiding her gently to the living room, "what I'm asking is what was it all about? How did an argument turn so nasty?"

"She...look it's done now; can we just leave it?"

"I need to understand. I don't need details; I just need to understand better."

Serena stared at her fingernails and bit her lip.

"Please, Serena."

After a moment of silence, Serena nodded and spoke, "Amy got caught in the sixth form toilets messing around with someone."

"With who?"

"Not saying."

"Was she smoking?"

"No."

"Was she doing drugs?"

"No."

"So, what was she doing?"

"Dad, please."

"Ok, ok," said her dad frowning, "go ahead. No more interruptions."

"Amy got caught in the toilets. The teacher that caught her told Amy that someone had snitched on her. She thought it was me."

"Was it you?"

"Dad no!"

"Ok. But why did she think that?"

"Because apparently I'm the only one she talked to about what she was doing."

"She didn't tell anyone else?"

"No, I don't think so. I'm probably the only one she told, but I wasn't the only one who *heard* about it."

"Who else knew?"

"Dad, I'm not telling."

"Serena."

"I'm no snitch."

"This could get you out of trouble," said her dad folding his arms.

"It won't. I got into trouble for fighting. Telling you, or anyone else, who grassed on Amy won't change that. I'm not a snake, dad."

"Ok," he nodded and took Serena's hand in his, "you know in the adult world, when you grow up, if you know something that will help someone or protect you, you have to say it."

Serena rolled her eyes.

"Seriously Serena, promise me when it's important enough, you'll say something. You'll step up and say something."

Serena shook her head at her dad but couldn't help but smile at him. She nodded.

"Good," he said standing up, "now go clean yourself up, and I'll make us some hot tea."

"With extra sugar?"

"Yeah, ok, extra sugar," her dad laughed, "don't get too comfy, I'm not going to make these next three days easy for you at all."

Serena looked at her face in the mirror; her bottom lip was swollen and under her right eye was a scratch that stung. She gingerly washed her face, wincing at the stabbing pain from her wounds. She brushed her hair and felt with her fingertips where Amy had ripped a chunk of it out. She swore and tied her hair back.

"Three fucking days," Serena said to herself in the mirror, "can't believe it."

She looked down at her phone and frowned. It was lit up with notifications. Puzzled, she picked up her phone, unlocked it and read the dozens of messages across her screen.

Bitch!

Snitches get stiches!

Such a snake, you slut.

No one likes you, snake.

Hiss! Hiss! Snake bitch!

Kill yourself whore.

Message after message from students at school calling her a snake. Amy had managed to persuade everyone at school that she had been the one to speak to the teachers. Serena's hand shook as she frantically deleted the messages. Her eyes blurred as the tears formed and she sat down on her bed breathing hard.

"Fuck," she muttered.

"Serena, tea's done- come and drink it while it's hot," called her dad from the foot of the stairs.

Quickly wiping her eyes Serena sniffed, "coming dad, thanks."

She took one last look at the messages, still unread and undeleted, threw her phone on her bed and walked downstairs.

Chapter 22: Then

Serena sat in the careers guidance advisor's office holding a piece of paper which had the results from a careers questionnaire on it. Slowly, the words on the page began to blur; staring at the page without blinking didn't help.

"Serena are you ok?" asked the careers advisor, Miss Lee.

Serena nodded and looked up at the lady in front of her. Miss Lee was one of Serena's favourite teachers at school, and even though she didn't actually teach a lesson, she was someone many of the students preferred. She was a short, large lady with thick curly red hair, and she wore thick rimmed glasses that framed her very pretty face. She was always smiling, and her personality matched her curly red hair: bouncy. She was one of the few people that Serena had encountered who genuinely looked like they wanted to know how you were doing.

"I'm ok," said Serena shuffling in the oversized chair Miss Lee used for her appointments, "I've just got a lot on my mind."

"Mmm, I'd say more than your exams and what it says on that piece of paper," said Miss Lee motioning to the paper in Serena's hand with her head.

"Yeah, you could say that" said Serena, a small smile creeping its way onto her lips as she thought of Dominik, "did you want this?"

"No, it's yours," she said looking at her computer screen, "I have a copy of your results right here. Shall we have a look at what it says?"

Serena nodded.

"So, what do you think to the results?"

"A bit surprised really," said Serena looking at the paper in her hand.

"Why is that?"

"Well, it says one of my top jobs or careers is a midwife."

"And you're surprised because...?"

"Because, well I'm not really a fan of kids."

"Ok."

"But, well, I do like children, kind of," said Serena relaxing and feeling like she could spend all day talking to Miss Lee and say whatever she wanted to, "but I never thought of a career looking after them."

"Uh huh," replied Miss Lee curls bouncing as she nodded, "but you know, being a midwife isn't just looking after the baby, its mostly about the pregnant mum and making sure she's ok too."

"True."

"Yes, and I imagine, and I'm not a midwife so don't know exactly, but I imagine once the baby is born and the mother and baby leave the hospital, midwives don't see them too much after that. Just a few visits."

"Yeah, the midwife only came a few times when Dani was born."

"Dani?"

"My baby sister, well she's five."

"Oh, ok," said Miss Lee turning back to the computer screen, "the other results – what do you think to those?"

Serena laughed, "you mean where it says social worker or police?"

Miss Lee nodded.

"I think it's a bit much."

"Why is that?"

"Well, I never want to be a police officer. The job doesn't appeal to me."

"Ok, what about a social worker?"

"That's less crazy than police. But I'm not sure I want to be dealing with children and the horrible things they have to live with."

"Well social workers don't just deal with children, you know Serena. There are lots of different types of social workers out there."

"Really?"

"Yeah, sure. You can work with the elderly, or patients with mental health issues, addicts, adults with learning difficulties and quite a bit more."

"Oh," said Serena, "I didn't know that."

"Many students don't. So, would that be an option to think about for you?"

"Maybe."

"Good. But no to policing."

"No policing, maybe social care or being a midwife."

"That's a good start."

"I just don't know if I'm that kind of person."

"What kind of person?"

"The kind that has that sort of responsibility- you know, over pregnant mums."

"Well," said Miss Lee collecting more sheets from a printer and handing them to Serena, "it looks like most of your top compatible carers based on the questionnaire are in those which you care for or protect others."

"Oh?"

"Yes, look at the sheets I've just given you. There's more information about Midwifery and Social Care work for you. Have a read of them in your own time."

"Thanks, miss," said Serena flicking through the pages.

"Take them home, and when you get a chance, have a read of them. I'm not saying you have to follow those career paths, but they are worth looking at."

"Thanks."

Serena put the sheets into her school diary and picked up her bag to go.

"Wait Serena," said Miss Lee motioning for Serena to stay, "we've talked about what the results tell us, but we haven't discussed what *you* want to do."

"Oh," said Serena blushing, "sorry."

"Don't apologise, Serena." Miss Lee wheeled her chair closer to Serena, "what career ideas do you have for yourself? Do you have any ideas on what you think you want to do? Take your time answering."

Serena sat and looked at her hands as she thought. She had an idea but after the talk of social care and becoming a midwife, she wasn't sure she wanted to admit what she really wanted to do.

"Serena," said Miss Lee after a moment of silence, "whatever you're thinking, whatever you want to do, even if it's totally different to what the questionnaire said, you can tell me. Nothing to be scared or ashamed of, ok? I'm here to help."

Serena nodded, "so, what I actually want to do after I leave school and everything, is maybe work in the beauty industry."

"Ah, nice, any particular areas?" asked Miss Lee a wide smile appearing across her round face.

"Maybe like a make-up artist."

"Nice."

"But not like the people in shops or something, more like theatre or film make-up artists. I do like art, and I think I'm good with colours and styles, I think anyway."

"That sounds like a fabulous idea," said Miss Lee turning to her computer and tapping away at her keyboard again, "nothing wrong with that. Sounds exciting."

"Yeah, it's an idea," said Serena shrugging, I just don't know though."

"Well," said Miss Lee looking at her screen, "according to your school data and progress reports, you're great at art and your teachers say you're creative, so that would help you a lot."

Serena smiled and nodded. It was a lot to take in and she was becoming more and more excited as she sat there talking to Miss Lee about her goals and dreams.

"Looking at your grades," added Miss Lee, "you could do whatever you wanted. High enough for art for the next stages, and even sciences if you decide midwifery. Your grades are good enough to do whatever you want to do."

"Really?"

"Yes," said Miss Lee retrieving another sheet of paper from the printer, "you can pick and choose whatever you want to do. Your choice as long as you stick to the grades your teachers think you'll get."

"Really?"

"Yep- make up or midwifery...the choice is yours."

Serena laughed, "make up or midwifery. Thanks, miss."

"You're welcome," smiled Miss Lee as Serena left the room smiling.

Chapter 23: Now

"Sestra get out here now!" shouted Olli shoving open the bedroom door loudly, "Tia is bleeding. You needed."

Serena's eyes shot open immediately as she sat up in bed.

"Ouch," she gasped holding on to her ribs, the lasting souvenir Martim and Olli had left her with a week earlier.

Deep breaths she thought, *slow deep breaths, you can get through the pain. Tia needs you.* She stumbled to her feet, wincing as the cold from the floor jolted up her bare feet and took hold of her ribs. Her lungs refused to work, and her legs wobbled. *Pills* she thought picking up the rapidly emptying tin, *I need pills.*

She swallowed them with the last of the stale water left in her glass and shook her head at the foul taste of rot in her mouth. She tongued her back teeth feeling where one of her teeth had chipped from the brutal punches Martim had doled out. The slow dull ache in her jaw spreading across her face and down her neck began again now she was awake.

"Serena get here now," shouted Olli barging through her room and looking at Serena shuffling towards the corridor, "hurry up, she's bleeding."

"What happened?" Serena struggled to speak.

"Ask David. He said she bleeds and to bring you."

Serena walked as fast as her tired and bruised body allowed, towards Tia's room where some of the other girls were standing. She looked at their faces, many of whom she didn't recognise. She looked towards Jasmine's room and her heart sank as she remembered that she had been chosen and collected a few months earlier. Serena remembered Jasmine begging and pleading to be allowed to stay, but Bishop wasn't allowing it. He was going to get paid a good amount for her and Serena was going to get a radio or something as a reward. A new girl looked at her with terrified eyes; Serena smiled trying to be reassuring but her battered body wasn't exactly a picture of safety.

"In here," Olli's hard voice cut through her thoughts, "Tia is in here. You girls," he called to the group standing and staring at the commotion, "get to your rooms and get ready. Party time starts soon."

Serena watched as the girls quickly moved towards their rooms, she steadied herself against the doorway to Tia's room, trying to catch her breath.

"Kurva," hissed David from inside the room, "in here, now."

Serena looked at the bed where Tia was laying down. Her eyes surveyed the horror in front of her. On the floor, next to the bed, were torn sheets stained with blood. *So much blood* thought Serena feeling herself wobble. Her hand moved to her mouth as she looked at the bed where Tia lay writhing in pain and moaning. The bedsheets were stained dark red, and the girl lay curled up, her arms wrapped around her stomach. David stood, arms crossed, towering over Tia and watched, his expression cold and emotionless.

"Look," he said pointing at the sheets on the floor and then at Tia, "she's bleeding."

"What happened?" Serena asked moving towards Tia, the ache in her body forgotten.

"She is bleeding."

"But why? Where is she bleeding from?"

"Where do you think, from down there."

"What happened?" asked Serena again her hands moving over the bedsheets that had been draped over her friend haphazardly.

David took a deep breath and walked to the wall opposite the bed. He leaned against the wall and fiddled with his belt buckle.

"She got pregnant," his voice was expressionless.

"What?" asked Serena her hand shaking.

"Stupid girl, she got pregnant."

"When?"

"I know yesterday."

"Why didn't anyone tell me?"

"I gave her medicine," said David ignoring her question.

"Medicine?"

"Yes, to get rid of baby."

"So, she miscarried?"

"Yes. I gave her the medicine – the pills. It would flush it out. We know she bleed it out but this time it is more."

"This time?" whispered Serena looking at her friend whimpering on the bed, eyes shut tight and sweat forming on her face. "This has happened before?"

"Yes, many times. Not for a year yet."

"Tia?" she said softly, "Tia, hon, can you open your eyes?"

"Mmm," mumbled Tia, her eyes slowly opening.

"It's me Serena, what happened?"

"I told you," said David walking towards the bed waving his arms, "pregnant. Pills. Blood. She not well this time."

"Of course, she's unwell!" snapped Serena as tears escaped, "she needs a doctor."

"Doctor said nothing to do now but wait. You fix her."

"Wait for what? How can I fix her? I'm not a doctor. I don't know what I am doing!"

"He said she needs cleaning, that is all. You clean her."

"Please go and get Bishop, or get the doctor back," pleaded Serena, "I'll clean her, but she needs to see a doctor. Please or she could die."

To Serena's surprise David nodded, huffed and walked out of the room. She turned back to Tia, and the bloody mess in front of her.

"Tia hon, can you speak?"

"Yeah," croaked Tia, "Serena my stomach is killing me. I can't stop bleeding."

"What happened? Why didn't anyone tell me you were pregnant?" asked Serena peeling back the covers and breathing heavy.

"Olli," said Tia rolling onto her back and allowing Serena to remove the blood-soaked sheets, "Olli said you were too busy."

"Why didn't *you* tell me then? Why didn't I know you've been through this before?" said Serena through sobs.

"My business," gasped Tia looking away and wincing as Serena lifted her top.

A moment of silence fell between the girls as Serena began to understand how the girls saw her now; that she was Sestra and now had preferential treatment.

"Serena?"

"Yeah?"

"I'm sorry."

"Don't apologise."

"It feels different than before. Hurts so much more. Something isn't right."

"I've told David to get a doctor."

"Doctor won't help."

"He will, he has to, otherwise you'll-"

Serena stopped herself but both she and Tia new what the next word was.

"It's ok, I'd rather do that then live this life."

"No, don't speak like that Tia, we're getting you help. You need a hospital. Say that back to me Tia."

"I need a hospital."

"Good. They will take you there and they will make you all better."

"They won't. Bishop says no hospitals."

"They will Tia," said Serena frantically placing a cold wet cloth on Tia's burning forehead, "if the doc can't fix you, they have to take you to a hospital."

"Do you have any pills?"

"No, Tia. The doctor has already given you something. He will give you the right medicine."

"No, the other pills."

Serena looked at her friend and her eyes welled up with tears and she shook her head.

"It hurts."

"I know," Serena whispered in Tia's ear, and she closed her eyes, "rest up. The doctor is coming."

Serena sat and watched her friend's chest slowly rise and fall. Serena's own chest felt like a rhino was standing on it. Serena spent the next few minutes switching between cleaning the blood and replenishing the cold wet cloth on her friend's frail body. Tia's moans were slowly easing and the blood flow had almost stopped.

"Sestra," said a voice from the door jolting Serena out of her daze.

Serena turned and looked at the surprise guest. Standing in front of David was the lady who had inspected the girls with Bishop a number of times since Serena's arrival. Mouth open, Serena stood, she didn't know what to do or say.

"Sestra, I have the doctor coming to help your friend. We will deal with Tia from now, you can go back to your room and ready yourself for the evening. Thank you for your help."

Serena noticed that although her accent was strong, so far, in the almost two years Serena had been trapped in this place for, she was the only one who spoke excellent English.

"Mrs Bishop, Tia is-"

"Marta, my name is Marta. We have Tia looked after now; you can go."

As Marta walked closer, Serena picked up the pile of red sheets and shuffled to the side, watching as she motioned the doctor to enter.

"Marta, she's bad. She needs a hospital now."

"We will decide on that in the morning," said Marta an edge in her voice, "tonight she can stay in observation with the doctor."

"She's really hot," said Serena meekly.

"Yes, we can see that. You have done enough, now you can go," she nodded to David to escort Serena out of the room.

"Serena?" said Tia's small voice making Serena stop.

"Tia, it's ok," said Serena forcing a smile, "they'll look after you. You're going to the hospital, you'll be fine."

Tia smiled and shook her head, "Love you."

She closed her eyes as the doctor quickly injected her with a clear liquid. Serena opened her mouth to speak.

"A sedative," said Marta blocking Serena's way back into the room, "It will help her sleep and we can look after her in the medical room. Thank you for your help."

Marta closed the door leaving Serena standing out in the cold corridor shaking and holding onto the ruined bedsheets.

"Love you too," Serena whispered, eyes wet.

Chapter 24: Now

Serena looked into the frightened eyes of one of the new girls the next evening still thinking about the pain on Tia's face as she left. She had taken the stained sheets to the laundry tub at the end of the corridor and had scrubbed her hands until they were red raw trying to erase the memory of Tia's blood. Now, after another handful of pills, and a feverish night's sleep, she was back sitting in a large room with the other kidnapped girls, in what had become a monthly ritual of trying on clothes picked out by Olli and the other men and readying themselves for the clients and buyers.

Serena's heart sank; in a normal world a roomful of girls getting dressed, putting their outfits on, applying make-up and getting their hair done, would have been a hub of excitement, music and giggles. But here, in this room, in this world, it was a subdued and sombre occasion. This was the evening the clients would inspect the collection of girls- new and old- and choose which one they would buy for themselves to take, or just have for the night.

Serena looked at the girl in front of her and smiled, "It's going to be ok," she soothed.

"How can you say that?" the girl sighed; her eyes already glazed over from the drugs she had been given.

She shook her head and sniffed; Serena guessed she wasn't any older than fourteen.

"What's your name?" Serena asked avoiding the question.

"Vanessa."

"Vanessa," repeated Serena softly, "I've been here almost two years. Girls have come and gone."

"Gone? Gone where?"

"Some of the clients will be looking at you. And if they choose you, you go with them and spend time with them in their homes. You'll be out of here."

Serena waved her arms around her. Part of being Sestra was making sure the girls cooperated with Bishop and his men, and although Serena hated herself each time she sugar-coated the real truth about what would happen to these girls in the collection, she knew it was easier, and safer for them all, to get them on board with her lies.

"What if I don't get picked?" Vanessa asked allowing Serena to apply some make up to her.

"Then you have to stay here with me," said Serena smiling.

"I think I want that," said Vanessa.

Trust me you really don't thought Serena as she smiled tightly at the terrified girl.

"Do you have a chaperone?" Serena asked biting her cheek at having to call the disgusting men that bullied the girls, chaperones.

"A what?"

"Chaperone. A man who looks after you here?"

"Yes, he is really sweet," Vanessa smiled.

"Sweet?" Serena raised her eyebrows in disbelief.

"Well, I thought he was when I first met him," said Vanessa her smile faltering, "he was so caring."

They always are thought Serena looking at this small girl in front of her.

"Young and fit too."

Serena began to feel uneasy.

"His name is Dominik. But I call him Dom."

The inevitable gut punch landed making Serena drop the brush she held in her hand. *Shit*.

"Are you ok Serena?"

"Yeah, just clumsy," Serena's laugh was strained, she picked up her brush, "so this new guy?"

"Oh, he's not new," said Vanessa blushing a little, "he's been my boyfriend for about 5 months now."

"Oh."

"Yeah, it's serious between us. We've slept together already."

Serena's breath caught in her throat, and she felt her face get hot.

"You and Dominik have already...?"

"Dom, yeah me and Dom have had sex."

"And then he brought you here?"

Vanessa's face fell, she looked at the floor and picked at the mini skirt she was wearing.

"I'm sorry," said Serena placing a hand on her shoulder, "I didn't mean to say it like that."

"It's ok, yeah, he's the reason why I'm here. But he said he'll look after me."

"Did he?"

"Yeah, he promised me. Gave me an expensive necklace too."

"A necklace?"

"Uh huh," said the girl excitement creeping back into her face, "it's this silver heart pendant and it has our initials engraved on it. He gave it to me when he said he loved me."

Vanessa leaned forward and showed Serena a pendant that looked all too familiar. She nodded and stepped back from the girl, the urge to vomit rising quickly from her core.

"Everything ok girls?"

Serena turned around as she saw Vanessa's eyes light up. Standing behind her was Dominik.

"Dom!" cried Vanessa running to him and wrapping her arms around his neck.

"Vanessa. Wow, you look beautiful as usual," said Dominik, his gaze locked in with Serena's.

"Thank you, Serena helped me."

"Uh yeah, that's her job now."

"Just call me *Sestra*," said Serena her jaw clenched, "it means sister."

"Sestra? That's pretty," said Vanessa smiling at Dominik standing awkwardly.

"Uh, are you two all done?" he asked clearing his throat.

"Yes, she's ready for them."

"Ok, Vanessa, go with that man over there, he's going to take you to the photo shoot."

"Ok. But aren't you coming?" her bravado dropping and fear beginning to manifest in her voice.

"I'll be there in a minute sweetie. I need to talk to Serena first."

"Ok," said Vanessa moving towards the doorway, "thanks Serena, see you soon."

Serena watched Vanessa totter away and felt her chest burn. She reached at the necklace around her neck, pulled it off and looked at it, then back at Dominik.

"Nice girl," she said surprised at how jealous she felt.

Dominik nodded.

"Bit young though, too young for this."

"She's sweet," said Dominik ignoring her comment.

"Sweet enough to give her a special pendant?"

"Look-"

"Take it back," she said holding her necklace out in front of Dominik as if it contained poison.

"Serena, keep it."

"I don't need it."

"I meant what I said when I gave it to you."

"I don't want it. It reminds me of a time I was weak and thought I loved you."

Dominik looked down at his feet. He was hurt; he took the necklace from her grasp.

"Serena, I do love you."

"Please don't Dom."

“I do. Vanessa’s just my job, but it’s real with you.”

Serena scoffed and turned away, Dominik’s hand reached out and held onto her arm.

“Let go of me,” she growled.

“We need to talk.”

“I don’t want to talk to you.”

“It’s about Tia.”

At the mention of Tia’s name, Serena turned; she was breathing heavy, and she felt suffocated, her skin was sweating but she shivered. She looked at Dominik, his shoulders slumped, and he was clicking his knuckles.

“What is it?” Serena asked feeling her legs weaken.

Dominik looked at Serena and then led her to the nearest chair, “you need to sit down.”

“No. I need to know what’s happened,” said Serena shrugging free from Dominik’s grasp, “is she ok? Did they take her to the hospital? Did she stop bleeding?

“Serena, no, they didn’t take her to the hospital.”

“Is she ok then?”

Dominik took a deep breath and paused. A few seconds in the real world, but in Serena’s mind, an eternity. She looked at Dominik, their eyes met, and he shook his head slightly.

“No, that’s not right.”

"I'm sorry Serena."

"You're lying."

"She bled a lot."

"No. No. No."

"Serena, they couldn't help her."

"Liar! They could have taken her to the hospital."

"It was too late."

"No! No. I don't believe it."

"I'm sorry Serena."

"No."

"She's dead, Serena. Tia's dead."

A primal scream escaped Serena's mouth; her whole body shook as she collapsed into a heap on the floor sobbing for her friend.

Chapter 25: Now

"You look like shit."

Serena opened her eyes and sat up slowly on her bed, "I need more pills."

"You need shower. You had daily amount," said Olli standing with his arms crossed staring at Serena from the doorway.

"I need more."

"No, get up."

"Please."

"No," repeated Olli irritated, "get up, more clients coming. You must get new girls ready."

"I can't without the drugs," moaned Serena. She shuffled towards Olli, weaving along the floor, her hands reached out to hold on to his broad shoulders. "Please Olli."

"Don't touch me," he growled pushing her off him. She stumbled.

"I need more, just to get through the day. There are so many girls, and Tia...she helped...and now...I need the drugs, I need pills."

Olli's face softened a little. Tia's sudden death had not only subdued the girls but also the guards that had known her all this time.

"Just two more," said Olli turning towards the door.

"That's all I need, thank you Olli."

He stopped, turned and looked at Serena, "get dressed, get clean, eat something and get the girls ready. I bring you pills." Then he left.

Serena walked back to her bed and picked up the small mirror she had been gifted by Bishop. Olli was right; she looked terrible. She felt it too. It had been a week since Tia had died and Serena was not coping. Tia had been there the longest; she was the one to help Serena at the beginning and she had been there every time one of the girls were bought and moved on. They had become good friends and allies, helping one another. But Serena couldn't help Tia in her time of need, and the guilt was drowning her. As the Sestra, Serena's life became easier but, the other girls' lives didn't- they suffered more as a result of her privileges and the hate the men felt for Serena was taken out on the girls.

She grabbed a flannel and some soap, another luxury only she was awarded, and trudged out of the room towards the showers. A small giggle to her right made her turn. Vanessa was standing at the doorway of Tia's room, grinning at Dominik who stood close to her with his hands on her hips.

"Hey, Serena," called Vanessa.

Serena took a deep breath and plastered on a smile, "hey. Hi Dominik."

He nodded.

"Did you hear the good news?" chirped Vanessa.

"No, what is it?"

"Dom's managed to get me Tia's old room."

Serena shot a look at Dominik. He smiled, pulled himself up straight, "I did."

"He said I could have it," Vanessa cooed over Dom.

"And Bishop agreed to this?" snapped Serena looking hard at Dominik.

"Yes. Said may as well use it as she won't need it anymore."

"We'll be neighbours," said Vanessa stroking Dominik's arm.

"Great." Serena turned and walked away.

Waiting in her room, on her table when she got back from showering, were two pills. She smiled; Olli had come through. She picked them up and looked at them for a moment in her palm. She picked one up and popped it into her mouth, then placed the second in her tin. *Need to start storing them again* she thought nodding to herself.

"Hey Serena," Dominik's voice came from the doorway.

"What do you want?"

"Bishop told me to give you this."

Serena turned to face Dominik. In his hand was a small flat parcel.

"What is it?"

"Not sure. He said it's a gift for being here two years."

"Not that I have a choice," she muttered and took the parcel from Dominik.

She sat down on the bed, ripped it open and tipped out its contents onto the bed.

"What is it?" asked Dominik moving to the foot of the bed, shifting from one foot to another.

"Still looking," she looked up at Dominik and added, "you can sit down."

"Thanks."

Serena began to sort through the contents; a card in an envelope with her name scrawled on it, and another sealed envelope. She picked up the card and opened it. Inside a card, not unlike a birthday card, from Bishop.

"Dear Serena, happy two years, Bishop." Serena read out the card to Dominik.

She placed the card down next to her and Dominik picked it up reading it and turning the card over in his hands. Serena turned her attention to the sealed envelope.

"What's in that?" Dominik asked.

"Maybe my passport and money allowing me to leave," Serena said sarcasm in her voice.

"Just open it."

Serena opened the envelope and pulled out its contents; a small collection of articles that had been cut out of newspapers stared up at her.

"Newspaper articles?" asked Dominik confused, "why did he give you these?"

"They're about me," said Serena breathlessly picking up the largest article and beginning to read it, "it's about me. From last week."

"Last week? What does it say?"

Serena read through the article, her lips dry and hands shaking. She placed it down and picked up another, read it and put it down too.

"What do they say Serena?" Dominik asked not daring to touch the articles that Serena still held on to.

"They're all about me, about my disappearance. This one talks about when I disappeared and questions about how I disappeared. It mentions that my dad and step mum are looking for me still and haven't stopped looking. It's about the investigation and that it's come to a dead end – no more evidence or clues to what happened to me."

Dominik placed a warm hand on her shoulder, an attempt to comfort the crying girl.

"Dom, they're still looking for me! The police are still looking. My dad, he's still looking. He hasn't given up on me."

Dominik was silent.

"This one says that even after two years my dad thinks I'm alive. He's offered a reward for anyone with information that can lead to me being found. He's got everyone looking for me. This is amazing. They're looking at CCTV."

"CCTV?"

"Yeah, going back over it. But they can't find anything."

"No, of course they can't," said Dominik, "Serena-"

"Dom you're not listening. They're looking for me but there's no CCTV!"

"I know."

"What?"

"I chose a place where there was no CCTV to meet you."

"They've tried tracking my phone," Serena's voice was small, "I gave it to you that day."

"I threw it in bushes near your school."

Tears flowed and Serena wept, "all this time, I thought they'd stopped looking for me. But they haven't. They just can't find me."

"Serena, listen."

"And I can't leave. You brought me here and I can't leave. They're looking for me but can't find me. Maybe Bishop will let me go?"

"He won't Serena."

"But I've done two years now, he can let me go. I won't say anything."

"He won't let you go Serena."

"How do you know?" screamed Serena standing suddenly and pacing the room, "why give me these articles then?"

"I don't know."

"To tease me? To torture me? To show me no matter what happens out there I can't leave?"

"I don't know," repeated Dominik picking up a small cut out that Serena hadn't read yet.

"If he lets me go, I can see my family. My friends. Everyone's still looking for me."

"Serena."

"Everyone- my dad, my step mum, my teachers, my friends. Amy, my god Dom, I bet Amy is still looking for me! I miss her so much!"

"Serena, you need to look at this."

"I can tell her I'm sorry when I see her. Tell her I'll never let anyone get in the middle of us again. I miss Amy. I miss my best friend."

Serena cried and banged her fist against the wall.

"Please, listen-"

"I want to see my family again!"

"Serena!" shouted Dominik, his voice bouncing off the walls in the cold room.

Serena stopped and looked at him. He was holding a small article in his hand. One she hadn't read yet. He looked pale.

"What?" said Serena walking towards Dominik, "what's that?"

"Another article."

"What does it say?"

"I..."

"Let me read it," she took the paper, "there's a picture of Amy on it. This story is about Amy, not me."

"Yeah."

Serena's head pounded as she read the headline. *Best friend of missing teen commits suicide.*

"What?" she muttered scanning the rest of the article.

"I'm sorry Serena."

"It says Amy...says that she killed...killed herself...it says she couldn't handle my disappearance. She's dead because of me."

"Don't blame yourself," said Dominik holding Serena in his arms as she sobbed, her heart breaking into pieces.

"She's dead, Dom. My best friend is dead."

Chapter 26: Then

"What are you giggling at so much on your phone?" asked Danika trying to read the messages that Dominik had sent Serena.

"Nothing, none of your business Dani," said Serena irritated at her sister's lack of personal space.

"Daddy," whined Danika, "tell Serena to call me my *real* name!"

"Serena, call her by her full name," her dad said watching the TV.

"Then tell her to stop trying to read my messages and stop being nosy," retorted Serena.

"Danika, leave your siter alone and stop looking at her messages," their dad said. Then peeling his eyes away from the TV, he looked at Serena and smiled, "what is so funny? You've got such a big grin on your face."

"Ooh, is it a boy?" Serena's step-mum Katalina asked giving Serena a wink.

Serena coughed, "uh, no...it's Amy. We're just chatting being silly, you know, girly stuff."

"So, you two have made up then?" asked her dad nodding.

"Yeah, she finally apologised, and I forgave her."

Serena bit her lip as she realised lying to her dad had become second nature and she had been lying to him more and more over the months since spending time with Dominik. He had insisted that she keep him a secret.

"That's good to hear," said Katalina, "you wouldn't want to throw away a friendship over some silly argument, would you?"

"Exactly," said Serena as her phone buzzed, another message from Dominik.

The truth in fact was that Serena had broken all ties with Amy since the fight; she had ignored all her texts, her phone calls and all of Amy's attempts to start up a conversation at school. Realising that in order for her to keep Dom a secret from everyone, Serena needed to cut all ties with her best friend. She did feel a pang of jealousy whenever she saw Alice and Hannah with Amy, but then she would remember all the messages that were sent to her from students at her school and knew that Amy wasn't to be trusted. Amy was messing about with the 'popular' crew at school; drinking, partying all the time and generally being someone Serena no longer knew. Amy had changed. And so had Serena; she was finally realising there was more to life than school and the people at school too.

She did miss having someone to speak to about Dominik. She hadn't been able to tell anyone in the months they had been dating for- he was a secret from everyone she knew, and he wanted it that way. It was a small price for Serena to have to pay to spend time with the man she loved.

Serena smiled at Dominik's last message: *I think you're the most beautiful person I've ever seen.* She put her phone in her pocket and stood up.

"I'm going to my room, dad. Going to do some work."

"And chat to Amy some more?" he asked winking at her.

"Yeah, of course," laughed Serena, "it's what us girls do. Good night."

"Night, don't stay up too late."

"I won't," said Serena leaving to kiss the top of her dad's head, "night Katalina."

"Night."

"Goodnight Dani."

"Danika. Night night."

Serena smiled and walked up the stairs, her phone in her hand before even getting into her room.

How beautiful do you think I am? She texted as she lay on her bed grinning.

So beautiful that I get hard just thinking about you.

Serena giggled and bit her lip. Over the last month or two things with Dominik had been getting more and more physical. They still hadn't had sex, but they had done lots of other things to satisfy each other.

That's sexy she replied.

You're sexy. And I love you, I love your lips, I love your butt, I love your body, and I love your mind. You truly are the real deal.

Aw that's so sweet. I love you too Dominik.

Serena lifted her head up and looked at her bedroom door; no one was there. She stood up and closed the door wanting more privacy. She pulled her jeans down so that her hips and her knickers were visible and took a photo of herself. Giggling she sent it to Dominik.

Oh my god, you're so sexy.

Dom...?

Yeah?

I think I'm ready.

Ready for what?

Ready for us to go all the way. Sex. I'm ready to sleep with you.

Wow, are you sure?

Yeah, why? Aren't you?

I am, but I think that's going too quickly.

It's been months Dom.

I know, I just don't want you to feel I'm pushing you to do it.

I'm not. I'm ready. Are you? Do you want to?

Serena sat there watching her phone, waiting for the instant reply she was used to when texting Dominik. She bit her nail as the notification *'Dom is writing…'* stared back at her. Her stomach was in knots and her skin began to feel clammy. Finally, her phone buzzed.

Of course, I want to, and I am ready. Really ready, but I want it to be special.

Me too.

So, what about we go away for a night or weekend together? Then we can…you know…

Weekend away? That sounds amazing, but how am I supposed to do that? My dad isn't going to let me do any of that.

What about after your exams?

But they don't finish for another 4 weeks!

We can wait that long. I want it to be special.

But how do I get away without my parents knowing?

What about your friend?

Amy?

Yeah, lie and say you're going away overnight with her.

Dunno if that will work.

I know you; you'll make it work. For me.

For you. I will try. Maybe say that it's a post exams night away in London or something?

Perfect, and then we can go away for a night in London. Spend the evening together.

Sounds perfect.

And you can meet some of my mates too.

You have friends?

Oi cheeky cow!

Serena laughed. She was dying to meet some of Dominik's friends, he spoke about them all the time. And a trip to London to have a special first time together sounded so romantic, almost like a fairy tale.

Ok, she typed as her face became hot with excitement, *I'll talk to dad and say that Amy and I are planning a post exams night and day in London – like shopping etc. I'll say that we are going with her mum, so he'll be more likely to let me go.*

That sounds perfect. I knew you'd be able to come up with a plan. You're amazing. Clever and beautiful...how did I get so lucky?

I think I'm the one that's lucky. You turned up just at the right time to rescue me.

Love you, Serena.

Love you too Dom.

On a different note...

Yeah?

When can I see you next?

Serena smiled and typed her reply.

This weekend?

Sure, same place, same time?

Yep!

Right, I have to go.

Me too, exams are next week, and I actually do need to study for them.

Night my sexy, beautiful, clever piece of ass! Lol.

Night to you too. Love you. xxx

Serena sighed dreamily and spread her arms and legs across her bed. Dominik was perfect and he loved her so much. And she loved him. She couldn't wait until the weekend. Everything else in between seeing Dominik was a boring blur.

Chapter 27: Then

Serena sat at the bench waiting for Dominik to show; her body was electric with nerves and her foot tapped uncontrollably. It was Saturday; the one day her dad didn't ask to know every detail of where she would be going and what she would be doing. The one day she knew she and Dominik could spend the day together without hassle and in private. Usually, they would spend the day in the park or walking around town, but today they had decided to go to Dominik's house. She had been there before, and met some of his family, or friends (she wasn't quite sure who they were), but today she had a surprise for him.

She looked at her phone and frowned. Dominik was late. He was never late. She found his number in her contacts and dialled. She held her breath as the phone rang and rang.

"Hello?" said a voice that wasn't Dominik's. It was much deeper.

"Uh, hello, is Dominik there?" Serena stammered unsure as to why Dominik wasn't answering his own phone. She heard the man speak in a language she didn't understand, a muffled conversation and it sounded like the phone was being passed around.

"Hello?"

Serena sighed, relieved, it was Dominik.

"Hi Dom."

"Serena?"

"Yeah, I'm calling-"

"I'm sorry Serena," Dom cut her off. He was rushing his words, "sorry but I won't make it today."

"Why not?"

"Something's come up."

"What? Can I help? Are you ok?"

"I'm ok," Dominik's voice lowered, "no you can't help, it's a family thing. My...uncle has arrived suddenly, and I need to help sort a few things out."

"Your uncle? What do you need to sort?" Serena asked suspiciously.

"Yeah, my uncle. Just family stuff. It's important and I need to be here, ok?" Dominik snapped.

"Ok, I just..."

"Look, my uncle is here, and it's family, and I need to sort this stuff out for him," Dominic continued as if he hadn't heard Serena's reply, "So, I'm not going to be able to see you today."

"I can come over and help?"

"No," Dominik sighed clearly hassled, "it's...private-family stuff. I need to be here."

"Ok, yeah...sorry. Will I see you tomorrow?"

"No. My uncle...he's here for at least a week, so I will be busy with him."

"Oh."

"You've got your exams to think about," said Dominik trying to add a lightness to his strained voice, "concentrate on those and I'll be in touch."

"Can I speak to you tomorrow even if I can't see you?" Serena hated how needy and pathetic she sounded.

"Yeah, we can chat. I'll call you though, ok?"

"Ok."

"I'll be busy helping my-"

"Uncle, yeah ok. No worries."

"Sorry," Dominik's voice softened, "Focus on your revision and your exams and we can talk later on."

"Ok, but when will you-"

"Look, Serena, I have to go now," the panic was back in his voice and the sounds around him became louder, "focus on your revision."

"Love you Dom."

But the phone call had ended. Serena's eyes welled up as she realised that was the first time Dominik hadn't said he loved her back. Serena felt lost and pathetic, she had no idea what she would do for the rest of the day. She had no one else to call. Wincing at the sharp pain in her wrist as she put her phone back into her bag, she looked at the small dressing and brushed away a tear. The surprise would have to wait.

Serena walked into her house hoping that her dad had taken Katalina and Danika out for the day. She wasn't in the mood to speak to any of them. She was in luck. There was a note from her dad in the kitchen counter saying they'd decided on a cinema trip and would be bringing back food for dinner. If she wanted to eat with them, she needed to text him. Serena had to admit, as much as she was upset that she wouldn't see Dominik this weekend, she knew the time revising and eventually getting a takeout with her family was a good consolation prize. She texted her dad.

Home now, going to revise here. Yes pls for dinner today.

You're home early her dad text back almost immediately, *all ok?*

Yeah, left notes here now can't be bothered to go back. Revising at home.

Good idea, that's my girl. Bringing home Chinese after movie, want your usual or something different?

Usual please. With extra prawn crackers.

Done and done. Be home around 5.

Serena grabbed a couple of cans of Tango from the fridge and trudged up to her room. She had about 5 hours of revising to get done before they came home. Plenty of time to revise for her first exam...maths. Her least favourite subject.

As she reached into her bag, her wrist brushed against the inner lining again. She flinched.

"Ow! Fuck," she hissed looking at her wrist. She began to slowly peel away the cling film and dressing wrapped around her sore forearm gasping at the pain she felt pulse up and down her arm. She looked at the brand-new tattoo she had done that morning. A red heart on her inner wrist; something that could be brushed off as a drawing with red pen ink, but also in a place that her watch could cover up once she was healed. It was discreet, it was small, and it was beautiful. It was for Dominik.

Serena was deep into her revision of algebra and ratios when she heard her dad call her from downstairs. They were home, which meant food. As she padded down the stairs, she felt her stomach growl in anticipation from the smell of a Chinese takeaway coming from the kitchen.

"Mmm, smells so good," said Serena walking into the kitchen and giving her little sister a hug.

"Will you sit and have dinner with us?" asked Katalina motioning to the dining table that already had plates on.

"Yeah, sure. I need a break from revising. Smells lush, and I'm hungry."

Serena grabbed some cutlery and napkins and joined her dad at the dining table.

"How's revision going?" Serena's dad finally asked after they had devoured the takeout.

Serena picked up a prawn cracker and snapped it in half and placed one piece in her mouth.

"It's going well," she said.

"Good to hear, first exam on Tuesday, right?"

"Maths, yeah. I've been doing that today," Serena smiled and dipped her finger into some sweet chilli dip and popped it into her mouth.

"Need any help?" Katalina offered, "you know I can-"

"What's that on your wrist?" cut in Danika as Serena reached for another cracker.

"What?" Serena said quickly dropping her arm.

"There," said Danika pointing, "what is it?"

"Nothing," said Serena, "just a drawing in red pen."

Serena laughed, trying to mask the panic that she felt.

"That's not pen." Danika insisted.

"It looks sore, Serena," said Katalina narrowing her eyes.

"It's a pen, got itchy. It's ok." Serena mumbled trying to pull her cardigan sleeve over her wrist.

"What is it?" continued Danika.

"Just a heart in red. Something I drew,"

"No, that's not a drawing Serena," said her dad his eyebrows raising and back stiffening in realisation, "that's a tattoo!"

"No, it's...I..."

"You've got a tattoo!" he cried, his hand reaching out to grab Serena's arm, "without my permission."

"No, dad...it's not...ow that hurts," Serena winced has her father's rough fingers swept over her fresh wound.

"What the hell Serena?" he growled letting her arm go and looking at her with fury, "when did you do this? It looks fresh. Is this what you and Amy have been scheming about?"

"No, dad. Listen, it's not like that. It's just a heart."

"You're too young to get a tattoo. What shop was it? Did Amy force you to do this?"

"No, she didn't."

"I don't believe you. She's such a bad influence."

“I wanted to do it,” said Serena sounding bolder than she felt, “it’s just a heart, no one can see it.”

“Why?”

“I wanted to,” Serena paused to think of a good explanation that didn’t involve Dominik, “it’s something I really like.”

“It’s horrible,” her dad snapped, his face was red, his eyes bulged, and his hands shook, “I can’t believe you would do this to your body.”

“Dad...”

“Get rid of it,” he hissed.

Serena laughed, “it’s a tattoo, it’s permanent, you can’t just-”

The slap across her face from her dad stopped her from speaking further.

“Anu!” gasped Katalina.

“Don’t you dare laugh at me,” he said ignoring his wife’s hand on his arm, “don’t talk to me. Get upstairs. I don’t want to look at you anymore.”

“Dad, please...” Serena sobbed.

“Now.”

Serena sat in shock, her face pulsed, and tears streamed down her face. She looked at Katalina who shook her head and looked away. Serena’s dad stood up abruptly, making everyone jump, and stormed out. Danika sat wide eyed, her lip trembling.

“Come on Danika,” said Katalina softly scooping up her daughter out of the kitchen.

“Katalina...” whispered Serena looking for an ally.

“Sorry,” said Katalina turning away from Serena, “this one I can’t help you with.”

Chapter 28: Now

"I don't think you should do this, it's too dangerous," whispered Serena, the urgency and panic clear in her voice, "they'll catch you."

"Not if you help us, they won't," said Becky a feisty girl who had arrived earlier that month, and who had already taken several beatings as punishment for not cooperating. "You can help us; you have some influence with them."

"No, I just-"

"They trust you," interrupted Becky leaning in closer to Serena so their conversations couldn't be heard by the guards, "Kerry said they listen to you."

Serena scoffed and looked over at Kerry, the last of the girls who had arrived with her. At the beginning, Kerry and Serena had become close but since being made Sestra and gaining privileges that the other girls hated her for, Kerry had kept her distance and they had grown apart. Kerry was now guarded whenever she and Serena interacted; only speaking to Serena when it was necessary and never joining in any small talk with her.

Kerry's haunted eyes looked at Serena; one of them was partly shut, a mix of red, green and purple, her face was swollen, and she lisped when she spoke- a reminder of who was in charge when she dared speak back to Olli the previous day.

"Serena, we need your help. Without you, we're trapped here."

"I can't help," said Serena unable to meet Kerry's eyes anymore and looking down at the floor, "and not because I don't want to. It's because I can't. The punishment would be...we can't escape."

"We can, we have a plan," said Becky.

Serena stared at Becky. Even with the remnants of bruises on her face, she was gorgeous; tanned skin, blonde curls cascading down her shoulders and she had striking green eyes. With an athlete's body and curves everywhere, Serena could see why she had become a prime target. She wondered how Becky had been trapped and taken but knew that she would be perfect for Bishop's collection. Bishop would be able to sell her for a very high price and probably put her in the auction instead to make more money.

"A plan?" Serena choked back some bile that had surfaced with the fear of escape.

"Yeah, Char tell her," said Becky nodding to another girl in their huddle.

Serena looked up at Charlene; a lean girl about 16 years old. She had a beautiful smile which Serena had only seen once since her arrival a couple of months ago, and she had long, red hair. Her skin was pale, but Serena guessed she was picked due to her slender figure and very long legs. Charlene's eyes darted towards the door, and she spoke quickly, and with an accent Serena guessed was from Manchester.

"Well," she whispered, "we plan to sneak out at night, once the main guards are gone."

"Sneak out? Do you even know where the doors lead to?"

"Yes," said Becky, "Kerry's been here a while and has tracked them. She thinks she knows a way out."

"Thinks?"

"It's better than being here and doing nothing," said Kerry her voice hard, "especially the way some of us are treated."

"Do you know what they'll do to you if you get caught?" said Serena ignoring the obvious dig at her.

"We can't stay here anymore, we have to try," argued Kerry.

Serena sighed, she couldn't believe she was hearing this, "so what happens once you're outside? We're in the middle of nowhere."

Becky nodded to Charlene to continue.

"Once we're out, we head in one direction, and just keep going until we find a town or something."

"A town?"

"Yeah, we don't stop at all."

"It's too dangerous," said Serena shaking her head.

"More dangerous than being raped and beaten and drugged every day?" hissed Kerry her voice rising with hate.

"Ssh," said Serena shooting a nervous smile at a guard who looked over at them suspiciously.

"I want out of here, Serena," said Kerry, "one way or another, I'm done in this life. Are you going to help us?"

"I can't...how would I even...it's too dangerous."

"Will you come with us?" asked Charlene softly.

Serena was stunned. Her heart ached to be out and free from this brutal life, but her brain needed her to survive. She looked down at her fingers.

"I can't come with you," she whispered.

"Then stay out of our way," snapped Kerry.

"Kerry," said Becky placing a hand on her friend's shoulder, a touch of warmth Serena hadn't felt in a long time and envied. She turned to Serena, "then help us get out."

"How?"

"Distract the guards. If they suspect anything, divert their attention away from us."

"How?"

"Tell them something different to our plan, whatever way you can."

"How will you get out?" Serena's voice was raspy, she needed water.

She looked afraid as other girls began to walk into the room to choose their uniform for the evening. Becky smiled and Charlene nodded towards Kerry. Serena looked at Kerry, her gaze dropped to what was in her hand.

A key. The master key.

"Where did you get that from?" Serena gasped her eyes widening.

"Traded it for this," said Kerry smiling and pointing to her face, "he just didn't realise that was the trade off."

Serena watched as Kerry, Becky and Charlene grabbed some clothes from the pile in front of Serena and walked out, her heart beating at the thought of escape.

**　　　**　　　**

Serena woke to her door being pushed open. Her eyes snapped open, and her heart began to beat fast. She sat up trying to adjust to the bright light that was streaming in from the outside corridor. She looked at the small clock that Bishop had given her for helping him sell one of the more difficult girls to the collectors. That and some more pills that helped in her trying to erase the part she played. 4.00am. Too early to start a new day and too late to help clean up after a collection party.

"What's going on?" she asked as Olli and Dominik stood in the doorway.

Serena recoiled when she saw the redness and puffed face of Olli's. He was angry. She looked at Dominik and he looked mad too. This wasn't going to be good.

"Kurva, bitch, get up now," bellowed Olli flicking the light in her room on, flooding the room in a bright fluorescent light that burned her retinas.

Serena did as she was told. She looked at Dominik who now walked towards her.

"Where are they?"

"What?" she breathed closing her eyes.

The slap she was expecting from Olli didn't come. The punch from Dominik dropped her to her knees. She looked up in shock at a blurry Dominik; he was shaking, his eyes were like thunder and his fists trembled.

"Get up," said Olli sneering.

Serena got up.

"Where are they?" Dominik asked again, his voice hard and filled with rage.

"I don't know what you are talking about," Serena whispered.

Another punch landed hard in her ribs. Air rushed out of her body and her chest sagged. Serena fell to the floor. She curled up and squeezed her eyes shut. The pain thundered through her body, and she struggled to catch her breath.

"Get up, now," hissed Dominik grabbing her arm roughly and pulling her to her feet.

Serena stumbled and was pushed onto her bed with force. She looked at Dominik through wet eyes, he seemed alien to her; like he has the devil in him. She had never seen him like this, she had never felt threatened or scared by Dominik, not until now.

"Dom," she pleaded.

"Don't even think about lying to me," Dominik said stepping towards her and towering over her small frame.

"I don't know what this is about."

"Lying bitch," said Olli stepping next to Dominik, the pair of them looking more dangerous than they had ever before. He swung his giant hand across her face, "you know what happened to them."

"I didn't do anything. She asked me to help but-"

"She?" Olli said frowning.

"Yeah, she asked me to help them, but I said no," Serena breathed trying to refocus after Olli's powerful slap.

"What are you-" began Olli but Dominik cut in.

"Who asked you to help Serena? How many?"

"I...I'm not...it was..." Serena mumbled; her chest tightened up as she realised she'd said too much.

"Tell us everything," said Dominik, his voice hard, "now."

Serena broke down and began to tell Dominik and Olli everything. She revealed Kerry, Becky and Charlene's plan to escape and how they would do it, she saw Olli's eyed widen and then crease into a frown. He marched out of the room and began shouting at some of the guards along the corridor. Serena placed her face in her hands and sobbed. Dominik stood over her, his body rigid, his breathing coming out hard and fast.

"It's good that you told us," he said walking towards the door, "otherwise who knows what punishment you'd suffer too."

"What are you going to do to them if you find them?"

"*When* we find them," said Dominik turning to look at the mess that was Serena on the bed, "they will be punished in front of you."

"No, please no," whispered Serena.

"That will be *your* punishment for this disloyalty."

Dominik shook his head closed the door behind him, leaving Serena too shocked to move. She stared at the door, listening to the shouts and cries of the guards running up and down the corridor and allowed her tears to fall freely.

Chapter 29: Now

She wasn't aware of how long she'd been sitting in rigid fear, but Serena was ripped from her stunned silence when Olli crashed through her door, his face crimson and eyes wild.

"Kurva, get out here now!" he barked, baring his teeth.

Serena stepped off the bed and walked briskly to the door, but not quickly enough for Olli who grabbed her hair roughly and pulled her into the corridor.

"Let go," she cried out in pain. It was like a thousand needles scraping at her skin.

"Shut up bitch," said Olli pulling her harder.

"Where are we going?" she yelped trying to sound like she had any control or authority.

"To Bishop."

"What?" Serena stopped suddenly, her legs cramping.

"Move, kurva," said Olli now looking at Serena and yanking hard.

"Why are we going to Bishop?" she asked her hands holding on to her head, a futile attempt to stop the shooting pain.

"He will sort the problem. He has asked for you."

Serena's heart plunged to her stomach, if Bishop was asking for her, he also knew. Nothing could be worse, could it? The contrast from the harsh fluorescent lighting of the cold corridor to the warm soft lighting in Bishop's room did nothing to ease the dread growing inside of Serena. If fact, knowing that she had to face Bishop made everything much more terrifying.

As Olli pushed her into the room and shut the door with a thud, Serena slowly took in the scene before her. Standing in front of his desk, looking tired and dangerous, was Bishop; his arms crossed over his broad chest and his eyes glowered. Kneeling in front of him was Kerry; and next to her Becky and Charlene; their hands tightly bound behind them with cable ties. Standing rigidly behind the girls were Dominik, Alexander (Kerry's handler) and a new man Serena had only seen a few times and didn't know the name of yet.

"Ah, Serena," said Bishop looking at Serena standing by the door, frozen in her fear, "sestra, please join us. You are just in time."

Serena felt the sharp pain in her lower back as Olli shoved her forward. Stumbling a little, Serena looked at the girls; Kerry's head was held high, her lip trembled but she refused to look at anything other than Bishop, the fire in her eyes burned. Becky breathed heavy, her nose clearly broken, and blood dripped from her nostrils. Her eyes were smothered by the swelling of her face. But it was Charlene that made Serena look away and retch. Her face was nothing less than a mess; her eyes were almost completely shut and above one of them was a deep gash- a wound not inflicted by a hand but by a sharp object. Her lip was split, and her jaw jutted out at an angle that was not natural. She swayed on her knees as her arms bled with cuts and bruises and some of her fingers were bent outward, swollen, and purple. She shook in pain at every strained breath she took.

"Bishop?" Serena whispered as she walked towards the girls, her hands automatically reaching out.

"Don't touch them," said Bishop, venom in his voice, "come and stand here, next to me."

Serena nodded and stood meekly beside him.

"Now, Sestra," said Bishop slowly walking around the three kneeling in front of him, "I need your help."

"Help?"

"Yes," Bishop looked hard at Serena, "these girls were caught trying to run away. It seems that this one," he kicked Kerry hard in the back sending her sprawling face first onto the carpet, "this one stole Olli's keys."

Serena looked over at Olli who was red in the face with shame.

"Yes," Bishop continued as he glared at Olli, "and then this one," he grabbed Becky's hair making her cry out, "this little bitch kurva had the nerves to distract one of my men and lock him in a room."

Serena opened her mouth to speak but the sound of Bishop's fist slamming into Becky's stomach stopped her.

"The guard has been dealt with. He will no longer be working here," continued Bishop waving his hand dismissively, and turning to Charlene, "but this one," he stood close to her and spat in her face and grabbed her jaw making her cry out in agony, "this one, this whore of mine thought she could be brave and call for help!"

Serena's throat closed and the room span as she watched Bishop bring his huge fist back and crash against Charlene's face. The force would have broken her jaw if it wasn't already badly disfigured. Charlene's eyes fluttered as she dropped to the ground like a ragdoll.

Bishop turned to Serena, flexing his hand, his eyes wild, and her gaze following him as he slowly stepped over Charlene and closer to her.

"And now you," he said inches away from her quivering body, "you knew they were planning something, didn't you?"

"No...I...please..."

"Lies!" shouted Bishop as he punched Serena hard in the face.

Serena fell back, the large desk behind her was the only thing keeping her somewhat upright. Her face throbbed and she tasted copper on her split lips.

"You knew and you didn't tell."

Serena nodded, tears cascading down her rapidly bruising face.

"You are sestra and you didn't help the girls."

"I tried."

"Not try hard enough. You should have told Dominik or Olli."

Serena merely nodded.

"You let it get so far, and now your punishment is to choose their punishment."

Serena looked up at Bishop, confused. She shook her head trying to understand.

"I don't understand."

"You could have stopped this," said Bishop pointing at the three badly beaten girls, "now you chose their final punishment."

"But..."

"Don't worry, I will help. Three little girls. Three punishments. You choose which girls get which punishment."

Serena stared, mouth open, not daring to breathe.

"Punishment 1: one girl will be marked. Punishment 2: one girl will spend the night with some of my very special customers. Punishment 3: one girl will lose her beauty."

"What?" Serena couldn't believe what she was hearing. She glanced towards the men in the room, they were all looking down at the floor. Dominik bit his lip and sighed heavily.

"You choose; marking, an evening with my special customers, or losing their beauty."

"Losing the beauty?"

"Yes, we have some mixtures. The girl will lose her beautiful face, but she will live."

"I...I...can't choose this."

"If you don't, you will join them in all three punishments."

Serena's legs buckled and she fell to the floor. A nod from Bishop and Dominik was at her side picking her up.

"You have 2 minutes to choose," said Bishop moving to his chair behind his mahogany table, "or I will, and you will suffer too."

"Choose," whispered Dominik pleading with his eyes once she had stopped crying.

"I can't," sobbed Serena shaking her head.

"You have to," urged Dominik lifting her head up with his finger on her chin.

"One minute," boomed Bishop.

Serena shook her head and covered her face.

"You have lost me good money. I cannot sell these bitches now. They must be punished. You must choose or you will be punished too."

Serena looked at Bishop, nothing was going to change his mind. She turned to Kerry, Becky and Charlene; all three broken and bruised.

"Do it," said Dominik squeezing her arm.

"Do it," said Kerry as she looked at Serena, "you have to. Or he'll kill us all."

Bishop nodded, smiling, "this one is right. I will kill you all."

"Ok," Serena whispered, her throat catching at the bile that was forming. She stood up shakily and held on to Dominik's arms for support. After the silence in the room became too much she looked up at Bishop and nodded.

Bishop stood and walked to the fireplace and picked up a pole that was sticking out of the fire. Serena saw him smile as the end glowered a hellish red.

"Choose," he said walking towards Kerry, Becky and Charlene, "hold them," he ordered Dominik, Olli and Alexander. "This one?" he asked hovering the hot poker over

Becky's shoulder. She squealed and tried to move away but Olli held her tightly.

Serena shook her head.

Bishop shrugged and moved towards Kerry, "her?"

Serena followed his movements and looked at Kerry, their eyes meeting. Kerry looked at her and smiled softly. Serena nodded and closed her eyes as the sound of Kerry screaming in agony pierced her ears. The sudden smell of burning flesh made Serena turn her head and vomit.

Chapter 30: Now

The world became a steady haze of eat, sleep, rape repeat. She was allowed more of the white pills – in fact Bishop made sure more drugs were given to all of the girls. She knew this was to keep them subdued and obedient, but *she* needed them. She needed to dull the reality she was forced to live in now, so she didn't argue. The horror of that night burned itself into her mind and nothing she did could erase it from existence, she had to make do with the drugs helping her navigate through the days and months of hell.

Of course, the physical reminders of that night haunted Serena too; every time she saw Kerry, the smell of burning flesh surrounded her and held on tight. Kerry's punishment of 'the mark' had been brutal; a horrific scar clung to the side of her neck and snaked round to the top of her spine. Bishop had made sure it was visible- an ugly scar for an ugly act- he called it. The creases from the iron that branded her caused blisters to pulse every time Kerry spoke and moved her head. The pain crystal clear in her eyes. Serena tried to speak to Kerry a few days after she had been branded, and once the girls had been cleared from the doctor's room, but Kerry had avoided her at all costs and screamed maniacally when Serena had approached her and touched her arm. Alexander marched to Serena, pushed her aside and slapped Kerry in the face to silence her. The look Kerry gave Serena as she held her stinging face was enough to stop Serena from reaching out to Kerry again.

"Don't come near her again," threated Alexander, "you cost money. Who will fuck her now? Stay away, Sestra."

Serena had nodded and scurried away knowing the scream had caught the attention of everyone around them.

"Leave her alone," a harsh raspy voice said as Serena walked away.

She looked up to see Becky and Charlene standing together. Becky was holding and supporting Charlene.

"Becky…I…" but Serena couldn't say what she had practiced over and over again in her room. The words stuck in her throat as she saw the bruises across their bodies and faces, reminders of their punishment.

Becky looked torn, all the fight she had was gone- the night with Bishop's special customers. The kind of customers no actual woman would go for, the filthy, putrid men who would buy girls and unleash horrific acts of violence and rape on them until they were tired from all the torture. Dominik had reluctantly told her about these men and what Becky had to endure for almost 8 hours, and that he had been the one asked to make sure she was treated for her wounds.

"Fuck off Serena," Charlene hissed.

Serena looked away from Charlene; she had endured the final punishment. What Bishop has called so cruelly 'taking away her beauty'. He had burned her face with acid.

The jagged scars across Charlene's face were still red raw, her skin looked like it had melted away and her hair line was charred with blisters. Serena looked down quickly and carried on to the safety of her room.

Sitting on her bed remembering all so vividly, Serena cried. She allowed the feeling of helplessness escape and she sobbed hard for the life taken from her. Tears gathered on her lap and she felt her body shake with anguish.

I can't do this anymore, she thought to herself.

"I can't go on," she whispered to herself through sobs.

"You have to," a voice from the doorway startled her.

Serena looked up and saw Dominik standing there, his face formed with worry. He moved slowly into the room and carefully sat next to Serena. They sat next to one another, in silence, for what felt like an eternity before Serena finally spoke.

"What are you doing here?"

"I came to see if you were ok."

"No Dom," she said turning to face the man she had once loved and trusted, "no I'm not ok. I don't want to be here. I don't want to be Sestra. I don't want this."

"But it keeps you safe."

"And what about the others?" snapped Serena holding on to Dom's arms, her fingers digging in.

Dominik winced but allowed Serena to hold him tightly. He placed a hand on top of hers, "you have to think about yourself Serena. You have to think about surviving this."

"What's the point?"

"What do you mean?"

"If I survive this hell, what does my life look like? I'm still going to be trapped here, still be raped until they don't need me anymore, then what? You think they'll let me walk out of here? I'm on an endless road to nothing."

"No, Serena, you can't think like that."

"Why not? Can you say I'll be allowed to ever leave?"

"Serena...look-"

"See! You can't guarantee it, or anything. I've been here so long already Dom; I'm never getting out. I'm going to die here!"

"Don't..." Dom whispered stroking her hand.

"I'm done, Dom, I'm done."

Before Dominik could respond, a knock and scrape of the door opening further interrupted them. Olli stood, staring at the two of them and frowned.

"She needs to get ready," he said to Dominik but his eyes never leaving Serena.

"She will, I'll make sure she does."

"Why are you with her?" asked Olli walking into the room.

"We're just talking. I'm checking if she's ok."

"That's what I do. You check your own girl."

Serena watched, breathless as Olli turned to look at Dominik. The hate in his eyes matched the intensity in Dominik's stare. After a minute of silent staring, Olli growled and shook his head.

"Go get your girl ready. No need to be here *priyatel*."

"I'm not your friend," Dominik hissed as he walked towards the door. He looked back at Serena, "be safe Serena. Survive this."

Olli laughed and turned to Serena as Dominik left, "kurva, time to get ready for work."

Serena nodded.

"Did you want your extra medicine?"

Serena nodded and reached for the 4 pills in his hand.

"Good girl," he snarled, "what do you say?"

"Thank you."

"Ten minutes, then you check others are ready."

Serena nodded and watched Olli walk out of her room and shut the door; another privilege she had gained from being sestra- a closed door. Once the door was closed

Serena sat on her bed and took out her tin from under her pillow. She tipped its contents into her palm. Eight pills in total, including the four she had just been given. She sagged, she thought she had more stashed away. She'd lost count.

"Eight will have to do," she whispered as she shoved them all in her mouth and chewed.

Crunching down to break the pills in her mouth, Serena picked up her glass of water. Half full. She closed her eyes and drank, swishing the water around her mouth so she could swallow all the pills better. Laying down on the bed, Serena closed her eyes waiting for the nothingness to take her away from this place.

Chapter 31: Then

"Where are you taking me?" Serena giggled as Dominik picked her up from her house.

It had been a week since she'd been stood up by Dominik for his uncle. Serena has tried to focus on her exams, but she was missing Dominik, and she couldn't concentrate on anything. She had left him at least 10 texts and 3 voice messages ranging from nonchalant, to worried, to angry and everything in between. So, when he text her and said he wanted to take her away for a weekend, she was shocked.

At first Serena didn't want to hear his exciting plans or about a fancy weekend away, she wanted to know why Dominik hadn't been in touch.

"It's complicated," Dominik said sounding a little nervous.

"What happened to you? Where have you been? You just seemed to drop off the end of the world!"

"That's a bit dramatic."

"Who have you been with?"

“My uncle. I told you. I took him sightseeing.”

“Sightseeing?” Serena wasn’t convinced.

“Yeah, kind of. He wanted to see some things, so I took him. I’m sorry I didn’t call you.”

“Not even a text or anything!”

“I know babe, I’m so sorry. I want to make it up to you.”

“How?” Serena pouted even though she knew he couldn’t see her down the phone.

“I want to take you away for the weekend.”

“There’s so many things wrong with that sentence Dom.”

“Like what?”

“Like, number 1: my dad. He won’t let me go, he’s never even met you! Number 2: I’m in the middle of my exams, so I can’t just go. And also number 1 again to that. Number 3: you’re mad. I can’t go away for a weekend and not tell my parents!”

“Then lie.”

“What?”

“Lie to them. Tell him you’re doing some sort of revision weekend with mates. And then come away with me.”

Serena's heart ached with the realisation that she no longer had any friends. She had cut them all out of her life, as Dom has asked her to. Amy never even looked at her anymore, let alone talk to her. Everyone she would have called friends before, had chosen Amy over her.

"My dad won't let me, he will want to check which friend I'll be staying with."

"Don't worry we'll get someone to pretend. I'll get someone to pretend."

"A revision weekend? He won't believe it."

"You can try."

"I'm in the middle of exams Dom. I need to revise."

"But I need to see you."

Serena felt her stomach somersault as she heard Dom's voice crack.

"I'm desperate to see you too Dom, but-"

"Then come away with me."

"I can't."

"You don't want to, you mean."

"No. Dom, look I have to revise."

"Revise with me. Away with me, just us."

"Dom..."

"Look, I know I've upset you by not calling, but I want to make it up to you. I love you, Serena."

"I love you too," she sighed, "I'm just not sure I can."

"You're not even going to try?" Dom's voice had an edge to it now.

"I want to, but-"

"I get it. This is my punishment. Even though I've said sorry."

"That's not it, Dom. It's not a punishment."

"Yes, it is."

"I promise it isn't."

"Don't you love me anymore?"

"Don't say that! You know I do!"

"That's why you won't come away with me."

"I just can't come away."

"If you loved me you would."

Serena gasped. The hurt in his voice made her ache. She couldn't believe he would think she didn't love him. she did. With everything she was. She'd kept him a secret, from all of her friends. She cut ties with them. All for him.

"Serena, please? I'll make sure you revise, and I'll make sure you get to your exams on time. Promise. I just want to spend time with you – we've been together for what, six months now? I want to celebrate that."

Serena sighed and closed her eyes, her resolve fading away. She knew he was manipulating her; making her feel guilty. But she was desperate to see him and spend time with him. She missed him so much.

"Please?"

"Ok," said Serena biting her lower lip and frowning, "we can have a weekend away."

"Yes! I promise I will help you revise too."

"Ok."

"And your dad?"

"I'll tell him I'm staying over at a new friend's house. I'll need your help with that though, Dom."

"No problem."

"Ok, I'll speak to dad tonight."

"Thanks honey. I love you so much. You are just the best. Love you!"

"Love you too," said Serena smiling at the excitement in his voice.

"Right, I'm going to get things booked now."

"Ok."

"And babes?"

"Yeah?"

"Remember not to say anything, ok? That'll ruin everything I have planned for you."

"Ok,", laughed Serena, "I won't say anything." *Even though I'm not sure why* she thought.

"Excellent. Perfect. You're perfect Serena."

"Love you, Dom."

"Love you more."

** ** **

Serena looked at Dom hopping from one foot to another in excitement. She smiled and stepped out of her home.

"Where are we going Dom?"

"Surprise," he said looking back at the house and frowning. He pulled his hood over his face further, "is anyone in there?"

"No, don't worry Dom," Serena rolled her eyes, "no one knows anything about you. Not even my best friend."

"I'm your best friend. You don't need anyone else."

"Yeah," said Serena, "so where are we going?"

"It's a surprise," said Dominik walking off fast, "don't ruin my surprise by asking."

"Ok, ok," she said jogging to keep up with Dom, "can I ask how we're getting there?"

"Car. But that's all I'm saying, 'til we get there!"

"Car? Who's taking us? I can ask that can't I?"

"My...cousin is taking us. No more questions now, ok?"

"Ok," said Serena linking her arm into Dominik's to keep up with his pace, "no more questions, I promise."

"Good," said Dominik stopping and kissing Serena deeply, "this is going to be a weekend you won't ever forget!"

Chapter 32: Then

Serena stared up in awe as they walked up to a large house on the outskirts of London. The music booming from the house was almost smothered by the hum of traffic from a nearby motorway.

"What do you think?" whispered Dom from behind her. His arms wrapped around her hips, and he nuzzled Serena's neck, making her body tingle.

"It's...big."

"Yup," he laughed.

Serena turned to face Dominik, "I thought we were having a weekend away...just us? Somewhere I can revise too?"

"I know, and we will," said Dominik grinning and leading Serena inside, "and we will get some 'us' time. And you'll have time to revise. Just relax."

"Here?" Serena asked doubtfully.

"No, we've got our own hotel room," said Dominik squeezing her hand, "this is just the party first to help you relax a little. Bit of fun for now and romance a little later."

"Oh, ok," said Serena with a tight smile, "but who are all these people?"

Dominik looked at the small crowd of people filing up the living room, talking, dancing, smoking and drinking-having fun. He glanced at Serena a little nervous smile.

"These are some of my friends and some of my family."

"I'm meeting them now? Here? Like this?"

"Yes silly, a more chilled out atmosphere to make it easier. I want you to meet my family. I'm ready for that now. I want them to meet the girl I have fallen in love with."

Dominik swirled Serena around and caught her in his arms. Laughing, their lips almost touching he smiled, "I love you Serena," he whispered.

"I love you too, Dom," said Serena melting at his kiss.

"Dominik!" called a voice from across the room, breaking their moment.

Serena turned to see who had called Dominik, she followed him over to an older tanned man.

"Hi Steff," said Dominik grinning and hugging the man. He turned to Serena and smiled. "Serena, this is my cousin Steff. He lives here in London.

"Hi," said Serena shyly shaking his hand, "you live in this house? It's beautiful."

Steff laughed, “no, I don’t live this house, I live central London, this house is family house, yes Dominik?”

He spoke to Dominik but kept his eyes on Serena, slowly looking her up and down, making her feel uncomfortable.

“Uh, yeah,” shrugged Dominik ignoring the look Steff was giving Serena, “like we all come here for...uh, family gatherings.”

“Cool,” said Serena feeling a little exposed and out of place.

“I’ll leave you two to grab a drink,” said Steff finally looking at Dominik and raising his eyebrows, “then we can introduce you to the rest of the family.”

“Thanks,” she said following Dominik into a busy kitchen with drinks laid out in abundance on the dining table.

“You ok?” asked Dominik as they stood at the table.

“Yeah, just nervous. If I’d known I was meeting your friends and family, I’d have made of an effort,” said Serena pointing to what she was wearing.

“You look stunning,” said Dominik leaning in for a kiss, “beautiful as ever. Want a drink?”

Serena looked surprisingly at Dominik; he wasn’t usually this carefree and relaxed. There was always caution in his eyes whenever they were out together, and he especially hated when they were in crowded places. He was very secretive. She smiled, Dominik obviously felt comfortable around his family, and he loved her enough to introduce them to her now.

"Yeah," she said grinning.

"Excellent, I'll have some too. What do you want?"

"Dunno," said Serena looking at the table, there wasn't any wine -which was pretty much all she had tried, "you choose. Surprise me."

Serena watched as Dominik expertly poured different spirits into a cocktail shaker, mixing them with some ice.

"What's that?" she asked as Dominik picked out two small white squares, crushed them, and added them to the mixer.

"Just some specially made sugar cubes from where I'm from. Makes the cocktail delicious and sweet."

"Where are you from again?" asked Serena realising she wasn't sure exactly if they'd had this conversation before.

Dominik grinned and began to shake the container, wiggling his hips and making silly faces as he did. Serena laughed.

"Grab those two cups please," he said nodding at the stack of plastic cups. He poured the cocktail evenly into the two cups and handed them to Serena, "drink up."

"Both? I thought you were having one of these?" asked Serena frowning.

“I’m having a beer, I actually don’t like that cocktail, but I know you’ll love them. Try it.”

Serena took a sip from one of the cups and licked her lips, “mmm that’s delicious.”

“Told ya.”

“But I can’t have two!”

“Yeah, you can, down one now, and then carry the other one around with you. The first will help you loosen up and relax a little.” Dominik looked at Serena’s face still concerned, “don’t worry I’ll look after you. I’m doing the same, look.”

He downed the bottle of beer, threw the bottle into the overflowing bin, and picked another beer. He nodded to Serena to do the same. She shook her head in amazement and did the same. The bubbly drink tickled her throat as she swallowed, and she was able to make out the distinct peach and raspberry flavoured alcohol and a slight hint of lemon. Dominik was right; it was easy to drink down and was delicious. The sugar giving it a sweet kick at the end. Dominik handed her the second cocktail and watched her intently for a while. Serena thought she saw his smile falter a little.

“Done,” she said, “let’s go meet your family.”

Dominik pulled her into his arms and kissed her hard, his hands travelling up and down her back making Serena arch her back in response.

“You taste good,” said Dominik, his breath hot against her lips.

"You too," she said breathlessly.

"An hour or two here, then we go back to the hotel, ok?"

"Sounds good to me," murmured Serena feeling lightheaded from the kiss.

She followed Dominik into the dimly lit room where a group of men and women sat in the dark. The music thumped and as Serena looked around, she noticed some of the girls dancing and swaying to themselves. *They've had a few too many cocktails* Serena thought to herself smiling.

"Hey, everyone," said Dominik as the crowd looked at them enter, "this is my girl, Serena."

The next couple of hours were a blur for Serena; she finished her drinks quickly due to nerves, and tried to concentrate on the people Dominik was introducing her to. She remembered Steff and nodded to him as she was introduced to another cousin called David. David shook her hand and stroked her wrist with him thumb, holding on to her a little too long. Serena was also introduced to someone Dominik called his close friend; Olli. But Olli seemed too old really to be his best friend and when she was introduced to Olli, he leaned in to give her a kiss on the cheek and Serena was sure he sniffed her hair and felt a lick at her ears as he pulled away. He said something to Dominik in a language Serena did not recognise and judging by Dominik's reaction and the way Olli grinned at her, Serena was sure they weren't friends. She wondered how Dominik could be friends with this group of people; they all seemed quite strange. Something was off with them all.

Dominik took a seat on a sofa and Serena sat down on his lap giggling. The cocktails were working, and she felt quite drunk and dizzy. Dominik was grinning at her, and his fingers tapped on her thigh to the beat of the music.

"Having a good time?" Dominik asked Serena as his fingers traced her arms and neckline.

"Mmm," Serena nodded.

"Kiss me," he said and pulled her close for a passionate kiss.

"Ah, Dominik," said a deep voice, breaking the moment of passion, "you going to introduce to your girl?"

"Oh, sorry," said Dominik shifting in the chair so Serena had to stand. She blinked and looked at the tall blurry figure in front of her.

"I'm Serena," she slurred, "Dominik's girlfriend."

"Girlfriend, eh?" said the man looking passed Serena at an uncomfortable looking Dominik.

"Uh, yeah, this is Serena, my girl," said Dominik forcing a smile, "Serena this is Bishop, um Ivan, my...uncle."

"Serena," he said, "a beautiful name for a beautiful girl. Nice to meet you."

Serena smiled and nodded as Dominik's uncle took her hand and kissed the back of it, his sharp eyes staring hard into her own.

Chapter 33: Then

The soft rocking motion and a dull rumbling sound dragged Serena from a fuzzy dream.

As she slowly woke, the events of the night before began to form. She frowned *where am I? What happened last night?*

"Dom?" she blinked a few times, but the darkness around her didn't shift, neither did the sensation that she was moving.

"Dom?" she repeated a little louder feeling the start of a hangover forming behind her eyes.

Nothing.

Everything was hazy, and she was so sleepy. Was that someone crying? Serena tried to move her hands to her pounding head. Nothing. She willed her legs to obey her foggy mind. Nothing. She turned her head. All black around her, someone shifted next to her.

"Dom?" she whispered again, "I'm so hungover. Where are you?"

Her heavy eyelids closed and lulled her back into a deep sleep.

Chapter 34: Then

Serena's sleep was disturbed by a deep voice. Not Dom's.

"Vstarat," a foot nudged her shoulder, "get up kurva."

Slowly, Serena forced her eyes to open. Her head ached and her stomach churned dangerously. She groaned.

"Scoala," a different voice. It sounded louder and the nudge was stronger this time - a kick in her ribs.

"Ow," Serena cried out, her eyes opening widely then shutting again at the bright torch light in her face.

"Water."

Water? That sounded like something Serena needed. Her arm lifted, numb from laying on it for...how long? She didn't know. She opened her eyes again, wincing at the pain shooting through her head and slowly sat up.

"Take," the voice said gruffly.

Serena looked at the man holding a small plastic cup of water out to her; she didn't recognise him. Taking a sip of the lukewarm water, Serena looked around. She was only able to make out the glimpses of what was happening around her. She counted six flashes of light- six men holding torches. She looked at the many outstretched arms snatching up the cups of water hungrily. Girls, almost all around her age she guessed. None looked familiar.

Finishing her water Serena continued to take in the horror unravelling in front of her. Her eyes were still fuzzy, and she closed them allowing her hearing to take over. The dull rumble was still there, but the rocking motion has stopped. The growing sounds of crying out, and gruff threatening voices thumped against her head, adding to the aching pressure inside of her skull.

"Dom?" she called out again, "what's going on?"

She opened her eyes and as they adjusted, the growing panic in the pit of her stomach began to swell. What she saw made her shrink herself as small as she could possibly be. She turned as she heard a scream. A girl cowered holding her face, a hard slap making her cry.

"Hey," another called out, but she was silenced by a swift kick in the stomach. Her eyes bulged and she gasped for air.

"What's going on?" Serena whispered. She began to move, an attempt to stand but a soft voice and a clammy hand on her shoulder stopped her.

"Don't."

Serena turned and frowned. She felt a glimmer of recognition.

"What's happening?" she asked the girl.

"You were at the party, weren't you?" asked the girl shuffling closer to Serena.

Serena nodded, now knowing why the girl was familiar looking; she had been with one of Dom's friends. Dom.

"Dom," she said, "where is he?"

"Not here."

"I have to get out of here." Serena moved to stand but a sharp pain against her left ankle stopped her.

"Ow," the girl said frowning at Serena, "stop."

Serena looked down at her foot and her throat closed with fear. Her ankle was swollen and red raw, but that wasn't all that scared her, she looked in disbelief at the chain around her ankle and followed the links to the clasp tight around the girl's ankle too. She touched the chain with trembling hands.

"What's happening?"

But before she could do anything, a shriek demanded her attention. Serena watched, her hand to her mouth as the horrific scene in front of her unfolded. A girl cried out in agony as two men beat her; punch after punch, kick after kick rained down on the frail girl. The cries of the others around her died down one by one as they realised that the girl was no longer moving. Breathing heavy, one of the men leaned over her and grabbed at her wrist. A moment later he let it go. The hand dropped heavily on the ground, lifeless.

"She's not moving, she's dead," she whispered.

The man nudged the lifeless body. No movement. He shrugged and called out to another man. He said something in a language Serena didn't understanding and laughed. Scooping up the limp body effortlessly, he hauled her onto his shoulder and stepped across the others on the floor. The door opened and he stepped out talking to the men on the other side; the door closed behind him leaving the girls terrified and in complete darkness.

Serena curled up into a ball, she shook. The sound of crying echoed around her. She dropped her head onto her knees and wrapped her arms around her legs and wept.

Chapter 35: Now

"Is she ok?"

"I not know."

"Is she moving?"

"Nem."

"Breathing?"

"Da."

"She's alive?"

"Just."

"So, is she going to be ok?"

"Look, I not doctor."

"But you're the one who treats the girls. You should know."

"All I know- she is alive. I know not much else ok?"

"We need to get back to girls and client."

"You go, I'm staying here."

"She's not your girl anymore. You can't stay."

"Fuck off Olli. I'm staying."

"You'll have to answer to Bishop."

"I don't give a shit. I'm staying. You go."

"Suit yourself. Doctor, we need you."

Serena stirred; her head ached, her throat felt like sandalwood and her stomach felt like it was on fire. She moaned as her whole body pulsed.

"Serena," a soft voice next to her whispered, "Serena, I'm here."

"Dom?"

"Yeah, it's me, hon. I'm here."

"I need water."

As Dominik reached to pick up her glass of water Serena opened her eyes and began to sit up.

"Ow, fuck," she said falling back on pillows that smelt of bleach, "my stomach."

"Yeah," said Dom helping her to sit up a little, "it's going to hurt. Slow sips."

Serena sipped from the cup, her hands shaking a little and her breathing shallow. She looked up at Dominik who was sitting close to her his hands helping her balance the cup of water. They locked eyes and for a moment, Serena thought she saw sadness and guilt cross his face. She looked away and rested her head back on the pillow. They sat in silence for a while; the only sound in the room was Serena's raspy breathing and Dominik's foot tapping nervously.

Serena looked at Dominik and sighed.

"Dom?"

"Why did you do it Serena?" he asked looking at her with tears in his eyes.

"Dom...I..."

"Tell me why you did it?"

"You're angry?"

"Of course I'm fucking angry. What were you doing taking those pills?"

"I had to."

"Why Serena? I was so worried."

"Worried about what?"

"About losing you."

Serena laughed, and then coughed holding on to her stomach.

"Why did you do this to yourself Serena? Why?"

"I don't want to be here anymore," Serena said through gritted teeth.

"Serena, you can't do this. I was so worried."

"You're not listening to me, Dom."

"I'm the only one listening!" Dom cried standing up, "I'm the only one who cares about you in here. The only one that listens to you. The only one making your life better."

"Fuck off Dom," Serena hissed.

"What?"

"You are the reason why I am here. You're the reason why my life has turned into shit. You're the one who brought me here!"

"Serena-"

"And you have the cheek to say you were worried?"

"I am worried."

"But you did this to me. I've been in this hell for years. You took me and this is what I am living with."

Serena coughed and winced. Her throat burned from screaming at Dominik. Everything hurt. She reached for the glass of water and finished what was left in it and refilled it. Dominik watched her. Serena looked over at Dom.

"You did this to me, Dom."

"Serena...I'm..."

"Sorry? Don't. I can't hear that."

"Listen-"

"Go away."

"What?"

"Go away. Leave me alone. I don't want to talk to you."

"I'm not going anywhere, Serena, we have to talk."

"I don't have to do anything. Get out."

"Serena look-"

"Get out!" Serena screamed and threw the cup at Dominik.

Dominik raised his hands trying to bat away the cup. His face dripping, he looked at Serena, looked at the floor and walked out, shoulders down. Serena watched Dominik go and then collapsed back onto her bed and cried.

"Are you ok?"

Startled, Serena's head shot up at the sound of the voice. She looked around the small room and saw hers wasn't the only bed. The voice belonged to a frail looking woman on the bed to her left. She had long brown hair knotty and greasy, beneath the dirt and the bruises, a face that was once pretty.

"Who are you?"

"Libby. Are you ok?"

Serena nodded and leaned back on the bed.

"What's your name?"

"Serena."

"Where are you from?"

Serena looked over at the girl and looked down at her hands.

"Like before they took you?"

Serena didn't answer. She thought of home and her life before this and breathed heavy.

"Shit," said the girl sitting up and on the edge of the bed, "Serena yeah?"

"Yeah, why?" Serena closed her eyes, willing the image of her little sister out of her mind.

"I know you."

Serena's eyes shot open. She looked at the girl, her breathing quickened.

"You know me?"

"Yeah, shit. I've heard of you."

"What?"

"I remember you."

"From what?"

"The news. I saw you on the news. When you went missing."

Serena sat in silence. The gravity of what this woman was saying weighing down on her heart.

"Yeah, it was almost 3 years ago now. You went missing. It was crazy," Libby said her voice getting faster and her arms more animated, "everyone was looking for you; there were posters up, TV interviews, door to door searches...everything. But no one had a clue where you were. There were no clues or anything. You just vanished."

"They were looking for me?"

"Yeah, your family. I remember seeing your dad on the news. They didn't have any CCTV or anything."

"My dad..."

"Then they started saying you just left. Like ran away."

"No...I..."

"I remember seeing your photo in the newspapers. It's you. You're here."

Serena stared, tears falling down her face.

"They thought you died. Your dad knew you wouldn't run."

"I've been here all this time," Serena sobbed.

"All this time?"

"I didn't run away," Serena cried, "I didn't run. I was taken. Dominik...he..."

"I know hon, shh," said Libby limping over to Serena and laying a comforting hand on her quivering shoulder, "they did a TV interview."

"Really?" Serena said placing her hand over Libby's, "what did they say?"

"Your dad was on TV, with your mum."

"Step mum."

"Yeah, she was on there with your dad. They were saying how they knew you wouldn't run, but you'd been secretive and odd recently."

"Dom made me swear not to tell anyone," Serena remembered, anger building in her aching heart.

The two fell silent.

"Libby," said Serena sitting up and facing the girl in front of her, "how did you get here?"

"I was homeless," Libby said picking at a scab on her elbow, "a perfect target."

"I'm sorry."

"It's the way it is," said Libby shrugging but her voice faltering, "he offered help, I was dumb and believed him…and now I'm here."

"I'm so sorry," repeated Serena openly crying now.

Libby shook her head, unable to speak. Her tears flowing freely too.

"I have to survive this," Serena said eventually.

"How?"

"I don't know how. But we have to get home."

"Serena..."

"We have to try," Serena said holding on to Libby's thin arms, her fingers digging into whatever muscle was there, "I have to try. I need to see my dad again, see my friends again, see my home again."

Serena held onto Libby and the two hugged tight, only their shared anguish keeping them upright.

Chapter 36.

Serena stared at her room- nothing was different: the stained rug was still there, a small pile of clothes were still crumpled on the floor, and her bed was the same except for a new stain on the thin padding they called a pillow- a reminder of her failed attempt to rid herself of the hell-hole she was trapped in. The lamp, the table, the bin full of used condoms and blood-stained tissues-all reminding her of her expected existence. She gulped, her stomach still aching, and her body still not recovered from the trauma. A warm hand on her shoulder made her turn her head.

"Are you ok?" Dominik's voice was as soft has his hand.

She shook her head and hugged her shoulders tight.

"I'll stay as long as you need me to."

"You don't need to stay."

"I want to."

"You'll get in trouble."

"At this moment, Serena, I don't care. I just want you to be ok."

"And make sure I won't try and kill myself again?" Serena said moving away from Dominik and into the confines of her prison.

There was a long pause before Dominik responded.

"Yeah, ok, that as well. I found your tin, Serena."

Serena turned to look at Dominick, a flash of anger overwhelmed her senses. "Don't look at me like that Dom."

"I just...don't want you to...die."

"Then why bring me here?"

Dominik looked at Serena shocked and puzzled.

"Dom, you took me from my home. You brought me here," she said waving her arms around the room and herself, "whatever happens it's on you."

"I'm...sorry." Dominik hung his head low.

Serena stopped; her words ready to explode from her mouth. This was the first time in years Dominik had apologised to her. The first time he'd even acknowledged that what he had done to her was wrong.

"What?"

"I'm sorry. If I could take back everything I've done to you, I would."

"Then get me out of here."

"Serena, you're not the only one who is trapped in this life. I can't get you out. I can't get myself out."

"But I'm the one that's actually suffering," she said her voice rising, "I'm the one who gets beaten every day, I'm the one who gets raped every single day. Not you. You get to pretend to help us, pretend that you actually care-"

"I do care."

"Then get me out of here."

"You know I can't. It's not possible."

"Why?"

"I can't. I'll be killed for helping you. There's no way out for either of us, now."

Serena walked towards Dominik, with a growing confidence she'd not felt in a long time. She grabbed his arms and shook him.

"Why am I still here, Dom? Answer me! Why can't I just leave? Why can't we just leave?"

"They'll kill you too," said Dominik not answering Serena.

"Why can't I just die Dom?"

"Because I need you alive!" Dominik yelled, his face red, "if you die, I have to replace you. If you die, I have to go through all this again. If you die, I don't get paid!"

A stunned silence fell between the two in the room, the sound of heavy breathing was all that could be heard. Serena let go of Dominik and walked to her bed. Sitting down she looked at him.

"Answer me this then," she said her body drained of any other emotion except sadness, "do you get paid more because I am Sestra?"

Silence.

"I thought so," she said laying down on her bed, "leave me alone, Dom."

"Serena-"

"No, I don't want to hear anything more. Just leave me alone., I need to rest."

"No rest for you, Sestra," came a voice from behind Dominik. Olli stood, arms folded and grinning like he was about to deliver good news.

"Why are you here, Olli?" asked Dominik turning to face Olli, his eyes glaring.

"Get ready kurva," said Olli, ignoring Dominik's stare, "you've got client coming."

"But I've only just got back," said Serena feeling pressure building at the base of her neck. She closed her eyes and covered them with her hands.

"If you back in here, you are back to work. A whore's work is never closed. Just like her legs!"

Olli tilted his head back and laughed, a cruel demonic laugh. He didn't see Dominik's face flash with anger and wasn't ready for the impact of Dominik's body tackling him to the floor. Serena's head snapped up as she stared open mouthed at the sight of Olli and Dominik fighting- limbs flying about and struggling on the floor.

"Stop!"

She screamed as she watched Olli pin Dominik to the floor, his sheer size overbearing and powerful, his fist slamming hard against Dominick's face making his head bounce off the cold concrete. The commotion spilled it into the corridor and Steff and David came running into the room. They pulled the two apart; Olli panting heavily and red faced, and Dominik limp and only standing because Steff had a grip on him.

"What happened?" David asked holding Olli.

"Dominik and Olli, they just-"

"Not you kurva bitch."

"He turned on me defending his whore," said Olli watching Dominik being led out.

"Bishop will fix this," said David putting an arm on Olli's shoulder, "come with me, friend."

"Wait," said Serena, her body cold and shivering.

"Get ready Sestra," said David turning to look at Serena, hate in his eyes, "you have client coming in 10 minutes."

"But-"

"And Olli choose who can fuck you."

Olli turned to Serena and grinned, a small welt forming under his eye from the wild attack Dominik had unleashed on him.

"Olli, please," she whispered.

"Ten minutes, be ready. Don't worry, I pick a special one for you."

** ** **

"Ah, chocolate lady," came a voice from the doorway twenty minutes later.

Serena looked up to see a large man, belly bulging over his ill-fitting jeans and his greasy hair slicked back. He stood licking his lips and smiling at Serena, his eyes two dark dots on his acne covered face.

"You will have much fun with this one," said Olli standing at the door behind the man, "she likes it rough."

"Good, good," said the man edging closer to Serena as Olli closed the door, leaving her trapped in the room with him. Rubbing his hands across his belly and down to his crotch, "we have fun, yes?"

"Please, don't," she whimpered.

"Now, now chocolate girl," he said closing the gap between them faster than Serena could move, "you play nice, ok?"

He leaned in close and grabbed at her breasts roughly with one hand and pulled her close to him with the other. As he leaned in close to kiss her, Serena pushed his hand off her breast and stepped back.

"Bitch," he hissed pulling her close again, one hand gripping her face.

"Fuck off," Serena muttered, spitting in his face.

The man winced and punched Serena in the stomach, sneering as she crumpled to the floor gasping for air, he wiped his face on his dirty t-shirt and licked his lips.

"Olli said you like rough," he said unbuckling his belt and yanking it off his jeans, holding it folded in his hands, "me too."

"No, please," rasped Serena as she felt the belt whip across the air and slide across her outstretched arm.

Chapter 37.

Patting her on her thigh, zipping up his jeans and walking towards the door, the man chirped, "thanks chocolate girl," and walked out.

Serena lay naked and motionless, eyes closed trying to focus on anything but the searing pain that flooded her body. Even when the door scraped open again and she heard Olli's voice, she didn't move.

"Shit," Olli snorted, "David get a girl to help clean her up."

"Who?"

"The one in room three. Sexy Sonia- she was nurse."

A few moments later Sonia walked in a gasped.

"What happened to her?"

"A punishment. One of special clients," said Olli, "just clean her up."

"I need a first aid kit."

"Use, this- whatever is here, you can use," said David handing Sonia an old, half empty green bag with a faded cross on it, "that's all we have."

"Give her these too," said Olli.

"She won't take those."

"Then she suffers more. This will take pain away."

"Nothing will take this pain away," said Sonia as David and Olli walked out.

Sonia turned to Serena, breathed, and opened the green bag.

"Hey Serena," she said softly, "are you awake?"

Serena nodded and opened her eyes slightly.

"I'm not even going to ask if you're ok," said Sonia kneeling at the bed, "but I do need to know what hurts so I can help."

Groaning and wincing in agony, Serena slowly sat up on the bed; her skin was sticky and had dark patches forming across her entire body, "my back," she whimpered.

Sonia stood, looked over Serena's shoulder, and took in a sharp breath. Serena looked at Sonia's face and nodded.

"What-"

"The belt."

"These are bleeding. I'll need to clean these up. It's going to sting."

Serena nodded bracing herself for the inevitable piercing sting. She gasped and scratched at the blood-stained bedsheets with her fingers.

"Sorry," Sonia said dabbing as gently as she could with a cleansing wipe.

"It's ok," said Serena through gritted teeth.

"Why did he?"

"Because he's a monster, they're all monsters."

Sonia nodded and applied light touches of cream she found in the first aid kit.

"I'm cold."

"I'll get you a t-shirt," said Sonia walking to a pile of clothes on the floor. She rummaged around and finally found a large t-shirt Serena had acquired from Dominik in the first few months.

"Here, let me help you," she said as Serena stood and wobbled.

Sonia stood in front of Serena and helped her gently place the material over her shoulders and lacerations on her back. She looked down at Serena's back and gasped at what caught her eye on the bed.

"Serena," she whispered her voice cracking in throat, "you're bleeding."

"Oh," said Serena looking at the blood stain imprint left on the bedsheet where she had been laying down.

"Turn around," said Sonia softly.

Serena shuffled around moaning at her movements. Sonia put a hand to her mouth as she saw what Serena had endured. Bloody fingerprints stained her inner thighs and buttocks.

"What…" but Sonia couldn't finish her sentence.

"Let's just say, he used more than his disgusting dick," said Serena tears running down her bruised face.

"Oh my god, I'm so sorry."

Serena shook her head, "no point in saying sorry Sonia. Nothing we can do now."

"Let me make sure you're cleaned up and patched up, ok?"

Serena nodded. As Sonia cleaned and taped up Serena's wounds, Serena began to tell Sonia what had happened. She talked about how she had been beaten almost unconscious, then brutally raped. She detailed how when she had cried for him to stop, he had laughed had gone harder and whipped her with his belt again and again, commanding her to bark like a dog. She spoke of how he had groped at her body and bit her nipples until they bled and strangled her until she thought she would die. She explained how once he had tired of raping her, he had thrust his penis into her mouth and deep into her throat until she had gagged, and her eyes watered until he finished. Serena spoke of how once he'd guzzled down almost a full bottle of vodka; he poured the remaining liquid over her fresh wounds laughing at her cries. He'd turned her over onto her stomach, pinned her frail body down with his knees, spread her legs and pushed the bottle deep inside her ignoring her screams of pain and slapping her until she stopped crying and just lay in silence, slipping in and out of consciousness.

"My god," breathed Sonia, her voice catching as she wiped away more tears from her face. Her hands shook and she looked at Serena.

Serena, her face wet with tears of anguish, shook her head, "I'm not letting it break me this time. They can break my body, but I can't let them break my mind too."

Sonia opened her mouth to speak but was interrupted by the scraping of the door.

"You done?" asked Olli standing in the doorway.

"Not yet," said Sonia looking at the floor.

"Yes, we're done Olli," said Serena nodding at Sonia, "it's ok, there's no more to do."

"Are you sure?" asked Sonia frowning, her heart still beating fast from listening to Serena's ordeal.

"Yes."

"Then leave Sonia, go back to your room," said Olli, no emotion in his voice.

"See you later," said Sonia giving Serena a gentle hug, "be careful."

"I will," said Serena wiping her eyes as Sonia let go of her and walked out.

"Get dressed," said Olli ignoring the glares he was shot from Sonia as she walked past him.

"What's happening?" asked Serena looking down at the blood sodden tissues Sonia had left on the floor.

"Bishop wants to see you. 5 minutes."

Serena looked up at where Olli was standing, he'd gone.

"Please, no more," she whispered her skin prickling from fear more than the chilly air.

Chapter 38.

“About time,” said Bishop frowning as Olli pushed Serena into his office, “you can go now Olli.”

“Bishop,” said Olli nodding and leaving Serena standing by the door.

“Come in,” said Bishop nodding to an empty chair, he added, “sit.”

Serena obeyed. Her gaze darted around the room searching for clues as to why she was summoned. She gasped and held on tight to the chair when she spotted Dominik.

“Dom?”

Sitting in a plastic chair on the opposite side of the room to her, Dominik looked up at her and then quickly back to his hands on his lap.

“Your face,” she whispered, her voice catching, “what happened?”

“This,” Bishop’s hard voice made Serena jump, “this is what happens when my loyalty is broken. This is what Dominik gets as punishment.”

"For fighting Olli?"

"For siding with a whore."

Serena looked from Dominik to Bishop. Bishop smiled seeing that Serena finally understood.

"He argued with his brothers and me about you. That's unacceptable. So, he was punished."

"What happened?" Serena asked not really wanting to hear the details of his answer.

"He sided with a whore, so he was treated like a whore."

Bishop laughed as he watched Serena gasp and cover her mouth with her hands. Looking at the shell of Dominik sitting on the chair looking down at the floor, she felt a surge of sympathy.

"You beat him?"

"Yes, and more."

"More?"

"Let's just say, Dominik now knows how it feels to be with a man."

"You...you raped him?" Serena breathed heavy, struggling to keep herself from fainting. She held on tight to the arm rests of the chair she was sitting in.

"Not me," Bishop shook his head and walked over to Dominik. He pressed his hand on Dominik's shoulder, "one of our more...what is the word...unconventional clients spent some time with our young Dominik."

Dominik flinched and Bishop grinned. Serena looked at Dominik closely- his face was purple and angry deep cuts stopped his eyes from opening fully.

"No," she whispered crying.

"Yes. He broke my loyalty. He broke a rule. He must be punished. His loyalty won't be broken again, will it Dominik?"

"No," said Dominik shaking his head, his lips trembling.

"Good boy," Bishop said walking back to his desk and Serena, "you may go now Dominik. Go and rest. I will see you tomorrow."

"Yes," Dominik mumbled as he stood unsteadily from his seat and shuffled out of the room.

"Why did you do that Bishop?" Serena asked as Dominik closed the door behind him.

"Whore!" shouted Bishop striding over to Serena and looming over her, "if it wasn't clear your last client enjoyed himself, I would slap you."

Serena stopped and looked down, afraid.

"You are here for two reasons," continued Bishop slowly regaining his composure, "one- to see what you did to my boy Dominik, and two- to choose two of your girls to endure the punishment you cannot handle anymore."

"What?"

"Pick two girls. They will be the entertainment for a very special party that are coming in."

"I can't."

"You must."

"I'll do it."

"Looking like this?" laughed Bishop shaking his head and flexing his hands, "I cannot have my clients see my girls like this," he pointed his finger at Serena, "they need to know I have everything under control, so you pick 2 girls. They will take your place."

"Bishop, please..."

"Are you my sestra or not?" his voiced hardened and his face darkened with danger.

Serena nodded, too terrified to speak.

"Good, then you pick two girls. Any two, but they need to be strong and healthy. They'll need their strength."

Serena looked at the glee in Bishop's face, he was enjoying the turmoil she was going through.

"You need to show me your loyalty, sestra," he said suddenly very serious, "go and pick two girls and tell Olli you will get them ready and bring them to me."

Serena nodded, the scratches and the bruises no longer hurting as much as her heart did at what she was about to do.

"You may go," said Bishop sitting in his chair and looking at his watch, "they will be here in an hour."

Serena nodded and stood. Her feet dragged across the floor as if her body willed her to not follow the instructions she knew she had to.

** ** **

"Why are we here?" said Emma breaking into Serena's thoughts.

Serena looked up at Emma, standing next to Olli and Nina at the entrance to the prepping room. She looked at Olli confused.

"Why is Emma here?"

"Why not?" asked Olli already bored, "you have two girls you picked for, now get them ready."

"I didn't ask for Emma," said Serena looking at the fear across Emma's face, "Bishop said they had to be strong and healthy."

"They are strong."

"But Emma is hurt."

"She's fine now."

"She was limping."

"It was fake. She is fine, yes Emma?" Olli shoved Emma into the room roughly causing her to fall. He looked at Nina and she shuffled into the room quickly to avoid Olli.

"Yes," said Emma through gritted teeth.

"Ok, you got two girls, get them ready for clients. You have under hour before clients want them."

Olli slammed the door, leaving Serena staring at Emma and Nina. Both looked at her for answers. Serena shook her head and pointed to the tub with steaming hot water in it.

"You need to clean yourselves up," she muttered looking at the tub and not at the girls, "use the cloth and make yourselves clean. Once...once you're done come over to me to pick your clothes."

"What's going on Serena?" asked Emma walking towards her.

"Bishop needs me to get two of you ready for some clients."

"Why did Olli say you picked us?" Nina stood behind Emma; her arms wrapped around herself for comfort.

"I didn't."

"Yes, you did. Olli said you asked for us."

"I didn't ask for you Emma, you have to believe me," pleading Serena.

"But you asked for me?" asked Nina looking at Serena.

"I had to pick," said Serena, "I'm sorry, but I had to pick."

"Why didn't you just say no?"

"Because I can't!" cried Serena marching to the tub of hot water and picking up a cloth, "no one says no to Bishop! You know this. And I..."

"And you're sestra," said Emma bitterly, "so you do Bishop's dirty work."

"It's not like that," said Serena her shoulders sagging.

"Everything ok?"

The three turned to see Olli at the door grinning; he could hear everything they were saying. Serena pressed her teeth together; he was spying on her for Bishop- making sure she was doing exactly what Bishop wanted her to do.

"Yes, all good," she said smiling tight lipped, "just girls talking."

"Hurry and be ready," said Olli nodding at the girls and winking at Serena before shutting the door.

Serena stared at the door for a minute before she turned to Emma and Nina, both looking hard at her.

"See, sestra," hissed Emma, "doing what Bishop wants."

"It's not like that."

"It's exactly like that," said Nina standing next to Emma and nodding, "you get to choose who you want and-"

"Just shut up!" screamed Serena shaking, her eyes stinging, "I don't get to choose. But you're right about one thing- I am Sestra and no matter what you say, you will be getting cleaned, you will be getting ready, and you will be seeing clients together," she paused to catch her breath, "Just do what I've said ok?"

"Yes sestra," said Emma shaking her head at Serena and reaching for Nina, "come on Nina, whatever they've got prepared for us, we can handle it together. Just us."

Serena stood silent as the girls brushed past her and began to wash themselves. She slowly walked past the pile of clothes to the make-up table and sat down. She looked at herself in the small mirror Olli had left for the first time since her overdose and saw how her face was purple and green in places where she had been injured and how her hair was clumpy and unruly. She slowly picked up a brush and began to brush her hair, trying to untangle the mess in front of her. In the reflection she saw Nina and Emma together, whispering and wiping at their bodies; Emma dunked her head into the hot water and Nina giggled watching as water sprayed everywhere as Emma flicked her hair out and squeezed out the excess water. Serena smiled but stopped as she caught Emma's gaze burning into her.

"There's make up here," said Serena standing.

"We don't need your help," said Emma walking to the pile of clothes naked. Scars on her body mapping the hard life she had before being taken.

"Just wait outside for us, we've got each other," said Nina following Emma's lead and rinsing her hair in the rare hot water they were given.

Serena nodded, defeated, and walked out of the room.

"Why you out here?" asked Olli as Serena closed the door behind her, "they ready?"

"Another 20 minutes and they will be."

"You not helping, sestra?"

Serena looked at the grin across Olli's face and clenched her fists.

"No, they want to do it on their own," she muttered looking at the floor, "they don't want my help."

Olli laughed and patted Serena on her head, "you one of us now," he said grinning.

Serena didn't reply and stood focusing on her physical pain until the door clicked open and Emma and Nina walked out. She looked at them, but neither acknowledged her.

"Ooh, nice," Olli said looking at them up and down and licking his lips, "you ready?"

Emma nodded, her bravado from earlier slipping.

"Good," said Olli and ushered them down the corridor, he turned his head and looked at Serena who hadn't moved, "clean up and then go back to your room, sestra."

Serena watched Emma and Nina walk away, and she choked back a sob as she felt guilt overwhelm her heart. She turned and walked into the empty room, her shoulders sagging in despair at her life crumbling around her.

Chapter 39.

Serena walked into the hot and stuffy dressing room ready to prepare for a night with clients, and the chilly welcome she received from the other girls didn't really surprise her. She'd noticed over the past month that the girls had become less inclined to talk to her unless they had to and less likely to ask for anything from her. Any conversation was business like and not friendly.

Even though Bishop had ploughed a lot of them with drugs and alcohol to keep them obedient, whenever Serena walked into the room, the girls had enough awareness among them to become hushed and standoffish with her. Serena wasn't sure how she should be reacting to this change in temperature, but it was beginning to feel like a very lonely existence.

"What are you lot talking about?" she asked walking up to Kerry, Becky, Emma, and a few girls she recognised but didn't know all the names of yet.

She admonished herself for becoming so lazy with the new girls, she no longer wanted to get to know them as she understood within a few months they would be gone, one way or another. Making friends in this life was only going to end in heartache, so Serena now kept as many people at arm's length as she could; being as solitary as possible was how she survived and protected herself.

"Nothing," said Becky as she looked at the other girls, all avoiding eye contact with Serena.

"Oh," said Serena looking at each girl; memories of the way Amy used to make her feel resurfaced and an uncomfortable hardening in the pit of her stomach began to form.

"Just talking about typical girly stuff," added Emma sarcastically, "you know, boys, annoying families, silly sisters not leaving our shit alone, new dresses, nights out...things we should be experiencing instead of this shit."

"Oh."

"Yeah, oh. And you're helping them to keep us here."

"I'm helping to keep you safe and alive."

Becky scoffed. Serena winced.

"And the new mirror, the extra food, cleaner and warmer clothes that you've got is making *us* safe, is it?" hissed a dark-haired girl, her eyes all bruised and glazed, track marks forming on her arms.

"It's not like that," pleaded Serena.

"What's it like then, huh?" asked Becky standing up and walking towards Serena.

"It's...I...I make sure that..."

"Go on."

Becky stood menacingly in front of Serena, her hot breath reeking of alcohol.

"Becky, look-"

"Don't come in here and pretend you're on our side and that you care. I know first-hand that you don't. Kerry knows first-hand that you won't protect us. You only protect yourself."

"But..."

"Piss off sestra bitch," hissed Becky spitting in Serena's face.

Serena stepped back, her cheeks burning with humiliation.

"What's going on?" called Olli moving towards the girls from his vantage point near the door.

He eyed Becky who had moved back towards the girls, and then at Serena.

"Nothing," they all said in unison.

"Sestra?" Olli asked frowning.

"Nothing," stammered Serena turning to walk away and wiping her face.

"You," said Olli grabbing Becky by the arm, "you did that?"

He pointed to Serena. Becky pulled her shoulders back and nodded. There was fire in her eyes as she snarled.

"Mistake," said Olli and slapped her hard across the face.

The room stopped, shocked by the sound echoing off the walls. Olli looked around the room nudging Becky with his foot as she lay crumpled on the floor.

"No one messes with sestra," he growled, "she is sestra- you do what she says."

The girls nodded, and scattered, some brave enough to give Serena a glaring look as they walked off. Serena stood, now with Olli by her side, shaking.

"Thanks, Olli," she said.

"Shut up whore," he hissed as he grabbed her arm and walked her to the corner of the room, "I don't care they hate you, but the little bitches need to see."

"Oh, ok."

"You should go back to your room," he said, "stay out the way. I'm not protecting you always."

Olli slapped Serena on the backside, squeezed and winked at her. He walked away laughing, knowing the other girls in the room were watching. Serena looked down at her feet, grabbed the closest dress she could get her hands on, and briskly walked out of the room; eyes full of hate following her every move.

** ** **

"What was all that about?" asked Libby popping her head around the door of Serena's room.

Serena looked up from where she sat and shrugged, tears forming in her eyes.

"Becky's really got it in for you, hasn't she?"

"Yeah, but I don't blame her," said Serena picking up the small mirror and looking at her face; her skin was still a deep brown, but marks, pimples and scars dotted across her face and body.

"Don't they see you're in the same shitty position they're in?"

"Probably not, they just see these extras that I get."

"But you've been through hell. You've been here for years."

"It's ok, Libby, it really is," said Serena looking at Libby and forcing a smile.

"Someone should say something, I should say something."

"Don't!" snapped Serena, then adding softly, "honestly, it's ok. They go through enough, and I think Becky was drunk. I don't want to cause trouble or get them punished anymore."

Libby nodded. The two looked at each other knowingly.

"Serena-"

"Knock knock," interrupted Dominik walking into the room, hands in his pockets, smiling shyly.

"Hey," said Libby looking at Serena and raising her eyebrows smiling.

"Hello Libby. Hi Serena," said Dominik.

Serena flinched at the lisp in Dominik's speech; a reminder of the brutal beating he endured only a week or so earlier.

"Hey, Dom," she said softly.

"Can I speak to you about your client today?" he asked.

Serena's heart sank, "yeah, sure."

"I'll get going, leave you two alone to talk," said Libby moving back towards the door.

"Thanks," said Dominik.

"Stay," said Serena.

Dominik looked at Serena surprised.

"You sure?" asked Libby.

"Yeah, nothing to hide is there?"

Dominik nodded, Libby shrugged and walked over to the bed and sat down next to Serena.

"So," said Serena, "what news do you bring about my client tonight? I thought I wasn't getting one?"

"Oh, yeah, you have one now, I sorted it," said Dominik a little thrown that he had an audience, "he's an old friend of mine."

"Oh, great," quipped Serena, "a friend."

"Yeah," Dominik breathed heavy, "he's not violent, or horrible, or anything like that. Nothing like the others."

"Just likes to rape girls too?" Libby retorted.

Dominik looked at Libby like he has just been slapped in the face.

"What's the catch, Dom?" asked Serena ignoring Dominik's awkwardness.

"He wants to film you with him."

"What?" said Serena and Libby together.

"He wants to film you."

"Bishop won't allow it," said Serena frowning at why Dominik would risk another punishment for a client.

"I know, that's why this has to be a secret."

Dominik looked hard at Libby.

“Don’t worry, I’m not saying anything that’ll get Serena in trouble,” said Libby shaking her head and placing a hand on Serena’s.

“Why?” asked Serena.

“Why what?”

“Why does he want to film me? Why are you allowing it?”

“Does it really matter?” asked Dominik nervously looking at the open door, “look, I owe him- he saved my life before, so I owe him.”

Serena shrugged, “Ok, so he wants to film me?”

“Yes.”

“And only us three and he knows of this arrangement?” asked Libby curious.

“Yes, and he’d be in as much trouble as us if Bishop found out.”

“It’s too dangerous,” said Libby shaking her head. Turning to Serena she added, “I don’t think you should do this. It’s too dangerous for you.”

“Like I have a choice,” said Serena.

“You could tell Bishop,” whispered Libby.

“And get Dom in trouble? Again? No, I won’t do that,” said Serena glancing at Dominik who was sheepishly looking at the floor.

She stood up and walked over to Dominik and held his face in her hands. She smiled and Dominik's shoulders relaxed.

"He just wants to film me?"

"Yes, he's not violent or anything, just a little strange, he just wants to film you."

"That and pay to rape women," said Libby bitterly.

Dominik's face fell and again he looked towards the door. He looked questioningly at Serena. She nodded.

"I'll do it," she said.

"Thank you," said Dominik. He looked at Libby, "please keep this to yourself, ok?"

"I think we're both protecting the same person by keeping our mouths shut," said Libby nodding towards Serena.

"Thanks," said Dominik, "he'll arrive with the others, but I'll bring him to you."

"Ok," said Serena.

"Ok," said Dominik, he walked out of the room rubbing the back of his neck.

"He looked nervous," said Libby.

"He'll be punished if they find out."

"Why do it then?"

"No idea," said Serena, "but I feel like I can trust him when he says the client isn't a bad one like the others."

"I'm not so sure. Look at where we are."

"I trust him, Libby."

"But I don't," said Libby moving towards the door, "just be careful, ok? I don't think this is a good idea."

"I know, I'll be careful, I promise," said Serena smiling softly at her only friend in captivity leaving the room.

Chapter 40.

Serena's moment of solitary peace after Dominik's friend left her was interrupted by the sounds of shouts and screams in the corridor.

"Get out here now, sestra!" called Olli shoving the door open and pointing at Serena.

Instantly Serena felt her mouth become very dry. Something was wrong. Legs feeling like heavy trunks Serena dragged herself out of her room, fighting her instinct to run and hide. The screaming, like a wounded animal, echoed in the cold corridor and pierced her ears as she looked.

"Fuck." Serena said as she watched Libby scrambling and scratching at Dominik as he struggled to hold her back from a man in the centre of the commotion.

"Get bitch away!" he yelled, and then added something in another language.

Serena looked and realised it was a regular customer, one of Bishop's clients that enjoyed being rough with the girls. He was holding onto the side of his face, blood seeping between his fingertips; his face flushed and enraged. He was shouting at Olli and the other guards, and his eyes were wild as he spat at Libby, missing only because Dominik had managed to pull Libby away.

"Fuck you!" she screamed.

"Shut up!" cried Olli pointing at Libby.

"Look at what that kurva did!"

"Come close to me again and I'll bite your other ear off- you rapist fucking son of a bitch!" Libby yelled spitting on the floor, her lips stained with his blood.

"Get her out of here, now." Olli shouted at Dominik who was struggling to pull Libby away from her attacker, "Sestra, get her to your room."

"I want to see Bishop!" the man cried- a mixture of anger, embarrassment and pain in his voice.

"Fuck you! I hope you die!" screamed Libby as Serena grabbed one of Libby's arms and pulled her towards her room.

Olli signalled to David to take the bleeding man to Bishop. He turned to Serena and Dominik, "lock her in your room and then get back out here."

Serena nodded unable to speak.

"Stay in here," Dominik said as he pushed Libby into the room and pulled Serena away as he shut the door and locked it. The unsettling sound of her room being locked snapped Serena out of her mute state.

"What happened?" she asked Dominik and Olli.

"That fucking whore just bit the client," hissed Olli rubbing his hands over his face and head.

He frowned and looked down the corridor; a mixture of terrified girls and confused men stood at most of the doors. He rolled his shoulders and stood straight. He smiled. When he spoke, his voice was silky smooth, he chose not to speak in English, but in a language Serena had yet to narrow down. She frowned as she listened, only picking up a few words.

"What's he saying?" she whispered to Dominik leaning in close so he could hear her.

"Just that he's sorry about the noise and disturbing their fun. He…he's also said that she will be punished…and that their session is now free."

"Shit."

"Yeah, shit," nodded Dominik.

Serena knew what this would mean for Libby. Bishop would make sure that whatever the punishment, Libby would be making up the losses from the other clients too. Slowly, the customers began to shuffle back into their rooms with their girls, until Dominik, Serena and Olli were the only ones left in the corridor.

Olli turned to Serena, his smile and charm gone, "where is that kurva?"

"In my room," said Serena, "what happened?"

"We're about to find out," said Olli walking briskly to the locked door.

"What's going to happen to her?"

"That's for Bishop to choose," said Dominik looking at the floor.

"And I am sure he will ask your opinion too sestra," said Olli smiling and shaking his head.

He gestured towards the door and Dominik stepped forward and unlocked it.

As Serena stepped forward to enter her room, Olli placed an arm across, blocking her way, "not you,"

"It's my room."

"And she's now my problem."

"But-"

"Wait outside, Dominik and me will go in."

"Let me talk to her first," pleaded Serena feeling panic rising.

"No, we will."

Serena looked at Dominik for help but didn't find any. Olli pushed her further into the corridor and then he and Dominik went in, shutting the door behind them. Serena moved to her door and placed a hand on the cold metal. She leaned her head against it as she heard cried of pain and thuds through the door. Olli was laughing- that she could hear clearly. Tears rolled down her cheeks as she whispered, "Libby, what did you do? Whatdidyoudo? Whatdidyoudo?"

Minutes later, the screech of the door startled Serena and she jumped back, eyes wide. Dominik walked out, looking at the floor, his hands trembling at his side.

"Dom?" Serena looked at Dominik.

"Go get Bishop," said Olli to Dominik patting him on the back, "you did good, for a little boy."

Serena looked up at Olli standing so close to her she felt her skin itch. He looked down at her smiling and licking his lips, "clean her up," he said and walked off.

Serena turned and looked at the darkness in her room. She willed herself to move inside but the fear of what she would find in there terrified her and froze her there in the spot.

"Libby?" she called softly, her dry throat sounding scratched.

She heard Libby hiss with pain and unsteadily walked into her room.

"Libby?" she repeated.

"I'm sorry Serena," Libby said quietly as she sat on the floor, her back against the cold metal bedframe.

"Sorry for what?" Serena closed the door and turned towards Libby, "are-" but her words disappeared as soon as she saw Libby's face.

Libby looked up at her, tears falling down her bruised and swollen face, "I've bled on your bedsheets."

"Fuck that Libby," said Serena kneeling down next to her friend, "what did Olli do to you?"

Libby looked at Serena; her bottom lip was split and bleeding, a yellow-green bruise forming over one of her eyes, the other already swollen shut, and her nose was dripping with blood.

"What did Olli do to you?" Serena repeated.

"It wasn't Olli, this time," said Libby her voice unable to hold back fresh tears.

"What...?"

"It was Dominik."

"No, he wouldn't do that," Serena said remembering his shaking hands as he left the room.

"Olli made him."

"Fucking Olli."

"Yeah, fuck Olli. Fuck Dom. Fuck them all," said Libby laughing a little then wincing as her lip glistened with more blood.

"What happened?" asked Serena moving to tend to Libby's injuries.

"Dominik, I told you."

"No, I meant with the client."

"Oh, that fucker," said Libby through gritted teeth.

"Yeah, him."

"He got rough, and I just had enough. So I bit him."

"You *bit* him?"

"Yeah, he was on top of me, pinning me down and grunting in my ear, and just bit him."

"Wow."

"Yeah," she laughed softly, "bit a chunk of his ear clean off! He squealed like a pig and ran screaming and crying."

"Oh." Serena tried to suppress a smile.

"And that's when the others came to his rescue," Libby rolled her eyes, "Dominik grabbed me and pulled me away."

"I'm sorry."

"It's ok, I'm the one that did it."

"But...your punishment."

"I know. I'll take whatever punishment Bishop wants to give. I hate this place."

"I can try and make it better?" asked Serena knowing that she wouldn't change anything that was coming to Libby as punishment.

"Don't worry, hon," said Libby putting a hand on her shoulder, "I did it. I'll deal with whatever comes my way. Alone."

"That's good to know," said a female voice stopping the two in mid conversation.

They turned to look at the door and standing there with her arms crossed over her heaving chest was Marta, Bishop's lady. Serena stood up quickly and looked at Libby, then back at Marta.

"Marta," she said meekly.

"Sestra," Marta said, her voice hard and icy. She pointed to Libby, "have you cleaned the girl up now?"

Serena nodded; seeing Marta was unnerving and Serena silently wished it had been Bishop there instead.

"Good," Marta nodded, she looked behind her and said, "she's ready."

As Olli and Dominik walked in, Libby cowered.

"Ready for what?" she asked Olli as he grabbed her arm, and Dominik the other, and they pulled her to her feet.

"Your punishment, of course," Marta said shaking her head.

"What?" said Libby her eyes wide like a rabbit in headlights. She began to struggle.

"Come girl," Marta said waving her hand and turning towards the door, "Bishop wants to see you. He will inform you of your forfeit."

"Shall I come too?" Serena asked meekly.

"No," said Marta, "but I would say bye now."

Libby pulled free of Olli and Dominik, surged towards Serena and hugged her.

"Bye Serena," she said choking back tears.

"I'll see you later, ok?" said Serena squeezing back tears and trying to sound hopeful.

"I don't think we will," said Libby looking at Serena and smiling sadly.

"Don't say that," Serena breathed, tears threatening to escape.

"Ok, let's go," Marta snapped her fingers.

"Just stay strong, you'll get out of here. Keep fighting- you have to. I love you," said Libby rushing her words as Olli and Dominik dragged her out of the room.

"I love you too," mouthed Serena as they walked out. Standing in her empty room she allowed the tears to fall freely and sobbed at the barrage of pain she continued to suffer through.

Chapter 41.

"It's time Serena."

Serena looked up at the figure standing in the doorway, silhouetted by the harsh lighting behind him. she squinted, her vision blurred, and she blinked a few times, but the figure still shimmered with every beat of her heart. Like a pulsating statue.

"It's time Serena," the shadow said again.

"For what?" Serena croaked, her throat dry and raspy.

"You know for what?" laughed the shadow.

"I don't want to, I can't," Serena mumbled leaning her head on the wall, "I'm sleepy."

"You've been sleepy for a month."

"No."

"Yes, it's been a month since Libby-"

"Don't say her name!" Serena cried opening her eyes and clenching the bedsheet she was sitting on.

The shadow laughed.

"You can't hide in here anymore."

"Why not?"

"It's horrible in here," the shadow said crossing its arms but staying in the doorway, "it's so dark."

"I like the dark."

"No, you don't, you're scared of the dark."

"No, I'm not anymore. Wait. How did you know that?"

"I know lots about you. More than you want to believe."

"Leave me alone. I want to stay here, it's cosy."

"It's disgusting."

"It's comfy."

"It's suffocating."

"I can sleep here."

"You can't sleep in here anymore."

"Why?" asked Serena squinting and trying to focus on the shadow.

"Because it's time."

"I don't want to."

"You need to come out of this dungeon."

"But I'm here forever now. It's nice."

"You're numb in here. You're disappearing in here."

"I like that."

"No, you can't just disappear like the other girls."

"Why not, my life is over."

"Remember what Libby said."

"Don't say her name!" shouted Serena rubbing her face hard hoping the shadow would be erased.

"But do you remember what she said?"

"I'm trying to forget…forget everything."

"Don't forget it. It's time to fight. Get up and move."

"Why?" Serena mumbled feeling groggier now than before the shadow arrived.

"Time to fight. Keep fighting to get your life back. To leave this place."

The figure moved to the side and a burst of bright light flooded into the room and engulfed Serena, blinding her. Then everything shook.

"Serena! Serena! Get up now!"

"Hmm?" Serena mumbled as she felt a hand on her shoulder shaking her.

"Wake up dammit, Serena," came Dominik's voice, full of worry and urgency, "you need to get up."

"Why? What's happened?"

"Bishop and Marta are on their way. To see you."

Adrenaline hit as she heard those names, and Serena's mind cleared.

"Why?" she asked.

"I don't know. Just get up."

"I need a minute," said Serena licking her dry cracked lips and forcing her eyes to open.

The sudden sensation of cold water thrown on her warm face, jolted her. Crying out in surprise, Serena wiped her eyes and coughed.

"Finally, now get up and get ready. They're on their way."

"Dom, you're a dick."

"You need to get ready; you look rough."

"Like I said, a dick."

"Enough Serena," said Dominik holding Serena's face roughly in his hands, his face only inches from hers, "no more drugs for you today."

"I need them."

"No, you don't."

"They help me forget this life."

"No, they don't."

"Is she ready yet?"

Olli was standing by the open door, arms crossed and frowning.

"She looks like shit."

"She's still high," said Dominik struggling to get Serena to stand, "I...she needs more time. Can you get her more time?"

"I'll see what I can do," said Olli, "but no promises. Get her ready."

"Thanks," said Dominik. Turning to Serena he pleaded, "Serena, please work with me. You've got to get cleaned up before Bishop gets here."

Serena sighed, rubbed her face and opened her eyes to watch Dominik's panicked face. It startled her. She nodded and took the refilled glass of water he held out to her, gulping it down and coughing a little.

"Good," said Dominik looking at a more alert Serena, "that would've gone in your face if you hadn't drunk it."

"Thanks," said Serena smiling a little, "Dom, do you have any food? I'm starving."

"Um, yeah I do," said Dominik handing Serena a sandwich, "small bites or you'll be sick." He ran his hands through his hair and exhaled deeply.

"Dominik," Olli's voice made Dominik jump.

"Yeah?"

"Bishop said 10 minutes in office."

"Ok, thanks, Olli."

"Yeah, whatever," said Olli walking off.

Dominik turned to watch Serena; she had swallowed half of the sandwich already.

"Ten minutes," Dominik said picking up a small towel and a piece of soap, "come on, you need a shower."

** ** **

Ten minutes later Serena and Dominik were standing in front of Bishop and Marta. Marta sat in the armchair, her back straight and arms folded; her long red fingernails tapped lightly. Her face was flawless, skin silky smooth and her make-up light and natural except for her dark red lipstick. Next to her stood Bishop, hand in his pocket; his usual smart tie and shirt replaced with a more casual polo t-shirt – his muscles bulging from the sleeves.

They would make a gorgeous couple, thought Serena as she looked at them, *if only they weren't such disgusting people.*

"Serena, do you know why are here?" asked Marta leaning forward, her hands brushing invisible dust off the desk.

"No, I don't," said Serena trying to keep calm.

The drugs hadn't worn off yet, and Serena was struggling to keep her mind focused on what was happening in front of her. She had to force herself to ignore the blistering pain in her stomach and stand still.

"Dominik," Marta said ignoring Serena's response, "you can go."

Dominik nodded, and without a word, left the room. Panic crept its way over Serena as she watched him leave. The door clicked and Serena turned to look back at Bishop and Marta. She was alone in the room with them. No one else. Just her...and them. She swallowed and coughed.

"Take a drink," said Marta pointing to a glass of water in front of Serena.

Serena glanced at Bishop, who nodded. She gulped half of the water down.

"Feel better?" asked Bishop once she had finished.

"Yes, thank you," Serena said nervously.

"We need you to step up in your role as sestra," began Marta, "but you must be clean for it. Can you do that?"

Serena nodded. Swallowed. Ignored the pain.

"We need you to help us," added Bishop.

"Help you?" Serena's mind exploded- what more could they ask her to do?

"Yes," said Bishop. He looked at Marta and nodded, her signal to take over.

"Yes. We need you to inspect the girls."

"What?"

Serena's stomach fell. She swallowed down bile.

"Inspect the girls, like you have seen me do many times before."

Serena stood speechless. This was much more awful than she could have ever guessed. She remembered her first inspection and closed her eyes. Shivered.

"Serena," Bishop's voice was firm, scary and demanding, "what do you say?"

"Yes, um...I don't think I can do this."

"You can. And you will," Marta added.

"But why?" Serena's chin wobbled, she pressed her teeth together, grinding them trying to control the wave of nausea and emotions threatening to spill out.

"Because I have asked you to," said Marta.

"Because you need to learn," added Bishop.

"And because you're Sestra. That is part of your role," finished Marta smiling, tapping her nails on the desk.

"I...can't...they won't..."

"You can and they will," Marta said standing.

She walked slowly around the desk, standing directly in front of Serena, close enough for Serena to smell the mixture of coffee and mint on her breath.

"You don't have a choice," said Bishop walking around the other side of the desk and standing just behind Marta.

"You will help inspect the girls," said Marta tracing a long sharp nail around the contours of Serena's face, "and eventually you will do it on your own. You will do this or all your Sestra privileges will disappear."

She tapped her nail against Serena's dry lips and smiled.

"Understand?" asked Bishop smiling.

"Yes," said Serena shaking at what fresh hell she was being forced to endure, "I understand."

Chapter 42.

"Why are you doing this to us?" whispered a very young-looking girl in Serena's ear as she slowly inspected the row of new girls standing shivering and terrified in front of her. Their bodies stripped of warm clothes and comfort and only underwear hiding their modesty.

Serena looked up at the girl; her eyes were red and she was shivering, the fear clear across her face.

"I have to," she said quietly, looking at the ground and avoiding the girl's pleading gaze.

"It's her job," snapped Marta from behind Serena, making both girls jump.

Marta lay a hand on Serena's shoulder, "be confident. These girls must obey you."

Serena nodded, took a shaky breath, and looked directly at the girl, "I'm Serena, I'm your sestra. I look after you and you need to do as I say."

"You're one of them?" the girl asked in shock.

"I'm your sestra. I've been here a long time," Serena's voice faltered a little, "do as I say and you'll be fine."

“Can I go home, please?”

“Sorry…no.”

“Why?”

“Because…this is your home now. This is your life now.”

“But-”

“No more questions,” said Serena seeing Marta’s eyes narrow in disappointment.

“But-”

Serena gasped at the sting on her palm as she slapped the girl hard. The girl stepped back, her eyes wide with shock and wet, her hand raised to where Serena had just struck her.

“Do as I say. Step back,” said Serena swallowing the lump forming in her throat. She saw Marta nod, smile and walk to the next girl. “You’re wasting my time,” she added and walked on.

After the inspection was completed, Serena followed Marta towards her room. She could feel the gaze of the girls follow her, their silent glances of hate and careful movement into their rooms made Serena feel like she was going to throw up. Her hands shook and her face burned as the door shut, leaving her alone with Marta in her own room.

"Well done," said Marta patting Serena on the shoulder as she walked around Serena's room careful not to touch anything.

"That was horrible," Serena breathed her eyes stung with tears.

"It gets easier."

"I can't believe I slapped that girl."

"You had to show her who was in charge."

"But...I slapped her," Serena said sitting on her bed, burying her face in her hands.

"Look," said Marta standing in front of Serena and tipping her chin up to face her with sharp nails, "stay strong, the girls need to listen to you. If that means slapping one or two to show them who is in charge and who they must listen to, then it has to be."

"I'm supposed to protect them."

Marta snorted and began walking towards the door, "you do not need to protect the girls. You get them ready for our clients and ready for the catalogue. It's you getting them ready or the guards. Which do you prefer?"

"Me."

"Exactly. Now you have the night off, but the girls don't. Get them ready, then you can relax."

Marta walked out of the room, leaving Serena to curl up on the bed and sob and prayed she would be somewhere else when she opened her eyes.

The next few hours were a blur for Serena; she managed to get the girls to take their pills and struggled with the urge to swipe a few for herself but she didn't. The girls were ready, and she knew by the way Olli and the others were acting, that it was an important night- some of the girls would be sold so they needed to be perfectly presented. Once the girls were ready and Olli was happy with her work, she was escorted back to her room. She lay on the bed beathing through cramps and cold sweats, willing her mind to take her somewhere else. Her lonely hell was interrupted by a soft knock on the door. She frowned and sat up as the door slowly opened.

"Hey," said Dominik standing at the door.

"Hi."

"Can I come in?"

"Sure."

Serena watched as Dominik looked out in the corridor before closing the door. He turned to Serena and smiled softly but said nothing.

"You can come closer," said Serena shuffling on her bed and leaning against the wall.

"Thanks," Dominik walked to the bed and sat down. He turned to look at Serena, opened his mouth and closed it again.

"What's going on?" Serena asked, confused.

"I heard you had to inspect the girls," said Dominik softly.

"Yeah," said Serena looking down at her legs and playing with the hem of her skirt.

"Sorry you had to do that," said Dominik taking Serena's hands in his.

"Yeah, well I didn't have a choice."

"I know, I'm sorry."

"Why bother apologising, Dom? You can't help now anyway," said Serena her voice catching.

Dominik shifted on the bed and held her tight. She sobbed in his arms, and he held her, not saying a word. When Serena had cried as much as her body would allow, she stayed in Dominik's arms, holding onto the warmth.

"Serena," Dominik whispered.

"Mmm?"

"What if there was a way?"

"To do what?"

"Help you."

"Help me? What do you mean?"

"I mean help you to get out of here."

Serena's eyes opened wide, and she pulled away from Dominik, their noses touching. She saw that his eyes were as wet as hers. She stared at his face for a long time before speaking.

"What are you saying?" she breathed.

"What if I could help you out of here?"

"That's impossible Dom," said Serena shaking her head and moving away making space between them.

"What if it wasn't?"

"Don't talk like that Dom," said Serena placing her hands on his shoulders, "don't give me hope, don't joke. We'll be killed."

"I'm not joking," said Dominik glancing towards the closed door and lowering his voice, "I've found a way of getting you out. I have a contact and he can come and help you escape."

"What are you talking about? We'll get caught," Serena said confused.

"He...he can *buy* you. Like one of the clients."

"Buy me? I'll be killed. You'll be killed."

"No, it will be ok. He will bid on you and buy you from Bishop."

"Bishop won't sell me."

"He will for a high price. My contact can get you out. And get you home."

Home. Serena's throat closed up. He stomach lurched. He said home.

"You've been here too long now. You don't deserve it. I should have said no to bringing you here."

"Dom..."

"I need to fix this...this thing that I've done to you," continued Dominik, his hands shook as he cried hard, "I love you Serena and I know this is all my fault. I want to help you escape. Get you out. And now I can. I need to help you."

"Are you sure you can get me out?" Serena asked her lip quivering. There was a chance, some hope.

Dominik nodded, "I can get you out- my friend- my contact will buy you and then you'll be free."

"You can get me out of here?"

"Yes, I know that-"

Serena threw her arms around Dominik and hung on to him tightly. Her small yelps of joy were muffled in his chest. Dominik wrapped his arms around Serena and squeezed. He kissed her head. Her cheek. Her neck. He laughed through his tears too. Serena pulled away, held his face in her hands, and kissed him on the lips. she felt his body tense for a moment before relaxing into the embrace, kissing her back hard at first, then slowly and passionately.

"I love you," he breathed as their lips finally parted, "I love you."

His hands slowly moved down her back to her hips, he smiled as she gasped softly.

"Hey," he said kissing her lips tenderly.

"Hey," Serena murmured back, eyes closed and smiling.

"I'm sorry for everything that's happened. I truly am. What you've gone through...no one should ever go through."

Serena opened her eyes and looked at the sincerity on Dominik's face. Slowly, she lay down on the bed and pulled Dominik towards her.

"Be with me," she said smiling sadly.

"Are you...sure?" asked Dominik frowning.

Serena nodded and kissed him.

Chapter 43.

A loud bang on the door woke Serena from her deep slumber. The scraping of the metal made her jump and remember where she was.

"Shit." Dominik scrambled off the bed in a panic and wrestled into his jeans.

"What's wrong?" said Serena.

"I shouldn't be here," said Dominik pulling on his t-shirt.

"Wake up Sestra, you have work to-" Olli stopped abruptly seeing Dominik sitting on the bed pushing his feet into his trainers in a hurry.

"Olli," Dominik said standing quickly and pulling his t-shirt around his waist.

"Dominik," said Olli looking back and forth between Serena and Dominik, "what's this?"

"Nothing," said Dominik.

"He spent the night," said Serena at the same time.

"Spent the night?" Olli raised his eyebrows and folded his arms.

"It was my night off. What's wrong with this?" Serena said sitting up.

"You're not his girl, he should not be with you," said Olli not taking his eyes off Dominik who was looking uncomfortable and shifting towards the door.

"I'm leaving anyway," said Dominik.

"Good," said Olli.

"Dom...," said Serena.

"I meant everything I said last night," said Dominik as he stood at the door, "everything."

Serena nodded.

"Love time over," barked Olli, "Dominik get out, Sestra get up and ready."

Dominik nodded, looked at Serena and left. Olli turned to Serena, folded his arms and frowned.

"That was a big mistake."

"Why?" asked Serena suddenly feeling angry.

"You not his girl anymore."

Serena winced at his scorn.

"It was my night off."

"He has other girls to take care of. *His* girls."

Serena's face burned with jealously. Olli laughed at how upset Serena was at his comment.

"Get up, get ready. A new day. Special clients asking for you today."

Before Serena could answer or say anything, Olli laughed again and left the room.

"Fuck you," muttered Serena under her breath.

For the next few hours Serena tried to focus her mind on getting herself cleaned up and ready for the afternoon clients. All that she could think of was Dominik and his promise to help her. She believed his promises, and after they had made love, he spoke again about how he would help her escape. Serena smiled to herself at Olli's mention of a new client. Her stomach fluttered with hope.

"What are you smiling about Sestra?" Alexander, one of the guards, looking curiously at Serena.

"No reason," she said turning away from him.

Alexander frowned and then shrugged, "get the girls ready too. Once you done the afternoon clients you have them ready for tonight. Tonight is a big party night. You will see clients too."

Serena's smile faltered a little, she nodded and turned back to the pile of clothes and the huddle of girls in front of her.

** ** **

“So, when they come in, just nod, smile and do whatever they say. Don’t fight or struggle otherwise it’ll be worse,” said Serena remembering the searing pain of the cigarette burn on her inner thigh.

The girls had been given extra drugs to keep them lucid and to stop any rebellion or problems occurring; they were too high and drunk to do anything. Even Becky had been injected and plied with alcohol. Bishop needed the night to go well. Serena heard from snippets of the guards’ conversations that Bishop was losing clients to a new escort service which seemed legitimate from the outside so less danger for them. This left Bishop with only a handful of regulars, and the more depraved clients to conduct business with. Bishop wasn’t happy and tonight needed to go well for him. Which meant Serena had to keep the girls in line and cooperating.

“I don’t want to be here,” said a young girl that Serena had only recently learned her name was Mary. She breathed heavy and her eyes were glazed over.

“I know,” said Serena reaching out and touching her hand gently, “but until we can find a way out, we have to do as they say.”

“How long have you been here? A long time I bet as they call you Sestra.”

Serena forces a smile, “I’ve been here almost 5 years now.”

“Five years?” Mary asked shocked.

"Yes, but most girls aren't here that long?"

"What happens to them?"

"They..." Serena struggled to find anything comforting or positive to say, she sighed, "they...get sold on to one of Bishop's clients."

"Then what?"

"I don't know," said Serena, "just they are bought."

"They're sold?"

"Look don't worry about all that. You'll be fine. I'll make sure of it."

"How?" said Mary in disbelief.

Serena looked around her and leaned forward, motioning Mary to carefully do the same. Their faces, just inches apart.

"I think I've found a way out," she whispered.

"What!?" cried Mary.

"Shh," said Serena frantically looking around to see if Mary's outburst had caught the attention of any of the guards.

"Sorry."

"Look, I'm going to tell you something. But you can't say a word to anyone. Not a soul. Not one word. Promise?"

Mary nodded.

"If you say anything, we could all be in trouble. Like danger- physical danger, ok?"

"I won't say a word."

"Ok, I think I can get us all out of this hellhole."

"We're all trapped here, and the guards watch our every move. All of the time."

"There is a way. One of the guards can help us."

"Who?"

"I can't tell you that. I need to keep him safe too. Bishop would kill us all if he found out."

"I don't want to die."

"You won't. Look don't say anything but know I'm trying to help us all escape. Safely."

Mary nodded, a small, worried expression on her face.

"Ok," said Serena nodding too.

"When?" asked Mary after a moment of silence.

"Soon, not tonight, maybe not even this week, but soon."

Mary smiled.

"We have to get through tonight, ok? Without any problems. And then I can put the plan into action, ok?"

"Ok."

"Stay silent though- don't say a word to anyone about this or we'll never get out."

"I won't say a word, I promise."

"Good," said Serena moving away from Mary. She raised her voice so the other girls I the room could hear, "ok, let's get going. Make this a hassle-free night. Out through that door where Olli is standing and follow all of his instructions."

The girls nodded and in an almost eerie silence they quickly walked to where Olli stood, arms folded, watching the girls leave, occasionally grabbing at them and smiling when they squealed.

"Sestra," Olli called to Serena as the girls filed out, "Bishop wants to see you."

"Bishop?" Serena said a lump forming in her stomach, "now or after the clients have seen the girls?"

"He wants to see you now."

"Is everything ok?" asked Serena nervously, trying to see if Olli would tell her anything. Recently, any time with Bishop never ended well.

Olli laughed in reply and walked off following the final girl in the opposite direction to Bishop's office.

Chapter 44.

As Serena walked towards Bishop's office, her footsteps were the only sound echoing off the cold walls, she tried to think of what Bishop could want. As Sestra, she was given the privilege to be able to walk to his office without the need of an escort, but the silence and emptiness felt dangerous and put Serena on edge. She walked through the third and final door before arriving at Bishop's office. A guard she had only seen twice before stood in her way.

"I'm here to see Bishop," Serena said looking at the door behind his hulking mass.

"This door today," the hulk said pointing to a door opposite Bishop's office.

Serena looked up at him and nodded. The fear began to scratch at her legs as she walked towards the ominous looking door. She knocked softly, but the tinny sound was harsh against her ears.

"Go in," the guard behind her said.

He was suddenly very close to her, so close she could feel his hot breath on the back of her neck. Serena didn't turn around, and instead reached for the handle and walked into the room.

"Bishop?" Serena said softly as she walked into the dark room.

She couldn't see much; this room was a stark contrast to Bishop's normal office. There was a desk on the side of the room, with a few soft cushioned armchairs scattered about. The floor wasn't carpeted, instead a few rugs were spread about the desk and armchairs, leaving the rest of the floor laminated. A few lamps randomly placed around the area near the desk, but the rest was dark and only a slim streak of light from a small window at the furthest end of the room came through. It was odd. Serena frowned and took a tentative step inside, lightly shutting the door behind her.

"Bishop?" she said again only too aware that she was whispering.

"Ah, Serena," Bishop's voice came from the dimly lit desk area, "come in."

Serena walked towards the door and then stumbled a little when she saw Dominik sitting on the chair. He looked afraid.

Bishop ignored Dominik and looked at Serena. "How are you, Serena?"

"I'm...ok."

Bishop nodded, he looked at Dominik for the first time since Serena had entered the room.

"I've just been having a conversation with Dominik," said Bishop motioning to Serena to sit on the chair next to Dominik, "it seems you and he still have a connection. A bond."

Shit Serena thought nodding slightly and sitting down.

"He spent the night with you?" Bishop asked.

"Yes."

"And did you have sex?"

"You know we did," said Dominik frowning, "I've told-"

"Shut up," growled Bishop shooting Dominik a look that silenced him immediately, "I am talking to her." He turned to Serena, "did you have sex?"

"Yes," said Serena biting her lower lip, anxiety coming in waves across her body, "yes we had sex."

"You enjoyed it?"

"Sorry?"

"Answer me. You enjoyed the sex?"

"Um...yes," Serena felt a pressure on her chest.

"Good, good," said Bishop his face set and no emotion escaping, "as long as you and Dominik are happy."

"It wasn't like that," said Serena shifting forward in her chair, trying to compose herself and failing.

“Then tell me,” said Bishop turning his palms upwards and raising his eyebrows, “tell me what it was or wasn’t like.”

A silence fell in the room as Serena tried to think of something to say that wouldn’t end with Dominik being beaten and her being punished. She looked at Dominik who looked back at her; his eyes were glistening, his face flushed, and his lips twitched. Serena looked back at Bishop who sat waiting for an answer, hands clasped and leaning back in his chair. She took a deep breath.

“He came in to see if I was ok...after the inspection...and we began to talk.”

“About what?”

Serena glanced at Dominik and saw the slightest of flinches in his face.

“We...we talked about us. How we met, how we spent time together.”

“About old times eh?” said Bishop smiling scornfully.

“Yes,” Serena said through gritted teeth. She hated how much Bishop was clearly enjoying this interrogation of their night together.

“What else?”

“Nothing else. We talked, we...had sex...then we slept until Olli woke us.”

“So, you have feelings for Dominik again? The one who brought you to me.”

“I’ve always had feelings for him,” said Serena now looking at Dominik, “I love him.”

Dominik looked at Serena in surprise. Seeing her bravery, he sat up straighter in his chair and looked at Bishop.

“You love Dominik?” Bishop asked.

“Yes.”

“And do you love her, Dominik?”

“Yes,” Dominik said, reaching a hand out towards Serena.

Bishop nodded and sat silently for a moment watching Serena and Dominik hold hands. He brought his fingertips to his lips and closed his eyes, deep in thought. Serena and Dominik sat looking at one another and holding hands, waiting for whatever punishment Bishop was planning.

“Right,” said Bishop banging his hands on the table and smiling.

“You can’t punish us for being in love,” said Dominik.

“You can’t change us being in love with each other,” added Serena.

“No punishment,” said Bishop smiling, “no change, you are in love, no punishment for being in love.”

“What do you want then?” asked Dominik his voice small again and unsure.

"I would like you to show me how much you love each other."

The fear began to scratch at her skin again.

"Show me you love him," Bishop said shrugging his shoulders and tilting his head.

"I...don't understand," said Serena.

"No, please Bishop," said Dominik understanding Bishop better than Serena.

"Shut up!" shouted Bishop making both Serena and Dominik jump in their seats, "Serena, show me you love Dominik."

"I...how?"

"Please Bishop..."

"Give him a blow job."

"What?" Serena's eyes widened in shock.

"Please Bishop...I'm sorry...don't do this."

"Do it now, Serena," said Bishop ignoring Dominik's pleading, "if you refuse, you will suffer."

"Serena, no, Bishop, please," Dominik begged.

Serena looked at Bishop, he meant what he said. She needed to do this. She looked at Dominik, tears streaked down his face, his hands shook.

"Do it now."

"Ok, just don't hurt him," Serena said her voice catching and being replaced with sobs.

Serena moved off her chair onto the floor, she shuffled her way in front of Dominik. Looking up into his eyes, she smiled, and reached for his zip.

"No, Serena..."

"It's ok," she said softly sniffing and wiping away a tear, "it's ok, I love you."

"I love you too."

Serena undid Dominik's zipper, her vision blurred from the tears, her heart beating fast and aching at the same time.

"Good girl," Bishop said leaning his elbows on the desk, his eyes watching Serena's movements.

Serena took a deep shuddering breath.

"No!" shouted Dominik pulling away from Serena and standing up suddenly, "I won't let you do this to her. I won't let you do this!"

"Dominik-"

"I don't care Bishop! Do whatever you want to me, but we're not doing-"

A deafening sound echoed around the room and Serena placed her hands over her ears in shock. She squeezed her eyes shut and cowered on the floor. Then, sudden and complete silence. The only sound was Serena's heavy breathing.

"Dominik..." she heard Bishop say softly.

She opened her eyes and looked up. Dominik was no longer standing, no longer shouting at Bishop; he was crumpled on the floor, small gasps of breath escaping his lips, a strange gurgling sound coming from his mouth. She looked at Bishop and let out a scream. The smell of burning gunpowder filled the room. She looked back at Dominik's body. She crawled to him.

"Dom!" she screamed grabbing and shaking him. "Please wake up! Dom!"

Serena pulled Dominik's face towards her, holding his shoulders against her lap. She cried out his name repeatedly, patting him on the face, shaking him, trying to get him to open his eyes. But he lay there, lifeless and bleeding from his chest.

"Dominik," whispered Serena as she tried to put pressure on his wound, something she remembered seeing from a TV show years ago, "please wake up, don't go. I need you. I love you. Please wake up."

Bishop placed the gun on the table, stood up from his seat and walked over to Serena and Dominik. He looked at the lifeless body and turned to the door which had opened with the guard standing, waiting for his orders, not even flinching at Dominik's bleeding body.

"Take her," Bishop said to the guard, "she has an evening of entertaining to do."

"No!" screamed Serena as the guard grabbed her. She fought against him, but her frail and weak body was no match for his power.

Bishop leaned down and placed his hand on Dominik's face, the colour and the warmth draining quickly from his unmoving face.

"Don't you touch him!" screamed Serena at Bishop, clawing at the guard to release her.

"Get her out of here now," said Bishop looking at Serena struggling. He took a cloth from his pocket and wiped the smear of blood from his hand, "and get someone to help you clear this mess up."

"No!" screamed Serena as the door to the office was closed and the sight of Dominik disappeared, "I'll kill you Bishop! Get the fuck off me!"

Serena kicked the hulk, and he stepped back, his grip still tight on her arm. Serena looked up at him, "fuck you too!" she cried as he swung his fist towards her face.

Chapter 45.

When Serena came to, she was in a small room, full of smoke. She was laying on a stained sofa and her head pounded. As she looked up, she saw Stefan and David sitting around a tiny table, drinking beer, smoking and talking amongst themselves, barely taking any notice of her. She coughed.

"Ah, sleeping beauty wake up," said David grinning, "Benny really put you to sleep."

"I thought he broke you," said Stefan laughing and sucking on a cigarette.

"Where am I?" Serena asked sitting up slowly feeling dizzy and sick from the motion.

"In the guards' room," said Olli standing at the door.

"Want to sit on a chair?" asked Alexander grinning.

"There's a spare one now," said Olli bursting into fits of laughter.

"Fuck you Olli," said Serena standing, "I need to see Bishop, I need to see Dom."

The mention of his name made her choke back tears. The roar of laughter from the men died down and Olli stepped towards her, the smile and all the playfulness visibly gone from his face.

"Oh, no Sestra," he said towering over her, "fuck you. Your boy isn't here to defend you anymore. You've made Bishop kill one of his own. You have no one here now."

Serena trembled; she stepped back but the sofa was blocking her. The dark realisation that she was once again alone seeped into Serena's lungs.

"No one to talk to," said David standing up and shutting the door to the crowded room.

"No one to help you," said Benny stepping forward licking his lips.

"And no one to protect you anymore," said Olli tracing a finger down Serena's face, her neck and to her breasts.

"Please let me go," said Serena sensing the danger she was in.

"What will you do if we don't?" asked Stefan gulping down a beer.

Serena swung her arm to strike Olli but he was too fast, seeing her hand before she could hit him, he ducked out of the way. Then quick as a cat he reached out and grabbed her hand and pushed her onto the sofa.

"Hold her down," he said his eyes not leaving hers, "I think this sestra needs to learn a lesson by me."

"And a lesson from me too."

"And me."

"We will all get our turn to teach this dirty dark kurva a lesson," said Olli unbuttoning his jeans as David and Alexander held her arms and pulled at her legs, "one at a time."

"No!" screamed Serena but her mouth was muffled with Olli's hand as he loomed on top of her and pushed between her legs.

Chapter 46.

Serena woke to a steady beep. She moaned; everything hurt- her arms, her legs, her stomach and her face all swollen, bruised and crying out in pain. Slowly blinking and forcing her eyes open, Serena remembered what had happened that evening.

"Dom," she whispered.

"Ah, you're awake."

Serena flinched and instantly regretted it. She turned her head towards the voice.

"I won't ask how you are," said Marta sitting in a chair next to Serena picking at her nails, "I know what happened to you last night."

"You let them do this to me?" Serena croaked.

"No no my dear. That was you and Dominik. You two both upset Bishop."

"He killed Dom."

"I know, and I am sad too," said Marta standing up and moving towards the bed. Standing over Serena and looking her up and down she added, "we have a real doctor to look after you for today- well this morning. You are lucky he is in."

"A doctor?"

"Yes, one of our clients also helps us when we are in need. He is actually here to see Becky- you know her?"

"Becky? What happened?" Serena tried to sit up but collapsed back into the bed in agony.

"She...has an issue, which we are getting rid of for her."

"An issue? Getting rid of?" asked Serena.

"Nothing to concern you. Our doctor will check you over- make sure you have no broken bones, and then I am sure you will be fit for work soon."

Serena said nothing, the pain shooting through her body was mirrored by the hatred she felt looking at Marta and listening to her cold calculated words. They were humans, females, just like her, and she was so callous in dealing with them.

"Serena?" Marta asked after a long stretch of silence.

"Why are you here, Marta?" Serena asked, not masking any of the disgust she felt.

"Just to check you are still alive."

"Unfortunately, I am."

Marta let out a small laugh. She patted Serena on the shoulder and walked out of the room closing the door behind her. As soon as the door clicked shut, Serena closed her eyes and cried. She cried for the savage attack she went through at the hands of Olli, David, Stefan and Alexander; she cried for Becky and what this hack of a doctor was going to put her through; she cried for Dominik and the life he had led; and she cried for the hope that was snatched from her grasp when Bishop pointed that gun at Dominik. She cried until she eventually fell back to sleep.

Hours later, Serena woke to someone pressing down on her chest. She gasped and opened her eyes.

"Sorry my dear."

The voice belonged to a man in his fifties, balding with thick rimmed glasses and crooked teeth. He smelled of whisky and licked his lips. Serena recoiled in disgust.

"What are you doing?" she cried moving her hand to push his away.

"I doctor. Just helping you, Marta said," he said in broken English nodding, his face flush.

"I'm ok," said Serena forcing herself to sit up. She winced and gasped for air.

"You not," he said shaking his head, "your...ribs? They broke."

"Oh," said Serena leaning her head back onto the pillow.

"Let me fix it," he said smiling.

He leaned over Serena, pressing himself closer than necessary towards her, lifted her arms slightly and frowned. Serena cried out in pain at the movement.

"I need your top off."

"No," said Serena.

"I have to."

"I can't...it hurts too much."

"Ok," the doctor said nodding, then he went into his bag and pulled out a pair of scissors, "I cut this top, you can another one."

He looked at Serena. She nodded. As he cut her top, Serena closed her eyes, trying not to imagine his face as his fingers slid across her torso and trying to breathe through the pain. She opened them again once he stopped. He was looking at her breasts and licked his lips. he caught Serena's eye and nodded, looking away.

"I bandage you now. It will hurt. Sorry."

Serena nodded, a signal for the doctor to continue. She clenched her fists as he lifted her a little off the bed and pressed an ice pack against her ribs, whimpering only when she couldn't hold in the agony anymore. When he had finished, he carefully laid her back down on the bed, his hands lingering on her hips.

"You must take these," he said offering her a handful of pills, "take the pain away."

She snatched them quickly, popping them all in her mouth and swallowing without water, "hopefully it'll take the pain away forever."

Clearly not understanding her, the doctor looked at the door then back at her and smiled.

"Thank you," she breathed watching him carefully.

"It's ok. You rest, be better in a day or two."

"Ok."

"I come back for thanks?" he asked licking his lips and taking in every inch of Serena's beaten body.

Serena didn't say anything. She knew whatever she said, he would be back wanting his reward and payment for helping her.

"Ok," he said picking up his bag, "I go help get rid of...problem. You must rest. Sleep. I tell Marta for you."

Serena watched the little man scurry out of the room. As he closed the door Serena saw his silhouette in the frosted window being approached by another person. They spoke in hushed tones and not in English. The silhouette looked in Serena's direction, folded his arms and then appeared to nod. The doctor moved on. Serena quickly closed her eyes as she realised that the silhouette was opening the door. She pretended to be asleep as the figure moved to her bed and leaned in close.

"Get rest today Sestra," Bishop said, "tomorrow is back to work for you, a fresh hell."

Serena lay as still as she could, the pain in her chest threatening to explode out of her as she slowly breathed in and out. Her skin felt like it was on fire and blistering, and she kept her eyes closed until she was certain Bishop had left the room.

Chapter 47.

It took a few days for Serena's ribs to somewhat heal, and the pain meds she was given secretly from the girls was a relief. They heard what had happened to Serena with Dominik and were beginning to treat her like one of them.

"I'm so sorry about what happened to Dominik," Nina said as they stood in the changing room choosing their clothes for the evening.

"Thanks," said Serena, it was the millionth time she'd heard those exact words and she was numb.

"It must have been horrible," agreed Mary holding a red dress up against her bruised body.

"It's...I'm ok," said Serena, "let's not talk about it."

Serena reached down to pick up a skirt and shuddered in pain holding on to her ribs.

"Jeez hon," said Sonia, "your ribs aren't healed properly. You shouldn't be here tonight."

"I have to be," said Serena through gritted teeth, "I need to be."

"Just...take it easy, ok?" said Sonia placing a warm hand on Serena's shoulder and slipping her a pill without the guards seeing.

Serena looked at Sonia with thanks, nodded and walked away. She watched the guards and when they weren't looking, she quickly swallowed down the pill. Getting high was the least of her worries, what could they do to her now, that hadn't been done already? Serena watched the girls get ready, helping one or two of the newer girls who had been topped up with drugs and alcohol as they stumbled about. When they were all done, she nodded to Olli, who stood at the door leering over the girls, letting him know they were ready for the evening clients.

"Sestra," Olli sneered as the girls filed out and Serena followed.

"Olli," she said looking down at her feet and shuffled out of the room.

"You look good," he said winking at her, and then laughing at her discomfort.

"Olli," said Sonia interrupting Olli's fun.

"Yes kurva," he said not looking away from Serena.

"If you can't give Serena a night off-"

"I can't."

"Then, if you can't, then please can you give her someone gentle?"

Serena and Olli both looked at Sonia. She was standing straight and looked Olli square in the eyes. She wasn't afraid of him in that moment. Olli raised his eyebrows, moved his hand to his chin, grinning that Sonia and Serena both flinched away from it, and sighed.

"Ok, I get someone gentle for her. But just today because she is unwell."

"She's not unwell, her ribs are still broken and healing," said Sonia.

"Run along," barked Olli looking like he wanted to pounce on her and tear her to pieces.

Sonia nodded, flashed a quick smile at Serena, and walked away.

"You have some friends here," said Olli rolling his eyes and pushing Serena onwards towards her room, "I thought they didn't like you?"

"I thought that too," said Serena smiling a little.

Olli waited for Serena to walk into her room before speaking again.

"Sestra?"

"Yes?"

"Don't get too happy," Olli laughed as he walked away to collect the clients.

** ** **

It wasn't long before Serena's evening unfolded as it usually did. Olli kept to his word and gave Serena the clients who were not as rough as the others, but it still didn't stop her from gasping in agony as they lay on top of her. Two clients in, and the drugs were finally kicking in, and the drinks Serena had chased them up with, helped. Serena felt her pain wash away with every minute.

"Last client," Olli's voice interrupted her hazy bliss.

Serena nodded and slowly stood, her legs felt like jelly, and she struggled to keep upright.

"Are you drunk?" Olli asked frowning at her.

"I'm fine, just a little drink to help the pain," Serena said slowly trying to make sure she didn't slur.

"Sit down and wait for him kurva."

Serena nodded and sat back down on the bed, looking at her fingers blur in and out of focus.

"Hello beautiful," said a voice from the doorway.

"Knock when you are done." It was Olli's voice.

"Yes," the strange voice said again.

Serena slowly looked up from the bed to watch a large man walk slowly towards her, taking off his coat and pulling off his t-shirt.

"Hello beautiful," he said again.

"Hello."

"Olli said you like it rough, is that so?"

Serena frowned at him and shook her head.

"You don't like it rough?"

"No…I…"

"It's ok, not too rough." He winked at Serena and stood in front of her, he unzipped his trousers and pulled them down a little. "First, I think I want you to wake him up with your mouth."

Serena leaned away from him and shook her head.

"Suck me."

"No," she said trying to wake herself up a little.

The slap from the man across her face worked. Serena's eyes flipped open, and she gasped at the sting.

"Kurva, you will suck me," he said grabbing her arms and pulling her towards him.

"No! I can't!" Serena struggled.

A second slap caused Serena to fall across her bed.

"Bitch, whore," he snarled pinning her down with his body, "I go to have fun with you…I will enjoy you do as I say."

As Serena struggled against the weight of the man, her kicking and shouting barely noticeable without air to breathe, she looked towards the door. Something was happening out there. She blinked; black spots appeared. She gasped for air, her ribs crushing under the mass of the man on top of her.

"I...can't...breathe," she croaked gasping for air.

"You like that? I'm going to give it rough."

Serena focused on the sounds she could hear outside as he slid his hands between her legs.

Were they screams?

She blinked, this time her eyes wouldn't open.

Is that someone shouting?

She gasped for air, but her lungs were empty.

"I...can't..."

Then everything went dark.

Chapter 48.

Serena groaned; everything hurt but she wasn't sure why and couldn't remember how she got into this state. Eyes still closed, she frowned. The beeps, clicks, whispers and soft padding of footsteps felt out of place. She felt out of place. Serena slowly opened her hand and smoothed the fabric with the palm of her hand; it was soft. Strange. She wiggled her toes and to her surprise they were warm and were wrapped by soft cotton socks. She sniffed. Odd it was a mixture of bleach and lemon. No stench of urine or stale bodily fluids invading her nose. A building fear of the unknown, forced her eyes to open, allowing for small flashes of muted light to gently refocus her eyes and adjust to the room she was in.

"Serena?"

An unknown voice.

"Hmmm."

"Hi, are you ok?" How do you feel?

Serena groaned a little, feeling everything stretch, crumple, sting and burn all at the same time and all over her body.

"Can you look at me?"

Serena nodded and turned towards the voice. She frowned, she didn't recognise the face.

"Hello, Serena."

"Water," Serena croaked licking her lips.

"Thomas, get water. Call doctor she's awake."

Thomas? Who was Thomas? Doctor? Serena was so confused. Who was this woman? Who was Thomas? Suddenly she froze and held her breath remembering her prison. Eyes wide open, Serena remembered struggling for air...the man on top of her...suffocation...and eventual blackness.

"Calm," said the female voice again concerned, "you are panicking, get doctor."

"She's struggling," a male voice said.

"Ok, move aside," said a much deeper voice. A flash of white in front of Serena's face. "she having panic attack, we need to sedate her."

"No...please, no drugs. I don't like..." Serena gasped as she felt a pinch in her arm and the liquid was pushed into her body. It was comforting and warm...Serena slept.

When she woke again, Serena was able to focus on her surroundings better. Her head pounded less, and her breathing was steadier than before.

"Hello," the female voice was still there, smiling.

Serena looked at the woman; she was sat in a plastic chair next to Serena, she wore a simple grey suit with a baby pink blouse. Her hair was tied back, and she had kind eyes. Every time she moved, Serena smelt a pleasant floral perfume. Something about the way this woman looked at Serena, made her feel safe.

"Hi," Serena croaked.

"Have water."

Serena took the cup from the woman and noticed she had a wedding band on. She sipped slowly, thinking as she did. Handing the cup back to the woman, Serena closed her eyes. Eventually she opened them again and looked directly at the woman who has sat silently, patiently next to her.

"Who are you? Where am I?"

The woman smiled, "I am Natasha, a police officer. You here in hospital. You are safe."

"Your accent?" Serena said her muscles tensing at the familiar intonation of the guards.

"Yes...I...you are in Slovakia."

"Slovakia?"

"Yes, it is long story. I get a police officer that speak better English."

"You speak English."

Natasha smiled, "better than me. You wait."

Serena nodded as she watched Natasha get up and walk to the door. She spoke, in what Serena could now assume was Slovak, to a young man outside of the room in a police uniform. Serena began to panic, her breath was coming in short sharp bursts, and she felt her skin prick as the man followed Natasha into the room. She looked at him, and then back at Natasha. All feelings of safety gone.

"What's going on? Who is this?"

"It's ok, this is Thomas," said Natasha placing a hand on her arm, "he is police."

She nodded towards Thomas who stayed at the foot of the bed, smiled and sat back down on the chair.

"You're police?" Serena asked nervous.

"Yes," said Thomas nodding, "my name is Thomas, and this is-"

"Natasha."

"Yes. We're police officers."

"What happened to me?"

"Can you remember your name?"

"Serena."

"And your age?"

"I'm...20 now...I think. What happened? Why am I here, what did I do wrong?"

"Serena, you were found unconscious, almost dead and injured. Your ribs are broken."

"The man...he...I couldn't breathe."

"Yes," Thomas coughed a little and looked at the pillow instead of Serena, "those men were captured. Serena, there was a raid on the place you were kept."

"A raid?"

"A police raid."

"Some of them were police too," said Serena frowning and trying to understand the information being given to her.

"We are dealing with the corrupt police officers too. We are arresting all the men, some fought us and there were casualties."

"The guards?"

"And others."

"What happened?" Serena felt a knot form in her stomach; she needed to know but at the same time she was terrified and wanted to forget everything.

"A few men and guards tried to fight back and used the girls as shields in their escape. We rescued you and most of the girls too."

"Where are they?"

"They're here in the hospital. They are protected and recovering, like you."

"Who died?"

"A man, a guard we think. His identification said Oliver Rakol."

"Olli," Serena breathed.

"We will need to speak to you about all this when you are better. To fill in the gaps."

"What girl died?"

"I don't think you should know that."

"I'm their Sestra! I need to know," Serena snapped. Then looking at the surprise in Thomas' face, "I promised to look after them."

"A young girl. Her name was Kammi we think. We will look after you all now, you need to rest."

Serena closed her eyes, allowing tears to fall. Kammi was the girl she had slapped in front of Marta on her first inspection. She opened her eyes suddenly.

"What about Bishop? And Marta? They're the bosses-please tell me you got them?"

"Bishop?"

"Ivan," Natasha spoke for the first time since introducing Thomas.

"That's an even longer story. But in short, we have caught them both. We have seized a number of books, like catalogues with pictures of all the girls he has kidnapped.

And some passports too. We are working through them all now to see what we can do to track them down."

"Oh."

"Serena, you know you're safe now, don't you? We have several officers from the UK coming to help you all get home safe."

"How did you find us?" Serena said.

"Maybe for another time?"

"No, I need to know," said Serena shifting herself up to a sitting position on the bed, "how did you find us?"

"A video."

"What?"

"It was you. A video with you on. Someone saw it and recognised you as missing. The police managed to track the owner of the video and he eventually told them everything."

"Oh my god," said Serena remembering Dominik's friend with the camera fetish.

"Serena?" said Natasha said as she stood. She reached down and wiped away Serena's tears, "you're safe now."

Chapter 49: Two Weeks Later

Serena sat in her room looking out at the grey clouds through a small window. The sky was dark and gloomy allowing little natural light to come through; the blinds were almost fully drawn and the one lamp near the bed struggled to illuminate anything. Serena sighed and picked at fingers, her mind constantly going over the information Thomas and Natasha had given her. This wasn't the welcome home she had envisioned and dreamt of for many years, but the officers, social workers, and doctors all explained that she and the other girls that had been rescued needed to be somewhere safe and isolated from the press to readjust to life here, back in the UK. Back home.

"Knock, knock."

Serena turned to see a familiar face and smiled.

"Hey, come in."

"How you doing?" asked Becky walking into the room.

"Dunno. Ok, I guess. You?"

"I'm think they could've made the rooms a little less floral and sickening."

Serena laughed, "better than our previous accommodation."

"True," said Becky hopping onto Serena's bed since Serena was in the only seat in the room.

"I get why we need this...middle stage," she looked back out of the window, "away from the press. I know I need the space, but these last two weeks have dragged. I want to be home."

"I know what you mean," said Becky.

"Can I come in?" a sudden knock and voice at the door made Serena and Becky both jump.

"Doc, you scared us," said Becky her hand on her chest.

"Sorry, is it ok to speak to Serena?"

"Of course," Becky said winking at Serena and smiling, "see you later."

"Ok," said Serena, her voice wobbled a little still from the scare.

"I'll come by to see you later too, Becky."

"Sure. You know where I am."

Serena watched Becky walk out of the room and felt a pang of jealously. Becky seemed to have adjusted better and quicker than Serena. Serena desperately wanted to be able to get over her trauma that easily. She looked back out of the window.

"Little steps," said the Doctor as if she could read her mind.

Doctor Veera Patel perched on Serena's bed where Becky had just been sitting. She clasped her hands together and tilted her head.

"I know," said Serena.

"You went through so much."

"I know."

"It'll take a while to adjust. Everyone's different."

"I know."

"You'll be out of here soon."

"I know."

"Wow, you know a lot. Maybe you don't need me as much as I thought," Dr Patel joked.

Serena turned to look at Dr Patel and smiled sadly, "I think I'm going to need you for a long time."

"Eventually you won't, but until then, that's what I'm here for. So, how are you?"

"I'm ok," said Serena, "I'm happy but every sudden sound makes me jump."

"Of course, is it just sounds?"

Serena swallowed and shook her head.

"What else, Serena?"

"Any…male voices and…the accent…they…"

"Take you back to where you were kept."

Serena nodded.

"That will happen, but you'll find ways of coping and deciphering the dangers from what's safe."

"I know. I also miss my family. I want to see them, but I'm not sure I will cope. I'm so confused."

"That's ok," said Dr Patel, "we do try to integrate family to you all bit by bit. With what many of you victims have gone through, we try and keep male visits to an absolute minimum, and we try to make sure you ladies are ready to see them. For you, it's been a long time."

"I've no idea what I'd say to my dad," said Serena her hands shaking, "what would I say to him?"

"Maybe you don't need to speak. Sometimes on the first visit being in the same room as them is enough. Maybe a hug is enough. Or even a simple hello."

"He'll be so mad at me."

"He's not mad at you. He is happy that you're back in the UK and safe."

"How do you know?"

"I've spoken to him, briefly."

"What?" said Serena. She turned to look at Dr Patel and her lip quivered, "what did he say? Is he ok?"

"He said he misses you and wants you home," said Dr Patel, then added softly, "he's not well though Serena. You need to know this."

"What's wrong with him?"

"He didn't say, he's quite poorly though, so if we can get you seeing him soon, that would be good. He misses you and wants you to come home as soon as you're ready." Dr Patel stood up and took a step towards Serena, "and he's definitely not mad at you."

Serena sobbed into her hands, the thought of seeing her dad again and holding him was overwhelming.

"Sorry," she said as Dr Patel handed her a box of tissues from the bedside table.

"It's perfectly fine and normal to cry," she said, "clearly it's too much to see your dad so soon...but what about your step mum and sister?"

Serena sniffed.

"Yes. Maybe just for an hour. They're desperate to see you."

"Are they really here?"

"Yes. They've come here every day since you've been here. But it's up to you when you feel ok enough to see them."

"I...want to see them. I think I'm ready."

"Ok. Now?"

Serena nodded.

"So, did you want me to bring them in here?"

"In here?" said Serena waving an arm around, "in this room of misery. No thanks."

"We have a conference style room, it's bright and airy. No comfy sofas or anything though."

"That will be ok."

"Right, I will go and let them know and then come to collect you. Is that ok?"

Serena nodded; her body tingled with nerves, seeing her step-mum and sister after so many years was a big step.

"Ok, I'll go get them."

"Um...wait," said Serena as the doctor was leaving.

"Yes?" Dr Patel stopped and turned to face Serena.

"Will you be there too?"

"If you want me to be there, yes."

"Yes please."

"Then I'll be there. I'll take them to a conference room and then come to collect you."

"Thanks."

"Are you ready?" Dr Patel asked hovering her hand over the doorhandle of the conference room.

"Yes," said Serena shaking her head no at the same time.

"They're here for as long as you want them to be," said Dr Patel putting a hand on Serena's shoulder and smiling, "be brave."

As the door opened Serena looked at the floor, unable to look up at the woman and girl standing on the other side of the room who were looking just as nervous as Serena.

"Serena," Dr Patel said standing by her side giving her shoulder a squeeze, "look who's here to see you."

Serena nodded, and slowly lifted her gaze to the two people standing. She gasped as she saw Katalina, looking tired and much older, her hair cut short, and her sister, Danika, taller, leaner and with matching piercing eyes as Serena. Her chest felt like it was exploding. She opened her mouth, but nothing came out. She allowed tears to fall down her face as she locked eyes with Katalina. Her hands shook and her chest rose and fell with aching happiness.

"Serena!" cried Danika breaking the silence and running towards her.

Danika's arms wrapped around her waist in a tight hug. Both sisters squeezed each other tight and cried. Serena looked at Katalina who walked towards her, her eyes wet and lip trembling. Serena nodded and Katalina embraced Serena and Danika together. The three stood like that and cried, holding on to one another tightly.

"Serena," said Danika her voice choking with sobs, "you're home."

Chapter 50: Two Months Later

Serena felt nervous standing at the gates with a bouquet of flowers in her hands. The cold wind nipped at her bare knees and the long coat she had on wasn't keeping out the cold morning air. Danika stood next to her, thick jeans and jumper underneath her big coat; the only colour were her red gloves and scarf. Both shivered.

"Let's go," said Serena.

She hunched her shoulders, took a deep breath and walked along the path behind the gates. She kept her eyes on the ground ahead, walking quickly and breathing heavily, her sister following behind. She twitched and tensed at every voice she heard. By the time she stopped, she was sweating, out of breath and her hands were clammy as they gripped onto the flowers tightly.

"Hey," she said softly, "I bought you these. Your favourite."

She bent down and placed the flowers at the base of the cold white marble headstone. The wind whipped up a few stray leaves from the bouquet and tossed them along the grave and along the path, crossing other headstones but not stopping at any of them. Serena closed her eyes and breathed; calming herself and focusing her mind the way she had been taught to by the survivors' councillor. She swallowed as Danika took one of her hands in hers.

"I'm sorry I didn't listen to you," she said looking at the headstone, "I'm sorry I didn't reach out to you. I'm so sorry I didn't tell you about Dominik. I'm sorry I pushed you and everyone away." She stopped to wipe away tears, "I am sorry I lied to you, I didn't know what I was doing. I was so stupid. I should've spoken to you when you reached out. But I didn't. I pushed you away and I can't fix that, not now, not ever. I have to live with this. I'm so sorry."

Serena released all her pain and heartache. He shoulders shook as she sobbed, and Danika wrapped an arm around her shoulders. A moment passed, then wiping her face Serena took a step forwards. She kissed her fingers and touched the letters engraved into the headstone.

IN LOVING MEMORY OF

AMY COGTON

A BEAUTIFUL SOUL UNABLE TO GROW.

"I love you, Amy," Serena whispered.

"She loved you too," said Danika gently stroking Serena's back and comforting her, "and she would never say it was all your fault."

"It feels like it is," said Serena looking at the white headstone.

The two sisters stood side by side in silence for a moment: the wind swirling around their feet and the clouds thickening. It was the first time she had managed to bring herself to visit's Amy's grave. Something she knew she wanted to do but was afraid of doing. She closed her eyes and pictured her best friend's smile. The peaceful silence was broken by footsteps behind them.

"I thought I'd find you here."

Serena turned around fast not believing what she could hear. The figure standing in front of her looked exactly the same as she had last seen, and yet so different. Serena noticed a walking stick and a limp as he stepped forwards.

"Dad," she whispered.

"Hi honey," he said.

Serena fell into his outstretched arms and sobbed.

THE END.

Thank you for taking the time to read my novel. I hope you enjoyed reding it as much as I enjoyed writing it. It is a tough topic but a missing teen in the news where I live and my overactive imagination made this a reality. And now you've read it.

Please leave a review on Amazon and Goodreads if you can spare the few moments it would take to do this for me.

You can find Maaya Brooker on the following social media channels.

Twiter: @maayabrooker

Instagram: @maayabrooker

Tiktok: @maayabrookerauthor

Email: maayabrookerauthor@gmail.com

Printed in Great Britain
by Amazon

27301324R00205